JUST JULIET

CHARLOTTE REAGAN

Inkitt

This book is published by Inkitt.com the Hipster's Library – Join now to read and discover free upcoming bestsellers

Website: www.charlotte-reagan.com

1. The first thing that caught my eye was Juliet James.

I hated driving in the rain. It was probably the worst thing ever. I *loved* rain itself, but I really didn't want to bother with driving when it was raining. And my poor baby of a car was old and the heater didn't work so I was freezing.

I sat at the stop sign, rubbing my hands together and blowing on them while I waited, occasionally tapping the gas to see if it would help with the heat issue. Apparently not. Cars zoomed past me on the opposite road, throwing water my way, but I ignored it. I was in no rush. School was so not worth my life.

I drummed my fingers on the wheel for a while as I watched the rain pour down and waited for the traffic to ease. Honestly, I had almost decided to skip school, but there was nothing to do at home. The electricity was sketchy, my laptop was dead, and I wouldn't have any new books to read for a while.

"Lena Newman, you are the most interesting person in the world," I muttered before reaching up and throwing down the visor so I could see myself in the mirror.

I didn't look half bad. My brown hair was down in waves, covered by a light gray beanie that sat almost perfectly over my ears. Jade green eyes lightly lined, freckles dusting my nose and cheeks, lips colored light pink. My outfit matched in a comfortable winter way, the beanie came paired with a scarf, and I wore a light white long sleeve shirt with jeans that were stuffed into knit snow boots.

It was my rainy day outfit. Warm and comfortable.

A shock of thunder made me push the mirror back up. I glanced around at the roads again before finally pulling out onto the highway. One more block, a right turn, and I was sliding into the very large parking lot of Grant High.

Fantastic.

It was oddly empty; I could tell a lot of people had decided to skip. I didn't really blame them—the water was coming down like God himself was crying, causing the roads to almost flood. It rained a lot in our little town, but not always so much at one time, and even though the roads were equipped for this amount of water, it was still a pain.

With a sigh, I rolled into a parking space as close as I could to the front doors. I sat there for a while chewing on my bottom lip and debating on how fast I would to have to run to not get completely soaked. I had an umbrella in the back seat, shoved somewhere unceremoniously, but I doubted it would be worth the effort to fight with it.

When my door opened I nearly pissed my pants.

A guy flopped into my passenger seat, closing off his own umbrella and shaking it slightly before the door slammed shut.

I think I stared at him for an hour before his appearance sank into my mind. Blond surfer hair, grassy eyes— "Quin," I breathed, hand over my heart. "Jackass. Don't ever do that to me."

He grinned and leaned across the car to peck me on the cheek. "Sorry babe. I was going to ask if you wanted to walk in together but I didn't want to stand out there while you thought about it."

I nodded slightly and after giving him a real kiss, he was out of the car again and going around to the driver's side. Honestly, he was too damn sweet to me. Our relationship had been on the rocks for months, but I kept ignoring it because he was nice. And we got along.

I turned my baby off, frowning as she died down, running my hand over the wheel. Quinton constantly made fun of me because I loved her like a guy would. Except I didn't know how to make her tick. All that under the hood shit was definitely guy territory

2

and I just didn't have it in me. I honestly respected the girls that did.

Break the stereotypes ladies, go crazy.

He met me once I got out and selflessly shared his umbrella with me. I huddled up close as we walked into the school. Noise assaulted me first. The comforting sound of rain pouring, and the lovely smell of fresh water suddenly turned into bad cafeteria breakfast and yelling teenagers.

The first thing that caught my eye was Juliet James.

My high school was just big enough that we had every clique imaginable and a lax dress code, but just small enough that new kids were hot gossip. The newest one had come strolling in on the first day looking like she'd walked straight out of hell. I'd never seen anyone like her—thigh high black boots, ripped up leggings, a much too large Sex Pistols shirt, and beautiful blond hair cascading down her back.

Juliet—whose name I had learned when she finally sauntered into my art class at the end of the day—was so beautiful it almost made me cry.

Today she was wearing black leggings that disappeared into barely-laced combat boots and a dark evergreen sweater, all which contrasted wonderfully against her pale, creamy skin. Her top was a size or two too large, dipping down to cover her thighs, the neck hanging off one shoulder, the sleeves covering her hands, even where they were lifted to hold up her cell phone. Her nails were short, covered in chipped black polish, which showed as her fingers typed away on her touch screen.

She was pretty in a simple way, because unlike her style, her features were simple. Rounded cheeks, pouty lips, large bright blue eyes. Her hair was light blond, falling down her back in damp waves, bangs swept across her forehead. She wore very little makeup except for what was dark around her eyes, making them stand out even more than—I was sure—they would on their own.

She peeked at me through her lashes, the corners of her mouth tugging in a smile, before she lifted a hand to wiggle her fingers in a wave.

Quinton nudged me to regain my attention before leading the way to our lockers. I hadn't even noticed the bell ring, but I let him steal a goodbye kiss before he raced off to class. I sighed and shifted through my books before doing the same.

History was first period, so I shuffled in and took my usual seat in the front. The spot behind me was quickly occupied by my best friend. I'd met Lacey Parker in fourth grade, when she'd very seriously told me I was allowed to be her friend because I was pretty. Looking back, that was likely the type of toxic shit parents told their daughters to stay away from, but in Lacey's defense she was just the sort of person who could get away with collecting friends because they were attractive.

She was quite gorgeous herself, for one thing, and everyone in school knew it—five-nine model tall, more thin than curvy but with the type of ass that rappers sang about in the 80s. She had flawless dark skin that was an amazing contrast with her perfect white teeth. When she smiled you could just almost hear a dentist commercial. Her hair was long and fell around her chest in large dark loose curls, and she often complained about what it took to maintain. Lacey was high maintenance all around though. She was Grant's token black kid for the most part, but for all our school's flaws, seeing color wasn't one of them.

Today she was wearing black leggings, a high-waisted teal skirt, and a white shirt that read *Paris* in elegant cursive under a fitted black jacket. She was a cheerleader, the most popular girl in school, and somehow managed to get away with hanging out with me instead of the other snobs. She was probably just so cool nothing could stomp her reputation down. Not even me.

Not that I was a complete social outcast. I dated a football player and my bestie was a cheerleader, but I floated somewhere in the middle. In all honestly, I think people just put up with me because they thought I was funny. Technically, I wasn't. Just sarcastic and bitchy, which evidently made for good jokes.

Lacey plopped down, opened her book and sat her elbows on the table as she narrowed her eyes. I spared a glance at her, but she was very obviously glaring at someone else.

With a sigh, I twisted sideways and pressed my back against the wall. "All right. Who has your attention?"

And then I saw her. Juliet. She was standing at Mr. Radford's desk, tucking blond strands behind her ear as he talked about some piece of paper she was holding. Pretty much everyone was looking at her. I could hear the gossip starting around us, but it was nothing I was ever really interested in hearing.

"Can you *believe* her?" Lacey was saying.

This usually wasn't odd talk. We liked making fun of other people, though hers was from more of an I'm-A-Snotty-Cheerleader perspective while mine was more of an I-Hate-Everyone issue.

I tilted my head and shrugged. "I don't know. I like her."

Lacey snapped her head around so fast I was actually surprised it didn't fly off her neck. I shrank in my seat, holding up my hands in defense as she gave me a glare I wasn't sure how to read.

"What?" I asked. "She's different."

Lacey scoffed and sat back in her desk, flipping the pages in her book with an irritated aura that meant she obviously wasn't paying attention to what page she wanted to be on. "She looks like a bitch to me," she grumbled.

"Takes one to know one," I shot back. Lacey just shrugged, obviously not bothered by my little jab.

I sighed and twisted around correctly in my seat, flipping through pages in my book before I found the section we were on. Someone passed the notes out, and I sighed in relief that they were pre-made—we just had to fill in the blanks. Best. Notes. Ever.

I stuck the end of my pencil in my mouth so I could chew on it absentmindedly while I watched Juliet move to sit in the very back desk, and then she was out of my view for good.

Out of sight, out of mind.

The rest of the day pretty much went on like that. I walked with Quinton to my classes, but we only had two actually together, so we usually parted at the doorway.

Third period I had an aide block, which put me working in the library. It was a slow, quiet job I'd had for the last few years, and often made me feel like Tibby in the first *Sisterhood of the Traveling Pants*—when she's stocking shelves and gets so bored she starts putting price stickers on her face.

Mostly I spent the time arguing with teenage idiots about how to correctly pronounce the word "library" (*lahy-brer-ee*) and restocking books and putting others back into their right place. I spent an insane amount of time spinning around in my seat while trying to balance a pencil on my upper lip.

And that was when she came in. I didn't even notice her, just heard her. And by the sound in her voice, I knew she was smirking. "That looks productive."

The pencil fell off of my lip almost immediately and I spun around haphazardly to see the devil herself leaning against my desk, elbows propped on it and chin resting in her hands. She smiled at me, green sleeves falling down to the crooks of her arms now. I could see the outline of a tattoo on her wrist— something that looked like a basic infinity symbol.

"You know," she said, "I don't think I ever got your name."

It seemed to take a moment to realize she was actually talking to me. I blinked twice, I think, before I answered. "Lena," I said finally.

"Cute," she decided, then smiled and gave a nod. "It fits you." Her blue gaze flitted around the room as she stood back up. "I'm Juliet, by the way."

I knew that, of course, but didn't bother to tell her so. Instead I just smiled back and, after a beat of silence, seemed to realize where we were. "So, do you need help picking out a book or something?"

"Actually, I work here next period," she answered, crossing her arms before leaning one hip against my desk. Or, *our* desk, I guessed, since it was about to be hers. "I can see that it's super exciting in here."

I grinned at her. "Oh yeah, party central."

The bell rang then, cutting us off, so I hopped out of my seat and wished her luck. Then I had just over half an hour of English before I was free for lunch. English wasn't my favorite subject, but I didn't mind it too much. Art was my favorite, which mildly irritated my parents.

They wanted me to do well in school for my future, understandably, but nothing really interested me.

A kiss on the cheek pulled me from my thoughts and I looked up in time to smile at Quinton. He had a football in one arm, his friends just around the corner. They were yelling about something, telling me to put him in his place, probably, but I ignored them like always and just grabbed my lunch.

"How was class?" he asked, tossing his football from hand to hand as he led the way down the hallway, with me just a step or two behind him.

I shrugged. "Fine, I guess. The usual first week stuff."

We filled the walk to the cafeteria with idle chitchat about our first week assignments, and then we went our separate ways.

The cafeteria was the one room where Grant's cliques were immediately noticeable. Quinton sat with the rest of the jocks, but I didn't actually *fit* anywhere like that. Constantly straddling between the worlds of Popular Friends and Aloof Attitude.

At the very back of the cafeteria was a table—rectangular instead of circular like the others—and balanced on three legs because the fourth was mostly useless. It was chipping on the edges. There gathered everyone who didn't have a label.

The middle seat was mine and had been since freshman year. Lacey always sat to my left. She never sat with the other Snotty Cheerleaders unless she absolutely had to, and even then, she usually pushed off their business for another time.

We had two other friends who joined us—on the opposite side of the table, to the right by herself, was Aikiko Fujimoto. She was a tiny thing with a dark pixie cut and innocent-looking eyes. She liked math too much to be a real human and was often quiet just because she couldn't stand people. She'd started going by Kiki back in middle school when she got tired of people

7

mispronouncing her name, and occasionally pretended like she didn't speak English to get out of shit.

Georgia Harris, who was taller than any of us, sat in front of Lacey. She had natural tan skin, sharp features, and long curly hair. A few years ago, Georgia had been that one girl everyone just *knew*. Then she'd gotten pregnant the summer between sophomore and junior year and had come back changed. She'd dumped most of her old crew, dropped her schedule down to half a day to get a job, and started chilling with us. She was a single mom to a beautiful biracial daughter and on good terms with the baby daddy.

Maybe we were a table of outcasts, but it worked for us.

Because of that, though, I really shouldn't have been surprised when *she* showed up.

A tray dropped harshly on the part of the table between Georgia and Kiki, and we all jumped at the foreign sound. Juliet flopped down in the seat without a word and went to eating as if she'd sat there her whole life.

I was still in shock when I heard Lacey speak. "Uh, what exactly are you doing?"

It wasn't unusual for random people to come sit with us. We were sarcastic, crude, and lacked filters—typical affordable high school humor. Generally, however, people made appointments to be at our table.

Juliet looked up slowly, her gaze focusing on Lacey with the most unamused, unimpressed look I'd ever seen. "Oh, how rude of me." She thrust out a fork-full of cafeteria spaghetti. "Would you like a bite?"

Lacey screwed her nose up. "I have my own, thanks," she deadpanned. But she didn't, really. She had a salad. Most people got both, but not Lacey. The salad was enough for her. Heaven forbid her waist grows past a size three.

Juliet's attention turned toward me. "Can I sit here?" she asked, as if I was the ringleader. I wasn't—Lacey was, because Lacey was the ringleader of the world—but for whatever reason, I just shrugged. We were the outcast table, after all. And no one else could really handle Juliet's level of...Julietness. I was sure of it.

"So," Georgia drawled. She always had a habit of making us realize how awkward our silences got. That didn't happen often either, which meant we really were surprised at Juliet's appearance into our group. She propped an elbow on the table and looked at our newest addition. "I'm Georgia," she introduced. "That's Kiki beside you. You evidently know Lena, and I'm sure you've heard Queen Lacey's name all over the school by now."

Juliet stared at her, took a drink of soda, then nodded. "Juliet," she replied as an introduction.

"Juliet?" Lacey asked with a scoff, which I should have seen coming. "What, was your mom a Shakespeare fanatic or something?"

Juliet's gaze hardened, and I could tell this wasn't going to end well. "Yeah," she snapped. "She was. She played Juliet on Broadway in London the year she met my father. And then she died a few years ago. Bet you're laughing real hard now, huh?"

No. She wasn't. In fact, she had gone so pale she could almost pass as Caucasian. There was silence for a moment, but Lacey eventually deflated. "I'm sorry," she said, and she meant it. Even Juliet must have realized that, because she shrugged and let it go.

For a while, no one said anything. Looks were shared, questions asked without mouths ever opening, but no one knew what to say. Juliet's confession had hit home for all of us, who still had mothers to go home to. Regardless of our relationship with them, they were alive.

Finally, Georgia broke it, asking Lacey about her latest boyfriend. Aaron Something. He was a college student. Lacey's relationships had always been Georgia's favorite topic—she loved her child, no doubt, but sometimes I thought she missed dating, and lived vicariously through Lacey.

Lunch came to an end not long after and I trotted off to Chemistry by myself, only to see Juliet slip in right after class had started. Just like she had in History, I watched her stalk off to the back to sit by herself.

Only twenty minutes after that, the electricity went off.

It was really only then I realized it was still storming outside. The thunder seemed oddly loud all of a sudden, as did the rain beating against the roof. I sighed as I looked up, only to hear Ms. Fran do the same.

"All right students, stay in your seats, I'm going to go see what I can do." The door opened and then she was gone, leaving us alone in the complete dark.

With a bunch of teenage boys.

I had never been so glad to have a corner seat in my entire life. I just sank, closing my eyes. At least I could get a nap, if nothing else. I found my thoughts wandering to a specific girl sitting about three tables behind me, though. I couldn't hear her talking in the masses, so I figured she was doing the same thing I was doing. Hiding.

Why couldn't I stop thinking about her? I hadn't even realized how bad the obsession was until noticing the only time I *hadn't* thought about her today was during library. And mostly because that job was like the prerequisite to having your brain scraped out of your head. I probably couldn't have even remembered her name during that situation. But now…

The door swung open and the little flashlight reappeared. "You can all go home," Ms. Fran announced, and tried to say something else but it was covered by the sounds of whooping and hollering from all the freaking idiots in the room.

With a sigh and a shake of my head, I began gathering my things.

I didn't wait around for Quinton as I went to toss what I could in my locker. Most likely he would still have weight practice, so it wasn't worth pushing through the crowd just to find him. The hallways were dark anyway. I'd probably trip on something.

"Hey bitch," Lacey greeted as she slid beside me, using the flashlight app on her phone to get around. "Going home?"

"Yes?" I answered. I was already planning a good time with some candles and *How to Build a Girl* by Caitlin Moran. Lacey said I had a weird book style; I said it wasn't my fault all she read was porn and thus couldn't appreciate good literature. Her argument was that erotica *was* the only good literature.

"Ugh, you're so boring," Lacey muttered, dropping her head against the locker so hard it rattled. "I'm going to Aaron's. They're having a blackout party. There will be booze and sex, I'm sure."

"And STDs, I'm sure," I rebounded mockingly. She glared at me, flipped her hair over her shoulder, and stalked off. Which I took to mean she didn't need a ride home. "Have fun, whore!" My parting words were met with a few snickers from people listening to us, and I was sure Lacey's middle fingers were high in the air, but I couldn't see them so it didn't matter.

Outside, the storm had really picked up. The sky was dark gray, making the world look duller, even though it smelled fresh. Rain was coming down hard, coating the ground in layers of water.

I sighed as I dug my keys out of my bag, deciding I'd have to make a run for it, when something caught my attention out of the corner of my eye.

Blond hair. Green sweater. Juliet.

I hesitated a moment before stepping outside and under the awning, looking her over. She was sitting on one of the half brick walls, still safely dry, knees pulled up, sketchbook resting on them, drawing calmly.

There were other teens rushing around us, laughing and darting out into the rain, but they all seemed to fade because I cared more about her. Before I even knew what I was doing, I was standing next to her, tapping two fingers gently against her forearm to get her attention. She looked up at me slowly, her hands subconsciously falling over whatever she was working on.

"Aren't you going home?" I asked.

"I'm waiting for my brother," Juliet answered with a slight shrug, picking at the edges of her sketchbook. "He gets out at four, I don't have a car, definitely don't want to take the bus. You know the drill."

11

"That's almost two hours from now. You're welcome to ride with me."

She seemed unsure and eventually shook her head. "I don't want to be a burden. I'm fine. I'll just draw. I like drawing in the rain anyway."

So did I, but not when it was falling this hard. "I offered, so chill, and get ready to make a run for it."

She considered me another few moments before eventually shutting her book, tucking it safely in her bag, and then jumping off the wall. She regarded the parking lot warily, and slid her hand in mine. "Lead the way."

I grinned, held onto her tightly, and took the first step.

2. "Remember, as far as anyone knows, we're a perfectly normal family."

Juliet lived on the outskirts of town—a good twenty minute or so drive, made longer by the condition of the roads. It was a quiet ride, but not uncomfortable. We talked about our day, complained about our wet clothes, but it was nice.

She was nice.

Her house was an older model, more rectangular than anything else, two stories, surrounded by trees. It was far enough away from its neighbors to give it an air of privacy, but managed to still look inviting somehow.

There were two cars already in the driveway—a small black truck and a seemingly new dark blue jeep. I slid in behind them when Juliet said I could.

"Thanks again," she said, leaning forward to get her bag off the floor by her feet. I nodded, rubbed my hands together for warmth, and then realized she'd made no move to actually leave. When I looked at her, she was biting her bottom lip and seemed unsure about something. "Do you want to come in?"

I blinked, surprised. I didn't have a huge social life, and out of my friends, I'd only ever been inside of Lacey's house before. I was more of a 'hang out with people at school' type of person. It took me a moment to realize I needed to answer, and I stumbled over my words when I finally did. "Uh, I don't want to intrude or anything."

"You won't," Juliet promised, her natural confidence sliding back into place. "I invited you. Besides, I kind of owe you at least some hot chocolate for the trouble of coming all the way out here."

I hesitated, but the longer I thought about it, the more inclined I was to agree. Especially considering the only thing I was looking forward to was whatever fast food I could pick up on the way home for dinner.

"All right," I agreed, and she grinned happily before throwing open the door and making a run for it, using her bag as a makeshift umbrella.

I laughed, killed the engine, and took off after her. The rain was lighter thanks to the coverage the trees provided, but I was still relieved when she held the door to her house open for me.

"Thanks," I breathed out with a slight chuckle when we were both inside, the door clattering shut behind us and locking away the last of the cold air. It was warm here, and I sighed gratefully as I took in my surroundings.

Juliet had one of those homes that opened up to a hallway first. Wooden floors, tan walls, not a lot of decoration except for a chalkboard sign hanging up that declared: *Remember, as far as anyone knows, we're a perfectly normal family.* It was lived in, obviously, coats hanging on the rack, shoes thrown in the corner. The walls opened up on the left and right sides, one leading to what looked like a kitchen and the other to what I guessed was the living room. The hall went straight to a staircase—that probably had more rooms behind it. The atmosphere smelled faintly of rain and pumpkin. It was homey, even right there in the doorway.

"Hey," a teenage boy greeted, coming out of the kitchen. He was tall, probably close to six foot if not there, broad shouldered but mostly made of lean muscle. His hair was light brown, short and messy where it dusted across his forehead, just over chocolate-colored eyes. He was dressed in a pair of plaid pajama pants that hung low and a white muscle top sporting a faded Superman symbol, no shoes. He looked vaguely familiar, though I couldn't place him.

14

"Scott," Juliet greeted as she dropped her damp book-bag by the door and knelt to start unlacing her boots. "You know you don't *actually* live here, right?"

He grinned and leaned against the wall, crossing his arms over his chest before looking my way. I offered a small wave as a hello. "Who's your friend?"

Juliet stepped out of her shoes and left them with the others. "Scott White, Lena…"

"Newman," I supplied when I realized she didn't actually know it.

She nodded and gestured to Scott, shooting him a look that clearly said, "There, happy?"

Scott didn't seem bothered by her in the least, and instead offered me a hand for a quick shake.

"You play football," I realized now that I had a name to put to the face.

"Yeah, I do. Quarterback for Bridgewood," Scott answered. "You a fan?"

Juliet rolled her eyes and walked past both of us to head into the kitchen. I considered following her, but Scott didn't move, so I stayed in the conversation I'd entered instead. "Kind of, I guess. I mean, enough that I recognized your name. My boyfriend plays for Grant. I really only know the game for him."

Bridgewood Academy was a private school about an hour away—half that from Juliet's place. The football teams were well known rivals, so much so that their distaste for each other often bled off the field. Not that I cared.

"Baby!" another voice called. Definitely male, theatrically whiny, most likely coming from the living room. I knew he had to be calling for someone specific, but Scott didn't seem bothered in the least.

"You're welcome to take your shoes off," he offered, gesturing to where Juliet's boots were. I nodded my thanks, moving over to toe off my own. "So, who is your boyfriend?"

15

"Oh, Quinton Barron," I answered, thankful that my socks were dry even if my clothes mostly weren't. Juliet and I hadn't been soaked, but we hadn't been spared by the rain either.

"*Baby!*" If possible, the unknown boy sounded even more annoyed now, like he knew he was being ignored.

Scott still didn't seem to care. "Yeah, I know Barron. He's a Linebacker, right? Not a bad player." It was polite, but in a distant way, which didn't really surprise me. Made me like him, though, for putting in the effort to be decent.

I shrugged. "So I've heard. I've also heard whoever's calling…" I trailed off at the fond but mildly annoyed smile that crossed Scott's face. The acknowledgement settled me—like at least I hadn't been imagining it or something.

"*Baaabyyy.*" This time, the voice came with an owner, shuffling his way out of the living room. He favored Juliet a lot as far as facial features went, the slightest masculine traits making them different. In contrast to her blond hair though, his was black, messy, and long enough in the front that I was sure it would cover his eyes if he wanted it to. Juliet's were blue, but his were almost silver, although no less striking. He was taller than me, though not by much, lanky but not in an unhealthy way. He was in pajama pants too, paired with an oversized hoodie, his arms crossed. "I'm hungry."

Scott sighed deeply and went to turn into the kitchen. Before he crossed the threshold, the boy was calling at him again, and Scott dropped his head back against his shoulders. "*What* Lakyn?"

"Love me!" he demanded, stomping his foot, a pout gracing his face that could only be described as adorable.

I saw the corner of Scott's mouth tug into a smile as he twisted around, crossed the few feet between them, cupped Lakyn's face, and swooped to seal their lips together.

Rationally, I knew it was coming. No teenage males who were *just friends* called each other *baby*, but the shameless display of affection sent me into slight shock. Even behind closed doors, my entire family was rarely affectionate.

16

But more than that, it was the *feeling*. Even as soft and gentle as the kiss was, it suddenly seemed like I was witnessing something private. Personal.

I'd just looked away when Juliet came back into the room. She glanced at the boys, and I swore her gaze got darker, more guarded.

She was holding two mugs that were slightly steaming, her body already poised toward the stairs. "You okay?" she asked.

When I nodded, she motioned for me to follow her, and I did so, leaving the couple behind us, who were bickering good naturedly by this point.

Juliet's back was tense, and I realized I'd messed up somewhere.

"I was just surprised," I tried, as way of explaining my reaction.

Upstairs was just a hallway, family photos lining the walls, some sitting on the floor still waiting to be put up. Rain still poured, pattering the roof, and the slight pumpkin smell followed us. She chose a door at the end of the hall, shouldered it open and let me in, and I knew immediately it was her bedroom.

Every inch of the walls were covered in hard rock band posters, nothing I really listened to but knew by name. They were dark in color, contrasting the curtains that covered the one window in the room, white silk pooling at the floor and blending into the plush black carpet.

All her furniture was white, but it was scuffed, scraped, dented, and old in a vintage way. She'd taken numerous sharpies to everything, drawing and writing in mostly black, but there were the occasional splashes of color. She had a four poster bed pushed up against the left side of the room, complete with the full frame and a sheer curtain that was currently pushed back. There was a lacquer tufted bench on the floor against it—one that matched the headboard and the side tables. The bed set was black shag, made up perfectly.

Everything was fairly teenager-basic. She had shelves filled with books, knickknacks, and movies, cluttered side tables, a dresser with a modest flat screen perched on top. Against the right wall was a large vanity, and definitely the messiest part of the room. Makeup and accessories covered every available surface, and jewelry hung off every curve of the intricate frame around the mirror. She'd scribbled on the glass in what looked like lipstick, around the edges mostly. Across the top I could clearly read *Just be a Queen.*

Juliet led the way in, depositing the mugs on the dresser before going through the top drawer. I followed her, unsure of what to do with myself, before she reached back and handed me a pile of clothes. Pajamas, I realized.

"Oh, you don't have to."

Juliet shrugged, gathering a pair for herself. "You're soaked— go ahead. We look about the same size. Besides, no one in this house wears real clothes once they get home anyway."

I thought about the boys downstairs, both clad in their own pajamas, and huffed out a laugh at how *relaxed* everyone was. My mother got tightlipped if I wanted to eat breakfast before dressing for the day, much less hang around the house like that.

"Thanks," I finally said.

Juliet, obviously not very shy, turned her back to me and pulled her sweater over her head, then tossed it easily into the white hamper next to her dresser. I stared for a moment, watching her long blond hair getting caught up in the wool, gazing at the inches of creamy pale being revealed.

I didn't know why, but I couldn't look away. I was captivated. Juliet was thin, only a slight cinch to her waist, but not unhealthily, more delicate, almost—all small bones and petite stature. Her lacy black bra actually fit the way most teenagers couldn't be bothered with and looked very sensual somehow. I could have only had the view for a few seconds before her hair fell back down, but those seconds seemed to last forever.

I felt my face heat as I pulled off my own outfit, which was clinging to my body, thanks to the water it'd absorbed. I tried to focus on just changing, but I couldn't put a finger on why I was so entranced with the girl in front of me. She was just different. Beautiful.

The pajamas she had given me were simple: a black cotton T-shirt that was a bit too loose and a pair of silk leopard pants. I smirked as I traded my jeans for them, felt them snugly fit around my waist. I was curvier than Juliet, no doubt, but they did fit.

Juliet herself was in a pair of loose fitting boy shorts when she turned around, a large *Jack Skellington* shirt fitting a few sizes too large, just like her sweater had. She took the mugs off the dresser and handed one over before propping her hip against the piece of furniture, finding her drink suddenly very interesting.

"So," I mumbled, and took a sip to steady my nerves. It was probably the best hot chocolate I'd ever had, and I was surprised by the smoothness and the hint of cinnamon. I quickly took a larger drink. "Oh my god!"

Juliet smirked, finally looking up at me. "Homemade. With a saucer on the stove and everything. Lakyn flat out refuses to have it any other way."

"Well, he's ruined me for baggies forever," I grumbled, taking another drink and sinking carefully onto the bench at the foot of her bed. The awkwardness was still there, and my fingers danced around the edges of my mug while I thought. "So, Scott and…is Lakyn your brother?"

She'd mentioned a brother earlier at school, but now she started to shake her head. She stopped, though, and then shrugged. "I guess he is my brother, now. But technically he's my first cousin. His parents…" She made a face, like she wasn't quite sure how to continue. "Weren't good people, and only got worse when he came out, and he couldn't stay with them. It got bad, so my dad took him in almost three years ago now. He and Scott have been together for about that long, so he's usually around, pretending to live here and whatnot."

When I didn't have a negative reaction to that, she slowly walked to sit next to me. I already felt my heart going out to the boy I hadn't even spoken to. I'd never even considered having a problem bad enough I couldn't live with my parents. "What about Scott's parents?"

Juliet shrugged slightly. "It's complicated. He's out, and his mom claims she doesn't care but he's not allowed to talk about it or even have Lakyn over. And I don't think his dad has spared Scott even a glance in a couple of years. School's pretty hard on them, too. This, our home—*this* is their safe place. Where they get to be who they are without any judgment. So if that makes you uncomfortable—"

"It doesn't," I said quickly. I didn't have a lot of exposure to the gay community, but I had a lot of exposure to Lacey, who was all pro-free-love and everything else. I didn't *care*. Gay, straight, whore, prude, whatever. If it made someone happy and didn't hurt someone else, do it. Life was too short.

Whatever was on my face must have shown that, because Juliet's gaze finally softened, and she gave me a smile and a nod.

"Juliet!" I heard Scott's voice call from somewhere downstairs. "Come help with dinner! Bring your hot friend!"

I felt myself blush again and brought my mug up for another drink. "So is Scott bisexual, or what? I've heard *plenty* of stories about Scott White scoring off the football field, if you know what I mean."

Juliet cracked up laughing. "Slander and lies," she said as she stood, offering me her free hand. "I mean, I know he slept with a few girls back in the day, but I doubt they're talking because it was probably bad. That boy is *full on* gay. Just wait, you'll see."

I snickered behind the rim of my mug as I followed her back downstairs. I could already tell my night was going to be much more interesting than I'd anticipated.

On the way, Juliet explained that the teenagers usually took care of dinner. She said it had started out as Lakyn's thing mainly, but had eventually spread to the rest of them. Her father worked late, and while her older brother didn't technically live with them, he was around a lot. And hungry, more often than not.

Juliet said I didn't actually have to help when I paled at the idea. I was a horrible cook—couldn't even handle a grilled cheese half the time—but Scott laughed and promised there was *something* I could do.

So that was how I became in charge of cutting chicken into bits.

It ended up being more fun than I expected. Scott and Lakyn were a cute couple, mostly because they couldn't seem to leave each other alone. Scott was a tease, constantly messing with the other boy, tugging at his hair, nibbling at his earlobe. It was easy, it was normal. They seemed *happy*.

Scott was definitely the friendly one of the group. He was like an excited dog with a new toy when it came to me, interested in everything I said or did. Juliet stayed quiet mostly, hip-bumped me on occasion, threw in her two cents once in a while. Lakyn was the quietest. Kept to himself, buried in his hoodie, hair in his face. He didn't say anything to me, but when I took him the plates of chicken, he did smile and it felt oddly like approval.

Quinton called just as we were finishing up, and while I went through the trouble of wiping my hands off and grabbing my phone, I couldn't bring myself to answer it. I wanted to stay in the moment. Wanted to watch Juliet cross the kitchen, lift her foot behind herself to kick Scott playfully in the butt when she passed. It couldn't have hurt, but he still jumped around and glared at her.

I smiled and silenced the ring as she let out a girlish scream, darted around the island in the middle of the room. Lakyn had both hands full of food, his eyes going wide as Scott took off after her.

"Stop it," he demanded, but they weren't listening, pushing passed him roughly when one of them got too close to the other. He stumbled a few times, but the food stayed safe. Then he spun around towards me. "Lena!"

I felt something like pride swell in my chest at his effort to include me. "What do you want me to do?"

Juliet giggled, and then suddenly she was behind me, warm arms looping around my waist, holding me close, but more importantly like a human shield.

Scott drew up short when he saw his obstacle, glared again. "Don't make me hurt an innocent bystander, James."

"Can we just set the table, please?" I finally asked, trying my hardest not to give into utter amusement of the situation.

Juliet's arms tightened around me, and I also tried not to think about how comfortable that was.

"Yeah, can we?" she asked, and Scott looked like he was seriously considering it, but Lakyn's put-upon sigh finally made him back off. He shot Juliet a glare that clearly said they would finish this later, and took a plate from his boyfriend.

By the time we moved everything into the dining room, I had to admit it looked good. Chicken and cheese enchiladas, beans, rice, even sopapillas for dessert. "You know, for a house full of white kids, this doesn't look half bad," I praised.

Juliet chuckled while Scott shot me a grin. "See, I told you it would be okay if you helped. Nothing burned! Not even the house!"

I elbowed him in the ribs, because I felt like I'd earned that right.

The front door opening wasn't loud enough to be attention grabbing, but the voices that came through it were. Sounds of joking and laughter that made Juliet grin so brightly my heart fluttered. In a second she was gone, disappearing back into the hallway.

The dining room was situated behind the stairs, accessible from both the kitchen and the hall. It was a big room, with autumn-colored walls decorated with classic oil paintings. The outside wall was complete glass, but right now heavy drapes were covering the storm still raging outside. The main attraction was obviously the table, which was large enough to seat at least ten, but obviously only six places were set.

Juliet was back before long, two men following her. Her father was obviously easy to pick out. He was probably in his late forties, tall and broad shouldered, with a head full of short dark curls that were only just starting to gray. He had the usual scruff that came with forgetting to shave more than an actual design, and blue eyes that matched his daughter's almost perfectly.

22

He was still in what I assumed were his work clothes—a nice button-down shirt that seemed freshly untucked and dark dress pants—but barefoot like the rest of us when he crossed the room and immediately put Lakyn in a headlock. The youngest boy in the room started cursing immediately, but no one tried to help him.

"Who's this?" Mr. James asked as he saw me.

"New girl, Jules?" a man who I figured was probably Juliet's brother asked. He was a younger, green eyed version of their father, identical even down to their clothes.

My brow furrowed in confusion. I wasn't the new girl—Juliet was. I'd been going to Grant my whole life. Juliet's face reddened, both of the boys winced, and when Mr. James suddenly released Lakyn, he went right for Scott's hand.

Oh, I thought. Was it new *girl*? New girl as in...new *girl*friend. As in lesbian?

Juliet punched her brother in the shoulder once she recovered from the shock, and there was absolutely no playfulness about it. He leaned away from her slightly, expression wounded like he wasn't sure what he'd done wrong.

"Lena's just a friend, Rick," she stressed between clenched teeth. "Now can we eat?"

The room struck up the kind of awkwardness I remembered from lunch earlier as Mr. James shot his son a look. Rick shrugged, rubbed the back of his neck, then began to praise the dinner spread. Loudly.

Mr. James, on the other hand, just motioned vaguely toward the kitchen. "Scott, Lena is it?" When I nodded, he smiled. "Come here for a minute."

Since Juliet was pointedly not looking at me, I glanced at Scott for some reassurance. He smiled, then threw an arm around my shoulder and walked into the kitchen with me.

"Well, I'm glad to see Juliet is making friends. She was never very good at that," Mr. James said as he went to the sink to wash his hands. Scott chuckled, but I wasn't sure how to react, so I just smiled. "Scott, I know you drove here. Lena, I assume that is your '69 Camaro out there, because it better not be my daughter's."

I smiled despite myself at the very idea that Juliet could somehow obtain a car without her father's knowledge. "Yessir, it's mine. Do I need to move it?"

"No, no, you're fine," Mr. James promised as he left the sink to dry his hands. "But the storm has picked up and the roads are pretty questionable. As a parent myself, I'd rather you not be out there. Scott, let your parents know you're safe, all right? Lena, I can't tell you what to do, but if your parents are all right with it, you are more than welcome to spend the night here. Juliet has a queen-sized bed, so if you're comfortable with it you can stay with her. Or the couch is rather nice."

I blinked at him a few times in shock, at the idea of him letting me stay the night in her room. In her bed. With what was *probably* his at least somewhat gay daughter. "Are *you* comfortable with that?" I shot back, thinking of the heart attack my parents would have.

Mr. James was clearly amused. "Are you her girlfriend? Or dating her in any way, form, or fashion?"

"Um, no," I answered, and even though I was honest, it made something stir in my gut. She *was* gay then, which made sense, in an odd way. I'd known she was different. Interesting. Maybe that was why.

He shrugged. "Then I'm not worried about it."

Scott, seeming to take pity on me in this situation, chuckled and dropped his arm from my shoulders. "'Ight Mr. J. We'll call the parental units. Be there in a sec."

Mr. James nodded and left us alone in the kitchen. Scott pulled his cell from the pocket of his pajama pants, hit a button, then leaned his hip on the counter. I tried my father first, just because he was usually off work earlier, but by the time Scott was talking I was still waiting.

"No, Mom I'm fine... Yeah, it's just raining really hard... Grant... Yes..." He was different, talking to his mother. The cheer was gone from his voice, replaced by something guarded

24

and careful. Like he was choosing each word carefully. "Yeah I'll be home first thing... Yes, I will... In time for school, promise...yes ma'am. Okay."

I was calling my mother by the time Scott hung up, who sat and waited with me without seeming like an eavesdropper. I got her voicemail, unsurprisingly. "Hey Momma, it's me. I went to a friend's place after school and the storm picked up. Her father asked me to stay off the roads, so I think I'm going to stay the night here. If there's a problem with that let me know, okay? Love you."

"You okay?" Scott asked.

I nodded. My parents were good people, just busy. All the time. It was mildly annoying but could have been worse. "Are you?"

He shrugged, then stepped off the counter. "Come on, let's go eat."

Juliet's tension had faded by the time Scott and I sat at the table. Rick sighed gratefully when we appeared. "Finally, now we can say grace and eat!"

I'd never really said grace before, except a few times at church years ago, and was thankful no one decided to extend the honor to the guest. I took Lakyn's hand beside me, and reached across the table for Juliet's. Then we bowed our heads, and Scott started the prayer.

"Father God: thank you for this food, please bless it to our bodies, we ask in Jesus' name. Thank you for this family, which has been so good to each other and to me. Thank you for Lakyn, and how much he loves me. Still, somehow. Lord, I know you know he puts up with a lot."

There was a low chuckle around the room, and Lakyn squeezed my hand slightly though I doubted he realized he was.

"Thank you for Lena, because everyone knows Juliet could use a friend." I was pretty sure she kicked him for that one, but I couldn't see. "And thank you for the rain. So that we get to stay here. All. Night. Long."

He cracked up laughing and I peeked just long enough to see Mr. James scowling his way.

Scott's eyes were still closed, but he cleared his throat like he could see anyway, and finished with a very serious, "Amen."

There was no formality when it came to the actual eating. In fact, it was almost a fight to see who could get to the food first.

Once we were settled again, Rick pointed at Scott with his fork. "Why do we still allow this kid to say grace?"

"Because he's family," Mr. James answered simply before focusing on his meal.

And they were a family. Everyone joked, laughed, teased. They made fun of each other in good spirits, had inside jokes, and were just vibrant. Alive. Loud, but in a good way. It was always so quiet at my house. I was captivated by them so much that I didn't even realize I wasn't eating until Juliet flicked a grain of rice at me. I blinked a few times then shot her a look.

"What's wrong?" she asked, and though she sounded concerned her gaze was still guarded. The same one that had been there since Rick's *girlfriend* comment. "Don't you like it?"

I smiled slowly, not wanting to admit what I was really thinking about, and answered with, "Well, I helped cook it. I'm a little afraid."

That was met with a laugh, and soon I was roped into the conversation every which way. If I didn't get something, it was explained. And within just a couple of minutes, I felt like I belonged. Like I'd been there for ages, not like I'd just met Juliet the day before.

When everyone was done, I immediately jumped up to grab the dishes, the need to help almost overwhelming. Lakyn offered me a smile and laid a hand over my wrist, flicking his hair out of his face. "Don't worry about it."

"We have a system," Rick explained from the opposite end of the table as he piled plates on top of one another. "Half of us does the cooking, the other half does the cleaning."

Mr. James nodded in agreement. "You kids go off and have fun. Scott, Lakyn, behave."

Scott grinned in a way that was almost predatory as he wrapped his arms around his boyfriend's waist, dragging him off. Lakyn stuck his tongue out, but nodded at his uncle before they went off toward the stairs.

"It's almost gross how in love they are," Juliet muttered from beside me.

"I'm jealous," I admitted. "I don't think a lot of people are lucky enough to find that kind of love."

She glanced at me, and finally seemed curious instead of guarded. "You don't love Quinton?"

My nose screwed up. Quin and I had been together for almost four months, and while a lot of teenagers were dropping the L word by then, I definitely wasn't. "No."

Juliet nodded, like she either understood or didn't want to talk about it anymore. She held the door open when we reached her room, and I sighed as I walked inside, knowing the tension would reappear once we were alone. I went back to the little couch at the foot of her bed, sat and folded my legs under me.

Juliet busied herself with taking care of our wet clothes from earlier, pointing out where the bathroom was and letting me know I could borrow anything. Then she just bustled around, cleaning up stuff that didn't need it.

"It doesn't bother me, you know."

She was cute, all flustered. Her hands always going to tuck the loose strands of hair behind her ears, her cheeks slightly red, but her back was tense and I didn't like it very much. "What doesn't?" she asked softly.

I sighed. "If you're gay. It's fine, Jules. We can still be friends. I mean, we are friends?"

Juliet turned to face me, crossing her arms under her chest. "Are you sure? Because I understand if you're not. You can sleep on the couch. Don't have to talk to me again."

"I'm sure," I answered. She was just a girl, a very pretty girl, but just a girl. It was fine. "Now, can we watch *The Addams Family*? Because I saw it on your shelf and it really has been too long."

The grin that appeared on her face was the brightest I'd seen yet. She nodded once before leaving the room again, and I smiled as I got off the bed to set up the movie. When she came back, she helped me arrange pillows and blankets and killed the lights.

It was still raining. The day had been long and confusing. But at that moment—cuddled up with popcorn, a friend and a good movie—I'd never been happier.

3. Salmon. Caesar Salad. Cheese Potatoes.

My first night at the James' place had been amazing. I'd slept well, woken before Juliet—which wasn't surprising; I was an early riser—and shared my morning cup of coffee with Scott. We chatted easily about him and Lakyn for a while, before his boyfriend eventually came down stairs to sleepily burrow into his arms.

By the time I'd made it back upstairs, Juliet's alarm was going off, but she was refusing to get up. I'd taken her hands and pulled her out of bed and she fought me, but we ended up on the floor in a fit of giggles and it seemed like a good way for her to start her day.

It'd been fun, spending the morning with her. We did our makeup together and she let me raid her closet so I didn't have to wear the same clothes to school for a second day. We ate breakfast on the living room floor with the boys—just cereal, nothing fancy.

It wasn't like I hadn't spent the night at a friend's house before, but it was different at Juliet's. I didn't just feel like a visitor, I felt oddly like I belonged there. The knowledge that I wouldn't be going back immediately was a bit saddening.

As the week came to a close, I didn't see much of Juliet outside of school. The weather cleared up, so there were no more early days off, and everything was back on schedule. Which meant Rick was around to give Juliet a ride, and she lived just far enough out of my way I couldn't really find a reason to give her one myself.

The amount of time I spent trying to think one up proved that I was becoming mildly obsessed with her. It was hard not to. Juliet was *interesting* in a way no one else really had been to me before.

She was finally starting to get used to her new surroundings, which meant she'd make it to class early enough to actually chat with me before disappearing to the back of the classroom. She and Lacey still bumped heads a bit, but she got along really well with Georgia. Kiki didn't really talk to anyone, but even she was growing used to Juliet's presence.

She was crude sometimes, full of dark humor and biting sarcasm, but it was a personality style she managed to pull off without being overbearing. She didn't talk about herself much, not even when it came to her art, despite the fact that she carried a sketchbook everywhere which added some alluring mystery to her persona.

It didn't help either that the better I got to know her, the more attractive she was. I loved the way her eyes crinkled when she smiled, or the way the corners of her mouth turned down when she bit her lower lip in concentration. She ran her hands through her hair often, so she never seemed to bother with really fixing it all that much. With her style, though, messy hair worked. She smiled a lot, laughed rarely, and whenever she caught me looking she never seemed to mind.

I wanted to be around her all the time.

When Friday rolled around, she was the last one at the lunch table; her blond hair was pulled into a messy bun and dark smudges on the tips of her fingers said she'd probably been working on something art-related during her aide period. Lacey and Georgia were in some good-natured argument and Kiki was reading, so it was me that she greeted when she sat. "Hey."

"Hi," I replied, folding my arms over the English essay I was working on. It suddenly didn't seem that important. She noticed the movement, though, her brow furrowing as she picked up her burrito.

"Where's your lunch?" she asked. "I know I'm not *that* late."

Lacey sighed dramatically and abandoned whatever she was talking about to shoot a glare at me. "She *forgot to pack it*. Honestly, Lena, how you survive is beyond me."

Juliet looked mildly amused, but I could see the questions forming. Why didn't I just eat the cafeteria food, or did I want to share her burrito, or something else along those lines.

Before she could get there, I went ahead and answered her. "I'm allergic to beef. The calendar said we were supposed to have pizza today, which I actually kind of like, but apparently something got changed."

"Can you be allergic to beef?" Juliet asked, looking more curious than unbelieving.

"Eh, it's really more of an intolerance," I explained. "Like lactose intolerance, just the meat instead of the milk. People hear *allergy* and tend to remember that better though."

"Most people, not all people," Lacey muttered under her breath, sounding bitter enough that I actually pulled my gaze off Juliet in time to see what had caught her attention. Which happened to be my boyfriend falling into the empty seat at my right.

Lacey smiled so sweetly she could give Oscar-winning actresses a run for their money. "Quinton, long time no see."

Lacey wasn't Quinton's biggest fan, though I'd never really understood why. They hung with the same crowd and were technically in the same circle, but she'd never been fond of him. She claimed his *All American Boy, The Game Before Anything Else* attitude just rubbed her the wrong way. Which I understood, to an extent.

Likewise, Quin didn't like her just because she was a bitch.

"Lacey," he greeted, with a pinched look on his face that disappeared as soon as he swooped in to kiss me on the cheek. "Babe. Please tell me you're not doing that stupid essay over eating?"

"Allergic to beef, Quin," Lacey muttered with more sting in her tone than there really needed to be. "Allergic. To. Beef. Honestly, you should *know* that." She got up then, mumbling

31

something about refilling her drink with a dramatic sigh that was hidden to no one.

"Really?" Quinton asked, then shrugged when I simply nodded. Maybe *that* was why Lacey didn't like him very much. He never did listen to anything I said very well. "I guess it's never come up."

It had, but I didn't bother pointing that out. Besides walking to classes together, I hadn't seen much of Quin lately. We had different schedules and football season had just started. Which was exactly what he was talking about before he caught sight of Juliet. "Who's this?"

The question was directed at me, but Juliet—with obvious humor in her expression—wasn't having that. She leaned across the table and offered her hand just as Lacey returned. "Juliet James." It wasn't a polite introduction, not really. It was an *I am right here, dick* kind of move.

Lacey obviously approved, if the smirk she was wearing was any indication.

I really needed better friends.

Quinton recovered from the interruption with a well-mannered handshake, and then turned to me once more. "Can I steal you away for a moment?"

Lacey was stabbing viciously at her salad, Kiki was reading her book, Georgia just shrugged when I glanced at her, and I very pointedly ignored Juliet. Because I didn't want to go. I didn't want to get up from the table and waste a moment I could have had with *her*. I wanted to be with her over my *boyfriend*. It was ridiculous, and made me feel squirmy, so I nodded and gathered my things.

I knew my relationship was rocky; I wasn't an idiot. Quin and I had started dating in the summer, mostly because we were bored and both wanted someone we could drag to parties. Someone to cuddle up with and share a drink with. A summer fling, like what Danny Zuko and Sandy Olsson had sung about at the start of *Grease*. No one had expected us to carry it on through the school year, but we'd spent so much time together it'd seemed weird to cut it off.

32

"I feel like I haven't seen you in forever," Quinton said once we reached the locker hall. His hands went to my waist, pulling me closer, and I gave him a small smile before his mouth descended on mine.

His lips were chapped, hands worn and well-used even through the cotton of my T-shirt. He kissed too hard, the hair on his upper lip not yet visual enough to get him in trouble but still scratchy enough to make my skin uncomfortable.

These were things I already knew, of course, but he was nice and we generally got along. The little annoyances could be dealt with.

If Juliet could hear my thoughts now, she'd be giving me that *look*. The eyebrows arched, amused expression, slow head shake of a look that meant she was wondering why I was so delusional.

She wouldn't be in this position, I thought, as I slapped Quin's wandering hands away before the bell rang. He didn't let me go until the halls started to fill, then winked as he walked away from me.

I barely resisted the urge to roll my eyes.

My afternoon classes passed without anything horribly interesting happening. I shared most of those classes with Juliet, but given the habit of being at the back of the classroom that she had, I didn't see her much.

Last period we both had free, and I walked in just in time to see Juliet pulling a sketchbook out of her bag. She looked up and shot me a smile. "You all right?"

"Starving," I answered honestly. I'd had breakfast, at least, but not eating lunch was finally getting to me. Juliet made a face, dug through her bag, then came back and tossed me a snack-pack bag of chocolate chip cookies. "Holy shit, you are a goddess."

She chuckled and motioned for me to follow her as she used the side door to go outside. I went with her, happily digging my greedy fingers into the sack of goodness.

"Thank Lakyn," Juliet said as she sat down, balancing her sketchbook on her knees. She flipped to whatever she'd been working on probably all day and pulled a pencil out of the mess

33

of hair on top of her head. "Brat trained me to bring snacks everywhere I go. I would have offered them to you earlier but..."

"I honestly just got hungry," I admitted as I sat next to her, trying my hardest not to talk with my mouth full. "What are you working on anyway? Can I ask you yet? Has that Friendship Achievement been unlocked?"

Juliet glanced up at me through her lashes, seemed to consider it, then sighed and twisted the book around toward me.

The page she was working on was covered in the same model, a pencil outline of a faceless, too-thin girl. Each one was wearing a different outfit, from knee-high socks and an oversized shirt to skinny jeans and a complex jacket. Each one was creative, quirky, in a testament to Juliet's own style. Even without color, I could tell their originality.

"Fashion sketches?"

"You sound surprised," Juliet mused, and I shook my head quickly, but when I looked up she didn't actually seem offended. Just curious about my own reaction.

I shrugged and watched as she pulled the book back to herself. "I just didn't picture you as the fashion type."

"And what is the fashion type?" Juliet asked, the edges of her lips turning up in a smile as she glanced at me again. "Old women in fur coats with their noses held high? You know, *someone* had to design the stuff you buy at Target, not just the clothes on the runway."

"Point taken," I conceded, drawing my knees up and resting my arms on them. "You work on those enough I'm guessing they're not just a hobby?"

Juliet smiled again but this time she didn't look at me, instead focusing on the draw of her pencil against the page. "No, they're not," she finally admitted. "My mother taught me. Kind of, I mean. She liked to sew and liked patterns. And those *What Not to Wear* shows were her favorite. I developed an eye, I guess. Then I had some down time last year. A lot of it. So I just started drawing."

34

I knew there was more to the story, always seemed to be when it came to Juliet, but I didn't push her. She was sharing, and the way her shoulders were set said that one wrong nudge could send her over the edge. So instead, I just nodded. "Makes sense."

She worked in silence for a while, tilting her head from side to side for a better angle, before she asked, "Do you want to come over tomorrow? Scott's bringing movies. He said you and I could join in if we wanted. He and Lakyn have been together long enough they're not really stingy with their date time."

My stomach knotted up, disappointment coloring my otherwise decent emotions. Quinton had been right earlier—we hadn't seen a lot of each other and Saturdays were usually date night. "Um, I have plans. With Quin."

She nodded, opened her mouth to say something, but the bell rang. So instead we climbed to our feet, put our stuff away, and headed out.

I lost track of her in the hallways, but the feeling in my gut stayed.

***

I skipped the game that night. It was only the second in the season and I really wasn't feeling it. By the time Saturday morning rolled around, I had all the details from Lacey so that I could talk and act like I knew what had happened and what role my boyfriend played. I was a horrible human being, but I had my survival methods.

Quinton was usually possessive of our time, so I wasn't surprised at all when he texted early and asked if I wanted to do lunch. I figured he'd keep me for the whole day, but part of me was tempted to text Juliet and ask what time everyone was going to her place so that I could ditch my boyfriend and go see her.

After staring at my phone for several minutes with a blank text message open and Juliet's name glaring at me, I finally decided against the idea. It wasn't really fair of me. Besides, between school and sports, Saturdays were really the only days

Quinton and I got together. I could give him ten or so hours of my undivided, girlfriend attention.

So I put my phone away then hopped up and got ready, washing my face and brushing my teeth before I bounced to my closet to find something to wear. I ended up with a pair of black skinny jeans and a loose gray top. I did my hair up in a few curls, threw on some mascara and lip gloss, then grabbed my cell and walked out of the house.

Quinton drove a big red Ford truck, a newish model that was nice and shiny. He was very proud of it, but I'd always found it obnoxious. He had the door open for me already and was turning down the music as I climbed in. We shared a quick hello kiss, and then he pulled out of the drive.

"We're eating lunch with my parents, I hope you don't mind," Quinton said happily.

I did mind. I minded a whole hell of a lot.

"What are we having?" I asked, trying not to let the disappointment or the heavy sigh I was holding back slip into my words.

He shrugged. "Barbeque chicken and some steamed veggies. No beef, of course. Sound good?" He looked so fucking proud of himself, but it just irritated me.

I didn't care for his parents, mostly because they didn't care for *me*. But more than that, I hadn't expected to have to deal with them. It just made the fact that I wouldn't have had to had I just gone to *Juliet's*.

I wondered what they were doing; probably still sleeping. At least, Lakyn seemed like the kind to sleep until noon; I wasn't really sure about the other two. Scott was a morning person, but Juliet needed time to acclimate to her day. They were definitely still in their pajamas, a thought which made me smile.

I already had my phone out to text her when I remembered who I was with. For the second time in only a few hours, I sighed and closed a blank message, just in time to see Quin's place come into view. It was a big house—modern, well cared for. Had the white picket fence around the back and the garden in the front. Picture perfect.

He came and opened the door for me once he'd parked, kissed my cheek and led me inside. His mother smiled politely at my entrance, but his father barely glanced my way. It was fine—I was used to it. I lifted my hand in a general greeting.

"So Lena, how is school?" Mrs. Barron asked as she busied herself with setting the table. I made idle chitchat as Quinton and I sat, his hand resting on my thigh. His attention was glued to the football game playing on the television in the living room, and I forced myself not to say anything about it.

Conversation was awkward, and his inability to save me from it was starting to grate on my nerves. Just as I almost snapped—a quip about how he already played the damn game all the time, did he really need to watch it too? —my phone vibrated in my pocket. I let go of Quin's hand long enough to pull it out.

Juliet James – 12:42 P.M

what time are you hanging with whatshisface anyway?

I fought back a smile. Unlike Lacey, Juliet hadn't expressed an actual dislike in Quinton, but she also never cared to ask about him either. Besides all that though, it seemed like even from far away, she knew I needed a distraction.

Me – 12:44 P.M

already with him actually

Juliet James – 12:45 P.M

bummer. miss u around here

Me – 12:51 P.M

miss u too. see u soon tho?

Juliet James – 12:53 P.M

course

I wanted so badly to text her back, but the Barrons had rules about phones at the table. No one gave a shit about the TV being on, though. I tucked my phone away without complaint, because I was a good person, and readied myself for an afternoon I wasn't really interested in.

The chicken was dry, the conversation stale, and no matter how much I wanted to ask for more sauce, I knew it'd be considered rude.

It lasted too long and we had to be excused before ever leaving, not that we went far, because Quinton wanted to finish watching the game. When I pointed out that it was recorded on his DVR and he could watch it at any time, he merely gave me a look like I was from outer space.

I settled on the Barrons' living room couch, enough space between me and my boyfriend for Jesus, and put the data plan on my phone to work. I went through Tumblr until I lost half my battery, killed my Instagram feed, beat my high score in Candy Crush, and had an interesting text conversation with Lacey before the game was ever over.

I sighed out of relief, but then Mrs. Barron was talking about some baseball movie that had recently come out, and asking if we wanted to watch it with her. The lie that we had things to do was right on the tip of my tongue, but Quinton was faster and already agreeing.

I sighed, settled down more into the uncomfortable leather of the couch, and opened up Facebook. Lacey was already declaring her newly single status, which happened at least once a month, although the amount of likes she generated made it seem like a

38

new thing. Georgia had uploaded pictures of her daughter at the park, which were adorable. But it was one of Scott's statuses that caught my attention, mostly because he'd posted it to Juliet's timeline via *Out Magazine*.

Scott White *posted on* **Juliet James'** *wall:*

Lol is this right???

Article: *What it's like to kiss a girl for the first time, explained in gifs*

Juliet James *commented***:** lol shut up asshole.

My thumb hovered over the article, heart beating fast like I expected someone to be leaning over my shoulder, but I was sitting apart from the others on the couch against the wall.

I clicked it, my mouth going dry. It wasn't a raunchy article or anything. The gifs were completely innocent, leveling from nervous to excited about the notions of a first kiss.

Oh she's cute. Please be gay. Is she flirting? Definitely flirting. She's leaning towards me. OMG AM I LEANING IN TOO?! This is kissing. We're definitely kissing. She's kissing me back. It's perfect. I love it. I'm going to do this for the rest of my life. Score.

I grinned, couldn't help it. It seemed odd to think about someone as confident as Juliet panicking about her first kiss. I wonder who it had been with, how old she'd been. Had she loved it or had it been horribly awkward like my first kiss?

Juliet looked like the type of person that would be a good kisser herself. She had such a pretty mouth—pouty bottom lip, perfect cupid's bow. Her lips were probably soft; she might even let me softly bite down on one of them. She'd probably twine her fingers in my hair, use them to tilt my head back when she moved closer.

My heart skipped a beat when I realized that at some point I'd stopped thinking about Juliet kissing *someone* and started thinking about her kissing *me*. Fantasizing about it, really.

I nearly jumped out of my seat when my phone buzzed, a text message coming up to cover the article. From Juliet fucking James herself, because *of course.*

Juliet James – 5:08 P.M

Are u suuuuure u cant come????? :(

My heart started up again, too fast, fingers stuttering over my keyboard and how the hell to *reply*. Torn between wanting to see her more than anything else, and realizing my mind had turned down a path that was hard to come back from.

Juliet James – 5:14 P.M

We're about to start dinner! ;) pleeeassseee

I bit my lower lip and glanced at Quinton. He was involved in the movie on the screen, the one I hadn't been paying attention to at all. I'd been bored for hours, and suddenly I missed the boys and Juliet like I was homesick or something.

Me – 5:20 P.M

Lol what are the movie choices for tonight anyway?

Juliet James – 5:22 P.M

Lol the Horror Sluts brought the new Purge, The Quiet Ones, and something called Happy Camp that doesn't look all that happy

Movies I actually wanted to see. With people I actually wanted to see. With food I would probably want to eat, and most likely hot chocolate for dessert. Homemade. My stomach growled and my heart hurt and I didn't even feel guilty.

Me – 5:26 P.M

And what is for dinner?

Juliet James – 5:28 P.M

Salmon. Caesar Salad. Cheese Potatoes.

Juliet James – 5:29 P.M

You can tackle the salad

Juliet James – 5:30 P.M

Don't even act like you don't want to

Juliet James – 5:30 P.M
;)

I barely managed to keep myself from laughing. Already the panic from earlier was streaming out of my veins. I missed her. I missed Scott and Lakyn. The Barrons' place felt small and uncomfortable and I knew I was going to lie before I even did it.

"Quin," I spoke up, shaking my phone slightly. "My mom says I need to go home."

"Oh," Quin said, his brow furrowing slightly. "Can't you stay until the end of the movie?"

"I already asked," I lied again, which was something I wasn't really good at so I hoped he bought it.

He seemed to, because as he paused the film and got up he promised he'd save the ending for me.

I didn't bother telling him not to, just said my goodbyes and went out to the truck. I bit the inside of my cheek to keep from grinning and sent Juliet one last text.

Me – 5:51 PM

be there in half an hour. don't start without me. that salad is mine xoxo

I was a terrible person, but I couldn't find it in myself to care.

4. "You like her, don't you?"

Juliet liked pet names, she used them with everyone. Each time someone ended up with a pet name, it was like Juliet marked her territory: This Person Here Is My Friend, See The Pet Name?

Lacey was *honey*, and it was mostly used sarcastically, though not always. Georgia was *darling*, and likewise Georgia called Juliet the same—they'd stopped using their real names all together. Kiki was *sweetheart*, every once in a while. Just about everyone was *hun*.

As for me, I was *babe*. *Baby*, occasionally.

No one else was. Just me.

It was not helping my obsession with her. I tried to convince myself that *everyone* got a pet name, but for some reason mine just felt *different*. Important.

Also, I couldn't stop looking at her mouth.

Or imagining her mouth.

On my mouth.

It was getting out of hand, really.

I was slacking in my classes all week because I was too strung up in my thoughts. I didn't really understand why, either. I had *feelings*, where Juliet was concerned, feelings that I was tempted to label as a crush. But honestly I wasn't even sure if that was the right word.

It wasn't a word I really understood, for one thing. Crushing, *liking*, dating in general wasn't something that had ever crossed my mind much. I hadn't even considered changing my Single

Status until the summer before Junior year, and only then because parties and whatnot had started becoming a "couple activity" and I'd been lonely. Lacey had always been boy crazy, I just hadn't really cared.

I was attractive, though. In with the popular crowd and I'd never had a hard time getting someone's attention for the night, or the week, or, in Quin's case, a couple of months. But I'd never really been much of a *dater*. There had been Marcus O'Malley for about two months last year, but we had really just hung out more than anything. And then Quinton, who really deserved something different than me. I'd never really been in a relationship because I *wanted* to be, but because it was convenient.

So sure, I played in the big leagues. I got the cute guys. The popular ones, the football players. The one's everyone else wanted, so I had to be lucky? Had to be doing something right.

But I'd never been captivated by *them* the way that I was captivated by Juliet. I cared too much about the way she ran her fingers through her hair, the way her head tipped back when she laughed, the pale skin of her throat when it was exposed, the way her favorite bra was lined in lace and sometimes her shirt fell just a little too far down.

I hadn't known anyone gay before Scott and Lakyn. Lacey had a gay cousin in his fifties, down the line and twice removed or something, but he was the closest I could think of off the top of my head. It wasn't something really talked about in my house. But sure, I could think back on some of my friends when I was younger and realized I probably cared *too* much. Wanted to touch their hair too often or kiss them on the cheek, even when we reached the age that it was sort of awkward.

But the draw I felt to Juliet was a different beast altogether. It was chemical. All consuming. Twisting my thoughts around and making my heart beat in weird patterns. I hated it.

"Hey!" Juliet leaned down on my desk in French that Friday, head tilted, amused smirk touching her lips as she watched me nearly fall out of my seat in surprise. "Daydreaming again, babe? Really?"

44

"Shut up," I muttered, managing to regain my composure somehow. Juliet still looked far too amused, and far too fucking beautiful. "What do you want, anyway?"

"Feisty," she muttered, but not leaving. "I just wanted to ask if you wanted to go to the Bridgewood game tonight?"

It took me longer than I'd like to admit to realize she was talking about football. I was about to state that I didn't even watch my own *boyfriend* play—why would I want to go to another school's game? I got an exasperated look for my trouble.

"Babe, chill. Quin's got his away game anyway, right? Besides, Scott's playing. There's decent hot chocolate, and you can hang at my place later."

I didn't really have a reason to say no, other than that I didn't particularly enjoy football. Grant's game was far enough away that all the important people had left after lunch and wouldn't be back until either late Saturday or early Sunday. Either way, it was not a date weekend. "All right."

Juliet grinned, all smug triumph. "Awesome. Take me home later? I mean, if you don't have anything to do. My place is closer anyway."

"Sure," I agreed, and she smiled again before the teacher came in and called class to attention.

She stayed in a good mood through the class, writing her answers down where I could see them, which wasn't productive to my learning but kept me from failing the paper. I'd missed out on most of the week's lesson, given my inability to focus. She owed me a couple of fucking grades since it was her perfect face that was distracting me anyway.

We didn't have a big assignment in art and Juliet claimed she'd hit a creative block, so she spent the period painting my nails for me. She only had black polish, of course, but I couldn't find it in myself to care. Her fingers were soft, and my hand fit so perfectly in hers, and it was almost more distracting than just looking at her. She was focused, lashes dusting her cheek, warm breath ghosting over my nails to dry the paint.

I hated her.

At least in theory.

The practice wasn't working out too well.

Once school got out, we hit up one of the local fast food joints for a snack, then headed to her place and spent a few hours on homework. Juliet and I made the fanciest sandwiches I'd ever seen for her brother and father's dinner, then washed up and left for the game.

We were early, but I didn't mind. Bridgewood Academy was a nice school, well-funded, known for prestige and generations worth of wealthy families. It wasn't somewhere I'd been often, even if it was nearby.

You had to pay to get in, and I shot Juliet a nasty look over it. She shrugged and passed a twenty through the window before I could really argue about it.

"I love how I just had to pay to watch a game I don't even like," I complained as I searched for a parking spot.

Juliet snickered. "That's why I paid, babe."

I gave her the finger, which she skillfully ignored. A moment later, we had a place to leave the car and were climbing out to be met with loud chants and cold weather. The noise on Bridgewood's side was obviously louder, and alone clued into where the home team was.

"You used to go to school here, huh?" I asked as Juliet led the way, returning more than one polite wave from the loitering teenagers. I'd never really thought about where she'd gone before Grant, but given that it was Lakyn's school, it made sense.

She nodded as an answer, offering no more information, before approaching a very nice looking concession stand. It smelled fairly decent, and I had to admit I was looking forward to trying something. Lacey always raved about Bridgewood's game night foods.

"Lena! You're here!" I grinned at the sound of Lakyn's voice and looked behind me a few rows to see him walking over with a guy twice his size. His friend had tan skin, dark curly hair, and a crooked smile; he was dressed casually in jeans and a football jersey, though his right arm was done up in a sling. Lakyn was still in his slightly oversized school uniform, although his shirt was untucked, his blazer was missing, a few buttons were undone.

"'Sup, dude?" I replied, holding my fist out for a quick bump when they got close enough. In the past few weeks, I'd managed to win his approval, which was oddly gratifying.

He shrugged at me before dropping his chin on Juliet's shoulder to stare at the menu.

"Hey Matt," Juliet greeted when she noticed we had company. He smiled at her, then glanced my way. "This is Lena, a friend from school."

Matt nodded in greeting. "A Grant High survivor, huh?"

"It's harder to survive this hellhole, trust me," Juliet grumbled as she stepped up to the counter. The girl working glared, but when Juliet just raised her eyebrows daringly, she wasn't quite brave enough to actually say anything. "I'll take two hamburgers—one with cheese but nothing else—a coke, sprite, and some chips."

She gestured for me to go next and I ordered a chicken fajita burrito with a Dr. Pepper, which were handed over pretty quickly. Matt got something himself, and then we headed to the stands together.

Juliet climbed all the way to the top and I followed, wondering what she was thinking as it only proceeded to get colder and colder. She stopped at the corner and nodded to me, so I sat down at the edge.

And that was when I got it. While it was still freezing, the double walls on this side of the stands effectively blocked the cold wind. I smiled thankfully at her and she just grinned in response, sitting beside me.

Lakyn hopped across the seats and fell to the row in front of me, leaning and resting his back on my legs. I didn't mind, he helped keep me warm and honestly I was just glad he liked me. I had a feeling not a lot of people were lucky enough to get to call him a friend. Matt sat next to him, and it became obvious pretty quickly who the *real* fans were. Lakyn really got into it, and

Juliet knew enough to argue with him on occasion. Matt zoned out at some point, occasionally forgetting he was actually eating something.

The darker it got, the colder it got, and the wind began to pick up. I was freezing, visibly, but trying to ignore the way my shoulders shook and how I absentmindedly ended up huddled against Juliet's side. I still didn't understand much about what was going on, but it didn't matter, really. I knew we were winning by about ten points or so when, suddenly, it was halftime.

Juliet took Lakyn with her to go get hot chocolates, and Matt saved our place while I went to my car to get the blanket I kept in the back. It had been left over from summer, and I'd never actually been so grateful for my laziness.

I made it back in time to meet Lakyn and Juliet, and we walked back up to our seats together.

Halfway, though, I could practically smell trouble as we met another group. I typically wasn't a judgmental person, but every high school seemed to have *those* girls. The ones who pushed the rules of their school dress code at events and ignored the weather in favor of being *noticed.*

Bridgewood's brand came in the form of three girls. The first, and obviously the leader, had perfect makeup and beautiful brown hair that was pulled back in an elaborate looking ponytail. The girls with her were bottle blondes, wearing dark lipstick and dramatic pouts of annoyance.

People at Grant called Lacey "Queen Bitch" on occasion, so I felt bad labeling Bridgewood's girl the same. Instead, I decided to label her Skank Princess.

Her gaze focused on me, one hand rested on her propped hip, and she smirked slowly. "Well, well, who is this?"

"No one," Juliet answered, and although her tone was bored, I could tell she was ready for a fight. Which was fantastic, really. I was friends with Lacey, I could handle this. No problem.

Skank Princess didn't even bother glancing Juliet's way. "New friend?" she guessed, tilting her head like she was considering something. "I'd run for the hills, if I was you. But Juliet does have her perks. She won't try to steal your boyfriend, at least."

Thing One and Thing Two snickered like that was the funniest joke they'd heard all day. Their leader grinned, obviously pleased with herself, and side stepped to block Juliet's way when she tried to move around her. I wondered briefly if she was ready to throw down as much as her expression claimed.

"That one might, though," Thing One stated, and I realized that she was looking over my shoulder at Lakyn. "He likes to get his greasy little hands on things that don't belong to him."

Lakyn snorted, slid his free hand in mine, and gave it a tug as he started up the stairs. Thing One scrunched up her nose and leaned away from him when he did so.

Juliet, on the other hand, was still facing off Skank Princess. Long enough that the brunette actually started to get uncomfortable.

"What?" she snapped. "See something you like, lesbo?"

Juliet smiled slowly. "I was just wondering how you get a head that big so far up your ass."

"Lube," Lakyn answered, and I choked on pure air.

Thing One and Thing Two looked scandalized, and Skank Princess honestly seemed like she might explode.

"Enjoy the game, Claire," Juliet said with a smile before she followed us. Matt was standing by the time we made it to our seats, good arm folded under his bad one, jaw clenched.

"What was that all about?" he asked.

"Claire was being a bitch. Nothing new," Juliet replied

"Yeah?" Matt asked. "Did you tell her where to stick it?"

"Better, Jules asked her how she got her head up her ass. Lakyn did the honors of answering." I grinned as I sat. Juliet joined me, and somehow we all ended up where we'd started. Although Lakyn kindly sat against one of my legs and one of Juliet's so we could all share the blanket I'd tossed over our shoulders.

I had never really been much of a tactile person, but Juliet was comfortable to be around. I didn't mind being pressed against her from shoulder to ankle. I loved the warmth radiating off her body and, once I finished my hot chocolate, it was all too easy to rest my head against her shoulder. Lakyn's warm weight was comfortable too, something that felt safe and friendly, though not quite the same as it was with Juliet. I didn't mind Lakyn leaning against me, but unlike him, I didn't want Juliet to move.

The ending of the game was fairly interesting, if only because Bridgewood was so far ahead they were mostly just playing with the other team. It was probably the most enjoyable football game I'd ever been to, despite the cold weather. We stood and cheered with the others when the game finally ended, and then Lakyn was gone, racing down the steps with Matt.

Juliet and I hung back to gather up the trash and fold the blanket. She smiled at me, shaking her head slightly. "I told you that you'd have fun."

I rolled my eyes fondly. "Yeah, all right, it wasn't awful." She stuck her tongue out at me and without thinking I popped off, "Don't stick it out unless you're gonna share it."

Juliet stopped dead in her tracks, expression shocked, and my heart slammed against my chest so hard I thought it might be trying to break out. In a weak attempt to cover, I started backtracking. "What? It's a thing. A saying. You know…funny?"

She stared at me for a moment, but the crowd in the bleachers was working on getting down the stairs and we were swept in it before she could reply. Which was fine by me. Because awkward.

Scott was still with the rest of the team changing, so we hung out for a while on the track and did some people watching. When Juliet spoke again, she moved straight past my earlier slip and told me a few stories about the people she used to go to school with, ranging from interesting to scandalous.

"Everyone seems to know you," I mentioned after I watched her wave to a few more people. Everyone was polite, but not exactly friendly, and it seemed wrong to ask her about her old friends, somehow.

Juliet shrugged. "It's a small school; everyone knows everyone. But the people I used to hang out with aren't really the school spirit types."

There was a story behind that, I could tell, but then she was reaching out to brush my hair out of my face and I was smiling and nothing else really seemed to matter. She smiled back, then something over my shoulder seemed to catch her attention. "Ah, there's Scott."

When I turned around, Scott was walking toward us, carrying Lakyn on his back. His hair was plastered to his forehead—there was dirt on the side of his neck, and the closer he got, the more he definitely still smelled like sweat. Lakyn didn't seem to mind, but my nose scrunched up.

"Lena! You came!"

"Hey," I greeted with a grin. "Good game!"

Scott grinned widely as he glanced down at me, mouth quirking into a half smirk. "Did you understand any of it?"

Juliet covered her mouth to keep from laughing out loud, but I ignored her and indignantly placed my hands on my hips. "I know that you scored the laziest winning touchdown I've ever seen!"

"Good girl," he said with a wink, before tilting his head back so he could regard his boyfriend. "What are we doing tonight?"

"Mm," Lakyn leaned forward, dark hair falling to cover half his face. "I'm thinking Call of Duty."

"Deal. I just need some damn food on the way back to your place. Girls, want to join?"

Juliet glanced at me, and when I nodded she gave the affirmative before we split off. The boys headed for Scott's jeep and Juliet went back to my car with me. Given our delayed exit we didn't have a long trail of cars to wait after, so it was fairly easy to get out of the parking lot.

"So Grant's better, huh?" I asked

Juliet leaned back in her seat, small smile on her face. I wondered briefly why she'd left to begin with. Lakyn still went to Bridgewood, so there was a reason why Juliet didn't, but now didn't seem the time to ask.

"Well, yeah. Also, I mean, you're there."

I grinned before I could even really process what she'd said, but once I did something fluttered low in my stomach.

Juliet leaned over the small space between us, her head dropping down comfortably on my shoulder, and perhaps for the first time, I realized I was in trouble.

***

September bled into October without anyone really noticing. Likewise, no one seemed to take notice in my growing obsession with Juliet James. Georgia and Kiki honestly didn't care, but Lacey's schedule stayed so busy with cheer stuff that she didn't have *time* to care.

Which made it even easier for me to spend all my time with her. Juliet was easy going, happy to pack up a bag of art supplies and chill at the duck pond when the weather was nice, or go see whatever movie was out just for the hell of it. She liked eating just about anywhere and was always game for impromptu dancing parties on some obscure back road. And, of course, there was always cooking and Netflix nights at her place, whenever I wanted to join in.

I found myself just gravitating toward her. The need to be anywhere she was, to have my shoulder pressed against hers, or our feet knocking together under the table. I wanted to talk to her about anything and everything and…

And I was starting to feel slightly guilty about it, mostly because of how much I was blowing my own *boyfriend* off to spend time with her. Using excuses ranging from *homework* to *plans we've had for weeks.* So by the second weekend of the month, I decided to take a Juliet break. It also happened to be a Grant away game so I didn't have to see Quinton either, but that wasn't the main point.

The main point was that I spent my Saturday in bed binge watching *The Walking Dead* until well past two in the morning. Which was when Scott called.

I thought about ignoring it, if only because I was on a Juliet Break, but it hit me that if he was *calling*, something might actually be wrong.

"Scott?" I answered cautiously.

"Lena, did I wake you?" Scott asked, sounding relieved. His words were slurred, but what got me was the way he giggled afterwards. "You know, 'cause it's pretty late."

I sighed and pinched the bridge of my nose with my free hand before I pushed myself into a sitting position. "Scott are you drunk?" At least nothing was wrong; no one was in the hospital or anything. Yet.

"No!" he replied quickly, defensively. Then he cracked up laughing again. "Okay, maybe just a bit. Um, are you busy?"

I was already out of my bed, grabbing an oversized Grant High sweatshirt to pull on and my winter boots. No way was I getting out of my pajamas this late, but it was also cold out. "Where are you?" I asked, already knowing where this conversation was going. I'd had enough calls from Lacey over the years that I could figure it out.

Scott rattled off an address between giggles, one I recognized that would be around the Bridgewood area. It was a residential address, so I guessed house party. Probably celebrating for the sake of celebrating.

"All right, give me half an hour and stay put. And Scott? Drink some water."

"Yes ma'am!" he answered, and I could actually see him saluting me. I shook my head and hung up without another word, then shoved my phone in my sweater pocket and grabbed my keys on the way out of the house.

Ever since I'd gotten a car my parents had made it clear they didn't mind if I went to pick up a drunk friend, but I had to leave a note just to let them know where I was, so I did before heading out.

Because it was so late, the traffic was light and I made it to Scott in half the time it would normally take. I'd been right when I guessed house party—the music was playing loud enough to hear it as soon as I turned onto the street. The three story house where the party was taking place had all the windows and doors open, streamers and toilet paper decorating both the house and the front lawn. Along with many, *many* red solo cups.

Despite being a fancy neighborhood, none of the neighbors really seemed to mind. The cops hadn't been called yet, anyway. Scott was sitting on the sidewalk outside, a cup clutched in his hand, wide grin on his face. He waved me down when he saw me and I shook my head before I pulled up to the curb next to him.

I watched him shakily get to his feet as I leaned over and pushed the passenger door open for him. "Do *not* bring that cup in here," I ordered.

Scott's brows wrinkled in confusion before he glanced down at the cup he was holding, then he shrugged and dropped it. It bounced against the ground, thankfully empty. I thought about telling him not to litter in front of someone's *house*, but one more cup really wasn't going to hurt anything at this point.

"Thanks, Lena," Scott finally said when he managed to get himself into the passenger seat and shut the door. His movements were slow and precise, obviously aware of how drunk he was and trying not to be. He managed to get his seatbelt on, even if it took a few tries. "Didn't think I should drive."

"Good boy," I praised, honestly proud of him. He sounded better now than he had on the phone—his words less slurred— but he definitely wouldn't have been okay to drive. "Where do you live?"

Scott gave me another address and then started talking my ear off. About everything. His day, his friend Zachary, who had thrown the party in the first place just because his parents were out of town. He talked about football, and then told me about his day again, and then asked me why I was wearing my pajamas.

It didn't surprise me that Scott was a happy drunk—he was a happy person, it was just amplified and sloppy now.

"Why aren't you with Lakyn?" I finally asked, realizing I'd never actually seen the two without each other since I'd met them.

Scott's head lulled on the back of his seat as he glanced at me. "We *can* spend time without each other, Len."

I held up my hands in mock surrender for just a second before placing them back on the wheel.

Scott grinned, then said, "I love him, you know? More than anything in the world. I love him. I always have."

"What, like love at first sight?" I asked before I could stop myself.

"No," Scott slurred, and shook his head until it seemed to make him dizzy. "No, it wasn't like that. It was more like one day I just knew. I just woke up and I was like...*this*. This is it. This is what everyone is looking for."

I couldn't help but smile, the corners of my mouth refusing to behave and stay down. The boys were affectionate, especially at home—it wasn't hard to see that they *really* cared for each other. But I knew Scott meant it. Every word.

"I'm going to marry him one day," Scott decided. "I don't care if it's legal or not, we're going to get dressed up and say vows and kiss in front of *everyone* and it's going to be great. We'll get officiated by a flying spaghetti monster if we have to."

"Flying spaghetti monster?" I asked, wondering if he'd fallen and hit his head at some point in his drunken stupor.

Scott nodded earnestly. "Pastaferin...Pastafarin...Pastafarianism! It's a real thing. Look it up."

"Oh, I'm sure it is," I mumbled, and turned down the street leading to Scott's house. He pointed it out for me—an impressive, large white two-story building. It was in perfect shape, one of those houses that screamed money and a need to show off.

"I'm really drunk, Len," Scott muttered as he undid his seatbelt, hand resting on his stomach. He did look a little green, but when I asked him if he needed to throw up, he just shook his head. Said he already had and he just wanted to sleep.

I walked with him to the front door anyway, watched him pull his keys free from his pocket and struggle to try and unlock the door before he finally turned a puppy dog look on me. I shook my head at him and opened the door, then let him lead the way inside.

The house was dark and quiet, and I prayed his parents were either out of town or deep sleepers.

I didn't bother to look around, just kept a hand on Scott's arm to make sure he didn't walk straight into a wall. He made it to his bedroom okay, flicked on the lights, then fell face-first into his bed with a groan.

"I regret everything."

His bedroom was way too spotless to belong to a teenage boy. It was simple and large, but there was nothing in it that really said *lived in*. Except maybe a few clothes that weren't quite in the hamper, and a backpack dropped by the door. The walls looked more like a shrine than anything he'd decorated himself—pictures and awards and banners. There was a TV and a gaming system that looked like it hadn't been touched in a while, movies and a few books. His bed wasn't made, but even it was simple—navy comforter and white sheets.

It didn't look like Scott. Wasn't covered in *his* things. He wasn't even a tidy person, which I knew because at the James' house, it was always easy to find Scott by following the trail of his shit. The only thing that looked like something he owned was a picture on his nightstand. It was him and Lakyn, innocently sitting side by side, not even touching but at least smiling. Mr. James had a picture of Scott kissing Lakyn's cheek hanging in his *hallway*, but Scott didn't even have one like that in his *bedroom*.

Scott grumbled something and the sound of his voice snapped me out of my thoughts. He'd somehow managed to kick his shoes off, but he was having a lot more trouble with his pants. Part of me thought I should look away, but instead I just moved forward to help him. He smiled gratefully, then somehow managed to wiggle under his covers and land his head on his pillow.

"Lena?" Scott asked with a yawn. "You like her, don't you?"

"Who?" I asked, since we hadn't actually been talking about anything beforehand.

"Juliet," he answered. "You like her."

I shrugged. "Of course I do. She's my friend."

Scott had a bathroom that connected with the corner of his room, and inside I found a cup that seemed clean, so I filled it with water. The medicine cabinet behind the counter had Advil, so I got a couple before going back to him.

He regarded me tiredly. "You know what I mean. You *like* her. You like her like she likes you. It's okay, you know, if you do. We can help you—teach you how to be gay."

He was laughing softly into his pillow, but I was too busy trying to control the pounding of my heart to really mind. I dropped the pills and the water on the table beside Lakyn's picture and decided not to deal with it right now. "Get some sleep, hun."

Scott nodded and curled up. "Thanks again, Lena."

"You're welcome." I turned the lights out when I left his room and made sure to lock his front door on the way out of his house.

It was three am by the time I finally started driving home, but I barely noticed how long it took because my mind was working like a broken record, stuck on a train of thought Scott hadn't really put there, but mostly called attention to.

You like her, don't you?

5. Fucking Zombies

I smiled to myself as I gently drew my fingers down Juliet's arm, loving the feeling of her soft skin under my fingertips. God, she was so perfect, too perfect to even be real. She still looked like she was sleeping, bundled in blankets, the sunlight streaming in and lighting up her bright hair. But the small smile on her face said she was awake, even if her eyes weren't open.

I pressed my face into her shoulder, inhaling the perfect scent of coconut and honey that lingered on her after a shower.

That broke the spell, and Juliet chuckled before I felt her fingers slide through my hair. She stayed there for a moment, then twisted in my arms until we were level, her touch moving from my hair to across my collarbone. "Are you awake?" she asked softly, and I smiled before tilting my face up just enough to look at her.

"Yeah," I whispered, and her lips pressed against mine in response. I didn't question it, didn't even think it wasn't normal. Instead, I just relaxed, melting into her touch.

Waking up was just cruel *for so many reasons*.

It'd been almost a week and Scott's question not only refused to leave my head, but manifested into fucking dreams. Fantastic.

I was grumpy by the time I got to school, which Lacey thought was hysterical if only because it made me bitchier than usual and more likely to snap at people. It didn't help that Juliet looked fantastic. I had already been obsessed with her, but Scott's voice in the back of my mind was only making it worse.

I liked boys—there wasn't a question about it. By stereotypical gender norms I was attracted to sharp jawlines and broad shoulders, chiseled chests and displays of strength. I liked the idea of spending time with someone who had a different view on the world, a different thought process. Male perspective.

But when I looked at Juliet, I liked the gentle curves of her body and the soft touch of her hands. I liked knowing that we thought the same, understood all things *girl* that boys often grumbled about not getting. There was a draw to her, a need to be around her *all the time*. I *wanted* to know what she felt like. What she tasted like.

At some point, maybe even the first time I saw her, I'd stopped thinking *wow, she's a pretty girl* and just started thinking *wow, she's pretty. I want her.* And it had happened without me even realizing it.

She smiled at me when I sat across from her at lunch, and all I really wanted to do was run my thumb across her lower lip. Ask her to be mine. Before I could even take the time to tell my subconscious to shut its *whore mouth*, the normally empty chair beside me pulled out and Quinton sat down.

Lacey rolled her eyes, Juliet's nose wrinkled, and I sighed. Georgia and Kiki took no notice of him whatsoever.

How had I ignored for so long that my friends disliked my boyfriend so much?

"Hey Quin," I greeted, doing my best not to lean away from him when he pressed a kiss to my cheek. His breath smelled like cafeteria pizza and it wasn't the most appetizing. "What's up?"

"Not much. I was thinking we could go out tonight. It's been a while." He smiled hopefully, and I felt another sigh coming on. He wasn't wrong, it had been a while, and it was an off week so he didn't have a game or anything.

But that also meant Lacey was free, and she'd asked me weeks ago for her attention.

"Uh, no, she can't. She's hanging out with me tonight, I got there first," Lacey chimed in, her expression clearly daring Quin for a fight.

Juliet was still paying attention to her food, but I could tell that she was half listening, probably ready to put in that I was hanging out with her on Saturday.

"Well, she's my girlfriend, Lace, not yours," Quinton pointed out. "In fact, if you swing that way, you're wasting your time. You could try with that one though." His head nodded toward Juliet and I felt my mouth drop. It wasn't like she'd walked around proclaiming to be straight or anything, but I also hadn't seen anyone call her out on being a lesbian either. Until now.

Juliet's eyebrows arched in that dangerous way they did right before she spat out a comeback, but Quinton just kept going. "Yeah, I know about you. The Bridgewood boys talk. So, if you two could just get together and leave my girlfriend alone, that would be great."

"Quin, I don't like your tone right now," I jumped in, before either of my more assertive friends could decide this was something they wanted to fight about. He wasn't joking around, and despite the fact that it was his suggestion, he sounded like the idea disgusted him. "What's your problem?"

"What's *my* problem?" Quinton asked, returning his attention to me. "My problem is that I haven't seen my *girlfriend* in forever. Now come on, you're going to eat lunch with me." Quinton's attempt at a dramatic exit would have been a lot easier if I ate cafeteria food and he could have just grabbed my tray and stalked off with it. Instead, his hands fumbled with my sandwich, chips, fruit bowl, and then my drink, which Lacey snatched before he could grab.

"I'm sorry, Quin, but I think I missed the part where you owned her?" Lacey's voice was overly sweet—a tone that everyone knew meant business—and Georgia let out a low whistle even though she was still trying to pretend like she wasn't listening. "My girl can be, sit, and eat wherever she wants, so fuck off."

"Well she wants to be with *me*," Quinton shot back. "So you fuck off!"

When I took a moment to actually look at him, I didn't recognize him. The Quinton I knew was light and easy, up to go on a road trip at one in the morning and down for jumping off a roof into a pool. Which was stupid, but fun—the reason why we'd gotten together in the first place. But this boy was desperate, and I'd turned him into that.

He and Lacey were arguing so much that she was standing up now, her hands flying angrily as she yelled, and across the table from me Juliet's expression was mildly concerned. I could tell it wasn't so much for the situation, but *for* me.

Lacey was taking her earrings off. Shit.

"Lacey! Lacey, stop!" I pushed between them as I stood and took my food back from my boyfriend. They both looked confused, but I placed the items on the table and nodded. "I'll go with him."

Quinton's grin was triumphant, and his shoulders relaxed. I readied myself for a conversation I knew had been coming for a while, but one I didn't want to have.

Even more than that, though, I didn't want to spend one more date with him, bored out of my mind, texting the person I really wanted to be with.

"Come on," I murmured as I led him out of the cafeteria and down to the closest empty hallway.

We could still hear the chatter of the lunchroom, but we were alone for the most part. He was confused, but I didn't let that bother me.

"Quin…we really need to talk."

"You're breaking up with me."

It wasn't a question, but the answer was still yes. Part of me felt like I was doing it for Juliet, but I wasn't. I wasn't even sure where I was with *all that*, but what I was sure about was that I had to do this. I had to do this for me, because we weren't right together—I'd known that for a while, and it just wasn't fair. Juliet or no Juliet, this had to happen.

He realized it quicker than I'd thought he would, and when I didn't deny his accusation, he ran his hands through his hair and laughed as he turned away from me so he could pace. "That's fucking great, Lena. Just fantastic. You don't see me for weeks, and then this? What, were you hoping that I would just forget about you the longer you stayed away?"

I sighed deeply and folded my arms under my chest. "I didn't want to do this at school."

"Then when, huh?" he asked. "Next weekend is an away game, so the weekend after that? Or do you have plans with your dyke friends then, too?"

"Okay, *that*, Quin! That's a *problem*. You just can't say shit like that about my friends! So what if Juliet's gay? So what if any of them are? What does it matter? Don't be cruel just because you're upset."

I went to walk past him, and his hand shot out to catch my arm. It wasn't rough, so I stopped, looked over my shoulder at him.

"When did we stop having fun together?" he asked.

I sighed. "Summer flings are called that for a reason. And we should have left ours behind with the good memories."

He let me walk away after that, and I took the moment to shake my bad mood off my shoulders. I only had half a day of school left, and it was the fun classes, then an afternoon with Lacey. Which meant a do-it-yourself spa day and probably some wine. Not a bad post break-up night.

"You okay, babe?" Juliet asked when I sat back down, and I shot her a smile and nodded.

There was a silence before Georgia took it upon herself to bring up a topic we could all talk about, and then lunch went on as normal.

***

My weekend ended up being fantastic. Lacey and I had a brilliant time painting our nails and making our skin as soft as we could. We put on facemasks and sipped amusingly at wine while we watched old episodes of *Grey's Anatomy* and got lost in someone else's problems for once.

I spent most of Saturday with Juliet, and because the weather was nice, we packed up some food, blankets and our sketchbooks to take to the park. We drew, and threw food at each other, and laughed. She let me go through her new designs and didn't chastise me for changing art styles when she flipped through my own book.

By Monday, the fact that Halloween was coming was undisputable. Decorations lined the hallways, people were talking about their costumes and I was in love with it all. Lacey, however, was stressed to the max. Which generally happened around any holiday.

"Zombies," she said at lunch time, dropping into her seat without any actual food. "They chose fucking zombies. We only have a week to prepare and— zombies!"

Georgia shrugged. "Could be worse," she mentioned, cutting up her meat-patty-thing that the school was trying to pass off as food. "They could have chosen to just be cheerleaders."

Lacey flipped her off, then stole one of my carrots to angrily munch on. I gave her a mildly amused look but didn't bother to stop her. "So, what are you going to do?"

She sighed and shrugged. "We all still fit into last year's uniforms so I guess we'll just splatter some blood on them and be done."

"Don't you guys get, like, your own costume committee though?" I asked, only because they usually did.

"*No*," Lacey grumbled. "Because that bitch Violet Whatsherface didn't get our name on the list soon enough. So we have to make them ourselves. And they chose *zombies*."

I winced, but before I could offer my condolences, Juliet spoke up, "What the hell are you talking about?"

"Grant Scaregrounds," Kiki supplied, not looking up from her Algebra homework.

Grant was a typically small city, but that had never kept anyone from celebrating to the best of their abilities. Holidays were usually a pretty big deal.

Scaregrounds was a voluntarily run haunted house, and the Halloween destination for the surrounding towns. Even Bridgewood often donated money rather than try to pull something off themselves. There was a building on the outskirts of town that often held temporary events, like festivals or family reunions, and for most of October and the first weekend of November it served as the Halloween attraction.

"The art and theatre kids get extra credit if they volunteer their skills or talent," I explained, then nodded toward Lacey, "as do the school leaders."

Really, everyone did, but the event was particularly beneficial for those of us that could list it on our college applications.

Juliet nodded. "Right, I remember seeing the sign up for it in class. We get to work on it during school, don't we?"

"Yeah, if you do it for an extracurricular," Lacey answered, sighing. "Which, technically, I don't because it would cut into my gym time."

Juliet hummed and looked thoughtful. "Well, if you already have the suits and don't mind them getting ruined, I could make something."

"Not by yourself," Lacey argued, but I could tell that she was interested. She wasn't against the idea of zombies; she was against the idea of a poorly done costume, and Juliet was offering her an out. "It's the other school as well, and most of the football players."

Juliet shrugged and glanced at me. "Have you signed up for anything yet?"

"Nah," I replied, shaking my head. "Couldn't decide what I wanted to do, probably just going to help paint sets and stuff."

"Or you could help me?" She flashed me a hopeful grin, and when Lacey threw in a pleading look of her own, there was really no way I could say no.

The cheerleaders brought us their suits and old football jerseys that afternoon, and by Wednesday, each of the guys had donated a pair of jeans they didn't mind ruining for the cause. Lee, the other high school, didn't deliver theirs until Thursday, but it was the complete bulk at least. Juliet and I had a good two hours to spend on them, thanks to our free period following art, and actually it was more fun than I could really remember having at school.

It didn't hurt that working on the costumes meant I got to watch Juliet in her element. Making them made something in her glow. She was super creative, and found a new wave of excitement each time she thought of a different design. She covered the uniforms in dirt, rips and tears. She splattered them with blood and stretched them out. I watched her face light up, watched her eyes shine, with each new idea.

By the time we were done, the Zombie Athlete Line was perfect—much better than anyone with our given budget and time frame could have expected. Lacey was absolutely in love with them, and gushed for at least thirty minutes while she took photos with her phone to send to the rest of the squad. Juliet just smiled, seemingly proud of herself.

***

I spent Halloween weekend at the James', along with Scott, who was apparently a permanent fixture in the house. Lakyn was as much of a Halloween enthusiast as I was, and we spent most of Friday in the kitchen baking an excess of pumpkin flavored treats.

We decided to hit up Scaregrounds on Saturday, which was a busier time but also meant higher energy. The boys had easy costumes but still somehow managed to be absolutely adorable. Lakyn had a Spiderman hoodie paired with some dark skinny jeans and knee high converse. Scott, because they were *that couple*, was in a Deadpool hoodie, dark jeans and lazily laced boots.

It was, without a doubt, my favorite thing ever.

Juliet, on the other hand, had to be complicated and demanded my help in achieving it. She was awful at sitting still while I did her skull face makeup, and got called a *little bitch* more than once, but it didn't seem to bother her too much. In the end, she looked amazing in her mesh gown with her messy blond hair. Very skeletal indeed.

I, myself, was a vampire with a red and black corset dress, smoky eyeshadow and pop-on fangs—even a blood trail at the corner of my mouth, thanks to makeup and skills. As a group, we looked good, and we were definitely excited.

Scaregrounds was the type of place that started the creepy as soon as it could, with signs lining the entrance telling guests to *go, run, turn around, save yourselves*. We were all practically buzzing even as we stood in line, and Scott kept a grip on Lakyn's hand just to keep him from getting ahead of himself.

Juliet shot a smile my way when it was finally our turn. Lacey was behind the counter and completely killing her zombie look. Her hair was pulled back in a messy ponytail, her makeup dirty and bloody, but she somehow still looked good. "Hey guys," she greeted. "What can I get ya?"

"Four Monster Passes," Scott answered, and ignored my attempts at saying I could pay by pressing a hand on my face and pushing me out of the way. Juliet caught me, even though she looked mildly annoyed about having to do so.

Lacey snapped a bracelet on each of our wrists—except for Lakyn's, because he generally refused to let anyone but Scott touch him—then told us to have a good time. We decided to hit the Mirror Maze first since the line was the shortest. It ended up taking us forever to get through, and we got lost more than once, but we eventually made it out.

We did the other attractions as well: the actual haunted house, which caused Lakyn to say more swear words than I was aware he knew, The Graveyard, which was mostly about finding candy, and the Clown Concert, which was fairly terrifying but amusing because I learned very quickly that Scott *hated* clowns.

The last event was called Zombie Apocalypse and was one of my personal favorites. It took place in the lot behind the building and was a large roped off area filled with barricades and obstacles. It was spray-painted to look abandoned and blood splattered and never failed to be a blast.

"Isn't your ex-boyfriend working this?" Lakyn asked as we waited in line, doing his best to finish off the caramel apple we'd picked up earlier.

Quin was working—most of the athletes were—but I shot Lakyn a curious look when he knew the right prefix to use.

Juliet talks," he explained.

"Traitor," Juliet muttered under her breath. "But he should be, so feel free to shoot him."

I shrugged and nodded, because really Quinton did sort of deserve it. We were next in line and I recognized one of the Grant High theatre kids was in charge. He was decidedly human in costume, but scuffed and tired looking. Definitely a survivor then.

"Where ya coming from, friends?" he demanded cautiously, gripping a prop shotgun tightly.

"Down the road," I answered, falling into character because that always made everything so much more fun. "We aren't looking for trouble, just a place to sleep."

The guy studied us all, then nodded. "Can you shoot?"

"Damn straight," Scott replied, and Juliet laughed but somehow managed to keep what I was sure was a gay joke to herself.

The rules were read out to us, and it was pretty simple. We all started out human, with capture-the-flag style belts and laser-tag guns. The zombies had on headbands that went off if they were shot, and the goal was to take them out. If the zombies managed to get a flag off the human, they were out of the game, but if a zombie got both flags, the human had to turn in their gun for a headband.

It was a fucking blast.

We got sent in with two other large groups, and then spread out. There was a countdown before the game started and then zombies came from everywhere. Lakyn and Scott were already long gone, but Juliet stayed by my side and we couldn't help but laugh as we ran toward the barriers, watching each other's back.

It got *intense*. We ran into Scott halfway through, who was yielding a headband across his forehead by that point. We screamed when he took off after us, haphazardly trying to shoot but knowing we wouldn't win. I wouldn't have been surprised at all to figure out he switched teams on purpose.

He separated me from Juliet though, who triggered the car alarm prop and sent me a horrified look before we both went the other way as fast as possible, knowing every zombie in the game would be descending on that one spot in no time.

On the way to a new hiding spot, I saw Quin on the sidelines, which meant someone at least had taken him out. I smiled to myself, but a quick count said the humans were probably going to be the losing team. Still, I kept my gun close as I kneeled down behind some old water containers and tried to keep a lookout for any threats.

Juliet came out of nowhere and launched herself at me. We both hit the ground, but it didn't hurt too horribly.

I laughed until I realized she was sporting a headband, then sighed deeply. "Shit, not you too!"

She grinned at me, blond hair falling around us both in a curtain. She was so close I could feel her warm breath across my cheeks.

"Change with me?" she asked softly, her fingers trailing down my sides until I felt them curl around the flags at my waist.

I smiled softly, nodded, and let her rip them free.

It was the first time I hadn't won Zombie Apocalypse since seventh grade.

6. "You don't sound enthusiastic about that at all."

Once November hit, I decided to do some research. It wasn't the first time I'd sat down, pulled up Google, and basically tried to figure out what the hell was up with me, but it was the first time I really started *digging*. I read through the labels, the differences between romantic and sexual attraction, accounts of what it *felt like* and articles on finding yourself. I watched *How I knew I was Gay* and *Coming Out* stories on YouTube, followed blogs, made notes and overused my urban dictionary app.

I tried to do other things, but I couldn't seem to make myself. No matter what I did, my head was spinning, and the need to define myself was almost suffocating. I wanted a label, even though there seemed to be a general agreement online that I didn't *have* to have one. I needed it because I needed an answer. Closure, in a way.

A few weeks later I ended up at the James' place, with Lakyn and Scott of course, and I realized I could ask Juliet, but the thought made me nervous, for some reason. It felt heavy and I couldn't manage to bring it up.

I was awake early Saturday morning, and as usual, found Scott in the kitchen. He was digging through the cabinets and looked disgruntled, which brought a slightly amused smile to my face. "What are you doing?"

"I want doughnuts," he replied, shoulders slumping before he turned around to look at me. "Want to go get some?"

"And coffee?" I asked hopefully. When he grinned and nodded, I pulled my hair up into a messy bun and followed him outside to his jeep. We listened to the radio for a while, but then I realized I actually had a gay friend I could question—Scott.

When the commercials came on and Scott turned the volume down, I took a deep breath to steady my nerves. My palms were sweaty, but I still managed to say, "Can I ask you a question?"

Scott side-eyed me like he wanted to make the *you just did* joke, but evidently my tone had been serious enough because he just gave me a slow nod.

"How, um, how did you know that you're...I mean—"

"Gay?" he asked, the corners of his mouth quirking up slightly, and just like that, the swirling in the pit of my stomach disappeared. He waited for my nod, then shrugged, his gaze staying on the road. "I don't know, really. It was something I just always sort of *knew*. The real problem was accepting it. It's easy to get away with acting straight when you're little, of course, because girls have cooties and wear a lot of pink and that's just gross."

I chuckled, because it was easy to picture an eight-year-old Scott saying those exact same words with *feeling*. He sighed, then kept explaining. "It was harder in junior high, because kids in my class starting *going steady* and there were girls leaving these cute little *check yes or no* notes in my locker. And there was this teacher, Mrs. Thompson, who always wore low cut shirts and would put her boobs right in your face when she leaned over your desk, and that was supposed to be my *thing*, you know? But there was this boy in third period I was way more interested in staring at, and I *knew* what that meant. I pulled it off mostly by being shy, or busy, and just started nodding along when the guys sat around and talked about girls. But then..."

"High school," I guessed.

Scott nodded. "High school. Everyone's a couple. Girls were begging for my attention, there's homecoming and prom in the near future and man, I was lonely. And horny." I laughed at that, and Scott sent me a guilty grin as he pulled the Jeep into the doughnut stop drive thru. "And I just wanted someone. But it was never a girl's ass I was watching down the hallway, or a girl's smile that caught my attention in class. It was never boobs I was trying to see, because I was too busy waiting for some guy's shirt to lift up enough that I could get a peek of his happy trail."

We paused our conversation only long enough to order enough doughnuts for everyone, which were passed out pretty quickly, and then loaded up on coffee. Once we left, Scott glanced at me again and, at my nod, continued his story.

"Of course, being on the football team has its perks. I got invited to all the best parties, with all the best booze and pot and impaired decision making. And I thought 'I can do this, I can be straight. Just get a little drunk and...'"

"It still wasn't a girl," I murmured, and Scott slowly shook his head.

"I tried, I did. But it was hard to stick to a plan when I couldn't even think straight—that was a gay joke, hope you appreciated it—and before long, it wasn't hard to find the boys who were looking at me instead of the girls they'd come with. And then it became easy to just pretend. I'd get a couple of hours a night with some guy and the next morning we'd both pretend it didn't happen.

"Anyway, it's the summer before my sophomore year and Lakyn-fucking-James shows up at camp. What people don't realize about him, because he's so quiet, is that he's actually an asshole. I always knew that—I mean, we go to Bridgewood, so the people you meet in elementary school are the people you will graduate with. So, yeah, I remembered that middle schooler sitting in the back of the classroom muttering snide comments under his breath. But you know, we were older, he was attractive. Flirty, sassy, and I *wanted* him. And I mean wanted him for more than just a couple of drunken hours. I wanted to know what music he listened to, and the toothpaste brand he liked, and what he looked like when he woke up in the morning. I wanted to argue about stupid shit and kiss him in the rain and..."

Scott trailed off and the slightest of blushes touched his cheeks. I smiled, I couldn't help it, and he laughed while he focused on driving. "Basically, long story short, I always knew I was the gay kid. That wasn't the hard part. The hard part was giving in. Especially at sixteen, with people I'd mostly gone to school with my whole life. My family, my friends...they already had this idea of who I was as a person and this one thing changed that. Lakyn and I snuck around for a while, but that kid went through hell. He's had it rough, and he was out. He'd fought his way out of the closet, and it wasn't fair of me to make him go back in. And he knew he was better than that, too. So he gave me a choice. And in the end, I chose him."

There was silence as we turned on Juliet's street, and I sat back and let Scott's story roll around in my mind. I knew enough just from bits and pieces I'd overheard in the last few months to realize none of my new friends had had things *easy*. Their lives were complicated and messy and *painful*. But I also knew they were some of the happiest people I had ever met, and they had a completeness to them most teenagers never did. I surely didn't.

Scott parked his Jeep, and although he undid his seatbelt, he made no move to get out. Instead he just shifted until he could face me better, and demanded a doughnut. I laughed and handed him a glazed before digging a chocolate out for myself.

"So, what's on your mind, Len?" he asked, expression open but tone knowing.

I sighed and picked at my doughnut before taking a bite, because even though I knew Scott White was the last person on the earth that would judge me, it was still nerve wracking. It would also be the first time I said anything about Juliet out loud, and that felt *final*. Decisive.

"Heteronormativity is a real thing; you know?" When I glanced up, Scott's expression was conveying that *yes, of course* he knew. I shrugged apologetically. "I never really thought I had an option before. Grant is such a heterosexual town; everyone is straight or so far in the closet they're touching fucking Narnia because let's be real."

Scott snorted.

"I just feel like I've been expected, all my life, to do the *normal* thing. Date the football player, get married, have two-point-five babies, be a stay at home mom and substitute teach when your kids start school. That's life."

"You don't sound enthusiastic about that *at all*."

"I'm not," I admitted, licking icing off my fingers. "And I was trapped in this loop of not falling for anyone because I didn't want to end up there. But then I met you guys. And I like it here. I like that. With you guys, *love* is a real feeling not just something Hallmark came up with. I like that when you talk about getting married, it's because you *want* to, not just because you're supposed to."

Scott's brow furrowed and he chewed thoughtfully before asking, "Was I drunk?"

I laughed. "Yes."

"Makes sense." He nodded and took another bite. "I still meant it though."

"I know you did." We were both quiet as we finished off our first doughnuts. "But I wasn't like you, Scott. I wasn't the gay kid. I was just the uninterested one. But now, I look at her and I just want to be around her all the time. I want to hold her hand and kiss her cheek. But what if I'm *not*, you know? What if she's just the best friend I've ever had and I'm blurring my lines because…"

"How long have you been sitting on this?" he asked.

I sighed. "Longer than I think I even realized."

Scott nodded. "And what have you done about it? Just thought yourself in circles?"

"Kind of?" I admitted, finishing off my second doughnut. "And did some Googling, which, actually, is a little overwhelming."

Scott nodded and grabbed us some napkins. "You know, most straight people, when they have a gay dream just Google 'omg does that mean I'm gay?!' And when it tells them they're just *ignoring some feminine or masculine part of themselves* they breathe a sigh of relief and move on with their heterosexual lives. I'm going to go out on a limb here and say that was not your response?"

"Uh, no," I replied, shaking my head. "I started *The L Word.*"

Scott's laugh sounded like it surprised him as he finally got out of the Jeep, grabbing the coffees while he went. "Come on, let's get inside before my nosey ass boyfriend comes looking for us. But Lena, stop panicking. I'll send you some stuff to look at later."

I stuck my tongue out at him, but followed his lead and took the doughnuts in.

Despite the fact that my world felt like it had shifted, something else felt like it had fallen into place, and as we walked inside, I felt better than I had in weeks.

***

True to his word, a few days later Scott filled my inbox with everything he had ever looked up himself. He wrote a note apologizing that it was mostly male-centric, but that if I dug through the attached links I might find something I could identify with. He sent a lot of stuff close to what I had found on my own, just better. Along with chat rooms and places to have more of a discussion than just an overflow of information.

I really liked the term *bisexual*, and the more I read and learned, the more I realized it added up almost exactly to how I had felt my whole life. Even things I hadn't realized I was feeling. I kept the label in my head for a few days, and each time I woke up and thought *I am bisexual*, it seemed to take a weight off my shoulders.

By the time Lacey started talking about hooking me up with someone new, I was using non-gender specific pronouns when she asked who I thought I might be into. It was then that I realized I had found what fit. I didn't *only* like boys, and that was okay.

"You know, I think Oscar might be single again." Lacey looked thoughtful as she tilted her head before shrugging and taking another bite of her salad. "He could easily be your type."

"Awesome possum," I replied, trying and failing to not show how greatly uninterested I was. It was nothing against Oscar—I was sure he was great. He just wasn't, well, *her*.

"You did not seriously just say *awesome possum*," Lacey muttered.

I shrugged. "Admit it. I'm the coolest person you know."

Juliet snorted and I scowled, kicking her foot under the table. She glanced up from her phone before she cocked a brow, daring me to try and kick her harder, most likely. Beside me, Lacey just laughed.

I shook my head and turned my attention back onto my lunch, muttering, "No one here appreciates how hilarious I am," before taking another bite out of my sandwich.

"It's mostly because you're the only one who thinks you're funny," Georgia quipped, a small smirk forming on the corners of her mouth—even if she was pretending not to be listening to the conversation.

Juliet laughed so hard she actually had to stop texting, sinking back in her seat and wiping at an imaginary tear.

I threw a potato chip at Georgia first, then glared at the blond beauty sitting across from me. I was pretty sure that just made her laugh more. "I hope you choke and die," I snapped.

Juliet flipped me off lazily as she pushed her chair back enough to cross her legs, not bothering to finish her food, even though she'd barely touched it. I didn't really blame her. The cafeteria fish sticks were probably worse than the ones in prison.

"Who are you texting anyway?" I asked, admittedly sort of irritated at not having her attention.

Juliet sighed and set her phone on her knee. "My brother. He wants to ask his girlfriend to Thanksgiving Dinner with my family, but he's worried that it's too soon. I told him he's being an idiot."

"Mm, no, I feel that," Lacey said, finally deciding Juliet was more interesting than my boy problems. "This one time, I decided to bring a boy home over a holiday..."

It was a story I'd already heard, and I knew Lacey was just talking for the sake of it, so when I caught Juliet's attention, I smirked at her and mouthed, *"Someone in your family is straight?"*

"Fuck you," she mouthed back.

I smirked slowly and muttered, "Don't joke."

Her eyes narrowed on me and I briefly wondered if she could hear my heart beating, because it sounded really fucking loud to me. Unlike at the Bridgewood game, I'd known what I said this time. It was flirty, intentionally so, because I couldn't stop myself.

"How long have they been together?" Lacey asked, which managed to pull us both back into the conversation.

"Almost a year," Juliet answered. She sighed as she picked her phone up again, shook her head and typed out a reply. "She's a sweet girl. Showed up at the dealership my dad owns at least eight times before Rick finally realized she was more into him than a car."

"Sounds like me, actually," Kiki put in. "I never know when guys are flirting."

"Why's he so worried though?" I asked. "Do you guys do something big for Thanksgiving?"

"Not really," Juliet admitted with a shrug. "My grandparents come down, and sometimes my aunt and her family join us, but it's like ten people total. And then Scott usually shows up at some point, so obviously it's not a classy event."

"Oh, my god, be nice." I threw a chip at her this time.

"Never." Juliet laughed as she brushed her shirt clean. "Anyway, what are the rest of you doing for Thanksgiving? Anything interesting?"

Kiki shook her head. "Nah, my parents aren't really into holidays, so I usually just enjoy the downtime. Watch some TV and stuff."

"Same," Georgia agreed. "I mean, we do the big meal and stuff, but other than that we all just chill. Actually, I think this year me and Rose might go over to Chris' place. He has a big family, and since she spent last Thanksgiving with me, it only seems fair. And I mean, he asked, too."

"Girl, really?" Lacey asked and Georgia nodded. "Boy steppin' up. Good for him."

"Good for Rose," Georgia answered. "What about you, Lace? Same as always?"

"Yeah," Lacey answered, and then, for Juliet's benefit, explained. "My dad's a pastor, so every year we do a big cookout at the church, and then donate most of the food to the homeless shelters in the city. It's actually fun."

Juliet blinked, slightly surprised. "That's really sweet."

"Yeah, well, I'm a sweet person," Lacey replied, flipping her hair over her shoulder.

"Sure, honey," Juliet said, and glanced pointedly at the finger Lacey shot her.

When Lacey turned the question on me, I just shrugged. "The usual."

"Please tell me your parents got some time off," Lacey asked.

My parents worked a lot—they always had. They were both career-driven and older than most of my friends' parents. I was an only child for a reason, because I'd been planned that way and they knew they wouldn't have time for more. It was fine—lonely on occasion, but I was well loved and cared for. I just didn't get to see them often.

"Yes, Lace, they took off most of the week, actually."

"Awesome."

"Possum," I muttered.

Lacey slammed her hand down on the table and pointed a fork at me. "I will cut you, bitch. Shut up."

7. Shit, I had said that out loud.

The first day of break Lacey and I got some much needed BFF time, which meant the mall and spending more money than we really had. I had set it up that way on purpose, because I wanted her not only buttered up, but distracted when I decided to share my news with her.

Scott made it a point to let me know that I didn't have to come out until *I* was ready. It was my decision and mine alone. Only I would know when the time was right. Which sounded right, and I knew I wasn't ready to talk about it with my parents yet.

But my best friend? I felt like it was something she should know.

But the more time we spent together, the more nervous I became. It wasn't that there weren't openings—there were plenty, I just couldn't bring myself to say anything. By the time we stopped at the food court, I had decided I was looking at the hardest part of all this the wrong way. It wasn't figuring out a sexuality different from the social norms—it was trying to *tell other people* about it.

Somewhere along the way, I had gotten used to the comfort of the James family—and Scott, by extension. Their home, their company, was so completely accepting that I had almost forgotten what it was like back in the real world.

A world that was full of expectations and context, judgment and hate, misunderstanding and ignorance. A world I had, mostly, been a part of up until just months ago. Dragging Lacey into that suddenly felt almost unfair, if only because I couldn't let her take baby steps. It had to be all at once, like ripping off a Band-Aid.

Rationally, I knew that Lacey was my very best friend. The girl had eaten bugs with me in preschool, punched Alex Washington in the nose when he tried to look up my skirt in fifth grade, held my hair the first night I spent throwing up vodka in seventh, and dragged my ass to church when I lost my sense of being in ninth.

Regardless of where I was in life, she would always be there, eating my food and sleeping in my bed, probably. We knew too much shit about each other to ever leave, no matter how bad it got. And really, liking girls wasn't that big of a deal.

It was just a deal.

And it shouldn't be all that hard to simply say, "Hey Lace, I kind of dig chicks."

Shit, I had said that out loud.

Across from me Lacey tried to—as casually as possible—dig her fallen chicken nugget out of her barbeque sauce without making a total mess. She popped the food in her mouth, chewed thoughtfully, then wiped her fingers on her napkin before looking at me.

I could see the war raging in her, torn between trying to figure out how to be a supportive friend, and how to deal with her own confusion of being bombarded with my sexuality crisis. I was rather proud of her for trying to stomp down the inner bitch I knew was constantly too close to the surface.

"So, you're gay now?"

I let out a sigh and shifted uncomfortably in my seat, deciding to focus more on the best way to saturate my own nugget before I answered. "I mean, not *now*. I don't think people just turn gay or anything. At least I'm a firm believer in being born that way. You know, like Lady Gaga says."

Lacey arched a very unamused eyebrow.

"There's a song about it!" I demanded. *"Born This Way*! You know it!"

The look was not wavering. If anything, she was glaring harder.

"It's sort of like a spectrum? Like a rainbow, you know, because, symbolism I guess?"

Nothing.

"And there's not just gay and straight, either. There's asexual, pansexual, and—"

Abort mission.

"Bisexual?"

Abort. Abort! Fucking abort, Lena, get the fuck out of there!

I couldn't run. There was nowhere to go. The food court was packed and Lacey had driven for once. I was trapped.

Lacey shook her head and turned back to her food. "Girl, please. I don't know what you think you're doing. I mean, is this a joke? Because if it is, I need to remind you of a very good point Georgia made not too long ago—you really are the only one who thinks you're funny."

"Wow." I breathed out a laugh, because even as bitchy as she was, it was normal bitchy. Lacey bitchy. Not "I'm about to friend-disown you" bitchy. Plus, she was still sitting there, so that must have meant something. "Thanks."

"'Sides, I know gay people, and you are not one of them."

There were surprisingly few things Lacey could ever do that pissed me off, but one of them was telling me what I was or was not. I'd always had a problem with that, regardless of who it was coming from.

"That's, like, the number one thing you aren't supposed to say to a friend who comes out to you, Lace."

Lacey sighed like she knew this conversation wasn't going to be over quickly, and abandoned her food in favor of folding her arms on the table. "Okay, look. I watch TV with you, right? I see you drool over panned camera shots of nice abs. And, uh, that year we went to Nina's birthday party, you were not at all shy about *Seven Minutes of Heaven* with Troy? Lord knows how long you two were even in that closet. And you date boys, Lena.

80

Cute, athletic, boys. That all sounds pretty fucking straight to me."

She wasn't wrong, but that didn't necessarily make her right.

I sighed, but I couldn't stop now. "You do know what bisexual means, right? I mean we can tear down the roots if you need it. Bi means two—"

Lacey threw a French fry at me. I responded by flipping her off.

For a moment, we were silent. Lacey never looked away from me, and it was like she was waiting for something. For me to laugh, or yell April Fools, promise it was a joke or that I was just testing her. So that she could call me a bitch and we could just move on.

But I didn't, because it wasn't a joke. It was the most serious thing I'd ever learned about myself, and I'd chosen to share it with her first because she was one of the most important people in my life. It felt too weird not to tell her.

I'd done enough research to know what she was doing. Reflecting, because something would always be different now. She was probably reevaluating every moment of our lives together, and I really hoped she wasn't basic enough to—

"You don't like me, do you?"

Whoop, there it was. Fucker. "For the record, that is the second thing you aren't supposed to say to a friend when they come out to you. And no, Lacey, Christ."

The emotions that flashed across her face were too fast for me to really keep up with. Relief, confusion, offense. "What?" she demanded. "Why not? Am I not pretty enough for you?"

"Oh *my god*, Lace, you are such a textbook case!" I shot at her, mostly through clenched teeth. I should have seen it coming, cut her off before she could go there, but I really had expected more from her. "Do you want me to be attracted to you?"

"No!"

"Then why are you so pissed?"

Lacey gave me one of her best glares, then huffed in irritation. "I just don't understand why you wouldn't be. I'm a pretty girl, and you just sat here and told me you liked girls, sooooo?"

I rolled my eyes and decided my chicken nuggets were really much better company than she was. "I don't like every single girl on the planet, Lacey. Fuck."

"Mm," she mumbled, and finally unfolded herself from her defensive pose to finish eating as well. "Fine, you can be a lesbian if you want to. Whatever. I'll support you, even if I don't understand why you wouldn't want to be with me."

"You are such a jealous bitch, Lacey Parker."

"Hells to the yes I am," she replied with absolutely no shame. "And that is Miss Jealous Bitch to you."

***

I spent Wednesday at Juliet's place, only because my parents didn't get off until late that night. My grandparents were coming over for dinner on actual Thanksgiving, and as usual, they were cooking the turkey. To take some stress off my parents, I offered to help out making a few of the side dishes.

My mother had given me an odd look, but when I gently reminded her that cooking was a normal activity in the James household, she'd given in. She didn't like to cook very much anyway, so I didn't feel like it was exactly a hard decision.

Spending time with my friends was, as always, a good time. Scott and Juliet were constantly in a playful fight about something, Lakyn was really just more worried about his food than anything, and I was thankful to be a part of it all.

Juliet and Mr. James left that evening to pick up her incoming family from the airport. She took Scott's jeep after begging him for half an hour and making serious promises on her life that she wouldn't hurt it. Lakyn did the honors of letting me know that Juliet was a horrible driver, and for some reason, it didn't actually surprise me that much. Mostly because she never seemed to mind when I drove us around everywhere.

I stayed at the house with the boys, sitting up on the kitchen counter and reading ingredients from an old cookbook. We were down to making pies for dessert, and the kitchen smelled like the most amazing place on earth.

Of course, we were all in our pajamas, because no one stayed in real clothes at the James' for very long. Scott had flour in his hair from where he'd run his hands through it, and Lakyn's cheek was marked, but neither of them seemed to care. As usual, Lakyn was glued to his boyfriend's side, not so much helping as stealing bites of food.

"So, Lena," Scott started, feigning nonchalance as he tried to keep Lakyn from getting into the cherries. The other boy made a sound of distress before trying to dart around him again, but Scott was managing to keep him back. "How's life?"

"Fine," I said, trying not to smirk or look up at him like I knew he wanted me to. "How about yours?"

The beat of silence lasted just long enough that I finally couldn't help but peek, and Scott was giving me the most deadpanned look I had ever seen on his face. It was too funny *not* to give him what he wanted at that point. "I really am fine."

"Oh, yeah, she's having a gay crisis, right?" Lakyn asked, trying for a slower approach at the cherries this time. Scott, at least, had the decency to look ashamed, even as he slapped his boyfriend's hand away again. Lakyn glanced at me and seemed to take pity on the other boy. "I threaten him and he tells me things."

"He withholds orgasms," Scott muttered. "I'm sorry, Len. I'm just not that strong."

"I hate you," I decided, and Scott shrugged in a way that said he could clearly live with that. "Lakyn, how much do you know?"

"More than he actually told me, mostly because you're actually not that smooth."

"Rude," I muttered. He just smiled at me.

"Good luck with Jules, though," he muttered, and this time, when he went for the cherries, was completely pushed back a few steps. He glared, but turned his attention back to me. "She's a tough one to get through to."

"Yeah," I muttered, then leaned back against the counters. "Why is she like that anyway? You know, guarded?" It'd taken me forever to learn even the few bits and pieces of Juliet I knew. I wouldn't label her as a secretive person, she was just selective in the information she shared.

Both of the boys were quiet for a while, long enough that Scott eventually picked up a cherry and dropped it in Lakyn's open mouth. He started working on the crust before he answered me. "Did you ever ask Juliet why she switched schools?"

I shook my head. I'd thought about it, at the Bridgewood game when she'd been telling me stories about her old classmates. Lakyn still went there, so I could only imagine there was a decent reason why only she had traded schools, but I hadn't wanted to push. "I figured if it was very important, she'd tell me."

"It is important," Lakyn confirmed. "She just doesn't like to talk about it. Doesn't like to talk about much, really."

"That's a family trait," Scott confided, shooting Lakyn a look, who responded with an innocent smile. "I'm not even really sure if I can tell this story. Not that I'm not allowed to or anything, I mean she told me I could if you ever came asking but…"

"It's complicated," Lakyn finished with a shrug. "I guess it's my story too."

He fell silent for a while, and I let him take the time to gather his thoughts. He was wearing his usual hoodie and boxer shorts combo, and I watched as the fingers of his right hand moved to his left wrist, rubbing at the skin I couldn't see. "I was a mess when I moved in here. Really falling apart. Ready to tap out. Uncle Ben refused to let me slip, though. Aunt Lily hadn't been gone for long, just over a year, so Juliet was healing, but she wasn't exactly *okay*. Neither of us were, really. I mean, she wasn't even my mom and I missed her every day."

Lakyn took a deep breath, but continued. "Jules has never really been a *let's eat ice cream and talk about our feelings* girl.

84

She keeps to herself, and when she's hurting, she likes to numb the pain."

"Alcohol," I guessed.

"And drugs," Lakyn added. "Not the really bad stuff or anything. Mostly pot, sometimes a few pills. She's lucky in that she doesn't have a very addictive personality so it was always just when she needed it. Which, back then, was a lot.

"Anyway." He sighed and tugged his sleeves back down over his fingers, leaned against the counter in front of him. "She spiraled pretty hard. She was always gone, sneaking out. Lost a lot of weight, shit like that. But then, one night, the cops called. She got picked up for vandalism. Spray painting, I think. The business owner decided not to press charges because he knew the family, as long as she promised she'd clean it up.

"Uncle Ben got really upset over it, but I think he knew she was just hurting. She's not a bad person, ya know? She was just stumbling. So he made her get some grief counseling, and some help for the substance abuse. It was only a couple of months, but by the time she got back…"

"Bridgewood is a gossip school," Scott put in. "Everyone knows everyone, and Juliet hung with the rougher side. Rich kids who pull against the system. I wouldn't go so far as to call them posers or anything, just rebellious. But, also the type people who only care about you as long as you're actually *around*. Juliet's absence meant she was free game, so people talked. About her family, about her secrets, about her sexuality."

"Rumors spread, and it got nasty," Lakyn said. "When she came back she was healthy, and people were trying to drag her down for that. She didn't really have any friends outside of me and Scott. She just didn't fit anymore."

"So she moved," I summarized. "To start over."

Lakyn nodded. "So, that's sort of why. I think she feels like once people really get to know her, they won't like her anymore, or something. Trust like that getting broken is not a particularly good feeling."

"I imagine not," I agreed. "Why did you stay at Bridgewood? Why not move with her?"

"Scott," Lakyn answered.

Scott snorted. "Don't let him play you like he's a self-sacrificing romantic. He stayed because of Bridgewood's Advanced Placement program. As long as he keeps working hard, he'll graduate the same year we do. Grant doesn't have that kind of set up."

Lakyn shrugged innocently. "That's part of the reason."

"Shut up, you little terror," Scott replied, shoving a cherry in his boyfriend's mouth. Lakyn didn't seem to mind too much. I laughed at them both and somehow managed to bring their attention back to cooking.

We had moved to the living room by the time Juliet and her father returned home, taking turns playing *Mortal Kombat*, and even though their entrance was quiet, it was still filled with the energy of family that hadn't seen each other in a while.

Lakyn looked up at the sound of new voices, but didn't seem too bothered to greet anyone. Likewise, Scott and myself stayed put. From my vantage point on the couch I could see Mr. James walk past the doorway with a small child in his arms, reverse piggyback style, fast asleep. Another man I didn't recognize was following him, with a small girl in his arms. She was awake, but just barely.

Once they were gone, Juliet was walking in, followed by an older woman who must have been Mr. James' sister, if looks were anything to go by. Lakyn was currently playing, but he looked up long enough to mutter a quick, "Hi, Aunt Crystal."

The greeting was returned, but all I really noticed was the way Juliet's gaze lit up when they landed on me. "You're still here."

"Yeah." I gave her a small smile. "Didn't want to leave without saying goodbye."

"That's adorable," her aunt decided, and her own smile was nothing but kind. "How long have you two been together?"

I felt my heart skip a beat at the unhesitant question, like it hadn't crossed her mind at all that Juliet and I *weren't* a couple. I heard Scott hide a laugh in a curse like he was directing it to his game, but I knew better, and it took everything in me not to glare at him.

Instead, my gaze was locked on Juliet, and she was looking right back at me. It seemed like it was forever before she said anything, but it could have only been moments. "Um, this is Lena and she's just my friend."

Crystal looked like she didn't quite believe her niece, but decided to go with it anyway. "Oh, *this* is Lena then? She told us all about you on the drive here."

Juliet seemed put out, but I couldn't help but smile, even if my heart was still beating too fast. "All bad things, I hope."

Juliet laughed and offered me a hand, which I took so I could be tugged off the couch. "Come on, I'll walk you out."

I wanted to keep her hand, but I knew that I couldn't, so I let her go and waved a goodbye to her aunt instead.

Juliet, of course, apologized once we got outside, but I just shrugged. "It's not a big deal."

She searched my face for a moment but then nodded. "Did the guys drive you crazy?"

"No," I answered with a laugh. "They're good company, I like having them around."

She smiled. "We like having you around, too."

My heart skipped again, and I knew it was because I didn't actually mind getting mistaken for her girlfriend. In fact, it was a nice thought, getting to be a part of her life like that. Some sort of solid foundation. "Goodnight, Jules."

"Night, babe."

***

Thanksgiving dinner was always a small event for my family. My father had a decently sized family, but they all lived out of state, so we rarely saw them except for the occasional trip or family reunion. My mother's family was smaller, and her brother was a perpetual bachelor who liked to travel and therefore was never around. So usually it was just my parents and my mother's parents who came for dinner.

"You made pie," was my mother's first comment when I came downstairs just before noon on Thursday morning. She was already dressed, comfortably in slacks and a light sweater, her hair done up in a simple bun. I smiled, and leaned in for a side hug. "And you're still in pajamas," she added.

The James family was really starting to rub off on me. "Yes, Mom, I made pie. Apple and pumpkin. Dad likes pumpkin pie, right?" I wasn't a big fan of it, but Scott was so he'd shown me how to make it. Like Lakyn, I preferred the fruit pies. Juliet and her father liked coconut, which had been some of the prettiest we'd made.

"Yes, he does." My mother picked up the pie in question, gave it a sniff. I tried not to be annoyed because I couldn't really blame her. I'd barely made sandwiches on my own before sleepovers at Juliet's place. "It smells...good."

"I'm sure it is good," my father announced as he came into the room. Like my mother, he was already dressed, and together they both looked very *autumn*. "Don't berate her for picking up a hobby, Margaret."

"I wasn't *berating her*," my mother responded, while I presented my cheek for a kiss from my father. "I'm just surprised, is all."

"I also brought potatoes," I mentioned. "And some green bean casserole. I wasn't really sure what that was, but it tasted really good when we were sampling it yesterday."

My mother laughed and set the pie down. "Now *that* sounds more like you."

I grinned, and together we ate a small lunch before starting to get the dining room ready for dinner. I filled my parents in on what had been happening at school, how my grades were, Lacey and what she was up to, and about my new friends. My father mentioned that I looked happy, and he was glad to see that.

Once my grandparents arrived, everyone was hungry and focused on the promise of food. The turkey was fantastic, and everyone loved the side dishes I'd brought along. The pies especially were a hit, and I shined under the praise that I received.

My mother saw her parents even less than she saw me, which meant they were all very enamored with each other. I didn't mind so much, as it gave me time to text Juliet, who was mildly bored but not unhappy.

She sent me pictures of herself, a video of her father waving hello to me, and pictures of Scott and Lakyn, who were busy being adorable and feeding each other food when they thought no one was looking. It looked like fun, and I found myself missing them.

But it was nice to spend some time in my own house with other people for once, so I sent her pictures back, with captions of "miss you, hope you're having a good time!". Then I put my phone away, smiled at my dad when he smiled at me, and got back into the conversation.

8. "Whatcha lookin' at?"

"Whatcha lookin' at?"

Lakyn's voice was soft and sleep heavy, but I still almost jumped out of my skin. I turned a glare on him, but he just smiled as he pushed his hair out of his face.

"Really, Lakyn? Personal space! Don't sneak up on me like that!"

Scott laughed as he came into the room, a warm plate of apple pie in one hand and a mug of what I was willing to bet was coffee in the other. "If Lakyn knew what personal space was I guarantee we would have never gotten together."

The smug look on Lakyn's face made it clear that was not a story I wanted to know. I shook my head, debated slamming my laptop closed but decided against it. It wasn't like the boys wouldn't pull it out of me eventually.

Scott settled on the couch by my feet, clad in only his plaid pajama pants and messy hair. He looked expectant as he took a bite of pie, waiting for an explanation he knew would come.

"Healthy breakfast," I commented instead.

"Deflecting," Lakyn shot back with a yawn as he sat on the arm of the couch beside me, leaning down enough to see what was on my screen. "'*Haunted Hollywood:* A fashion show from the top horror artists on the big screen' in the old SouthGate Mall on December 6th?"

Scott nearly choked on his pie and I sent my next glare his way, but of course he completely ignored it. "Oh my god. You're going to ask Juliet out."

"What?" Lakyn asked while I buried my face in my hands, though the movement made my laptop accessible and Lakyn wasted no time taking advantage of that, grabbing the device off my lap and pulling it into his own. I could hear him clicking through the open tabs. Little asshole. "This is adorable."

"What's she got planned?" Scott asked, sounding amused as I groaned in distress. It was out of my hands now, though. Literally. Which meant I had nowhere to run, and thus, no turning back.

Lakyn grinned at his boyfriend before he settled back and began to rattle off my plans. "Well, they'll have to drive to the city first, and if I know Lena, that means she'll be picking up our Jules like the gentleman—gentlewoman? —she is. Then the show, followed by what is probably going to be hot chocolate at *Cuppa Mocha*. Where they will most likely finish off the night talking about their feelings and shit—"

"You're an asshole," I complained as I stole back my laptop with a quick snap of my hands, throwing him yet another glare. "You look sweet and cuddly but you're actually awful and I hate you."

"People never believe me when I tell them he's a dick," Scott muttered absently, and he actually sounded slightly upset about that fact. "I'm glad someone finally sees it."

"Talk about our feelings." I snorted, rolling my eyes and putting a little too much focus on my computer screen. "You two are the most lovey-dovey couple I know. What the hell did you do on your first date?"

"We fucked," Lakyn answered without hesitation, falling back against the edge of the couch and tossing me a mischievous grin.

I looked over at Scott, waiting for him to give me the real answer, but he just smiled sheepishly and shrugged. "Actually, that's kind of true. And by *kind of* I mean—"

"I blew him in the movie theater," Lakyn supplied, running his free hand through his hair. "And then he got pissed, dragged us out before it even ended, and we fucked. I still don't know what happened at the end of *Ted*."

Scott gave his boyfriend a thoroughly unimpressed look. "We can rent it if you want to."

Of course it was no secret the boys had an *active* sex life but, wow, that was much more than I ever needed to hear. I shook my head as if that would make me forget. "I hate both of you," I decided.

"No you don't," Scott answered, so seamlessly that I actually almost believed him. "You love us. Not as much as you love Juliet though."

I kicked him and glared again.

He just grinned at me around his fork. "Speaking of which, where is the princess? Still sleeping?"

"Did you see how much pie she ate last night?" It was the last day of break, which meant there were Thanksgiving leftovers by the boatload. And pie, so much pie. I clicked through a couple of pages, finalizing my plans before shutting my laptop. "Of course she's still sleeping."

Scott considered that then eventually nodded. Lakyn took it upon himself to pull the X-Box stuff out, and an hour later Juliet joined us. She didn't say anything, simply fell down on the couch, curled up, and rested her head on my thigh.

We spent the rest of the afternoon being completely and totally useless. Juliet's extended family had left the day before, so no one was around to actually bother us. We finished off the rest of the pie and promptly regretted it, but since we hardly ever moved from the comfort of the living room, it could have been worse.

***

The first day back to school was a drag if only because no one actually wanted to be there. Even the teachers were on turkey hangover, which made the students even less motivated. The morning passed slowly, and by the time lunch rolled around Juliet was waiting for me.

"Dad sent leftovers for us to share," she explained, holding up a lunch box.

I happily walked with her to lunch, where Lacey was talking about a boy she'd met while volunteering and Georgia was extremely enthralled.

Juliet handed me a fantastic looking Thanksgiving pizza and a slice of pie, which surprised me. "I hid some," she explained, and winked.

I grinned and waited for a lull in conversation before asking Georgia how her break went. She smiled and responded, "It went good, actually. Chris' family is super nice, even let me help with a few things. And Rose was really excited about having both her parents around. Do you want to see pictures?"

We all did, of course, and let her know just how adorable her kid was. Georgia smiled proudly, and then asked everyone how their break was. We took time swapping stories, which weren't extremely interesting. Only Lacey had a few good stories, given how busy she had been.

My afternoon classes were with Juliet, which were all fairly laid back, and I was more than ready to go home. The end of the school day, however, meant that I had a question I had to ask her. Technically, I had all week, but I felt like the earlier I could do it the better it would be.

"Hey," I said as we were walking toward free period. "Do you want to go ahead and head out early? I can give you a ride home, no big."

Juliet shrugged as she threw her bag over her shoulder and pulled her phone out of her pocket. "Yeah, sure," she answered before sending off a quick text to her brother. She smiled at me as we changed directions and headed toward the parking lot.

On the way to her house, we stumbled across a radio station that was playing only nineties music, which of course meant we were belting every lyric at the top of our lungs, windows rolled down so hopefully someone would hear us. Backstreet Boys, Destiny's Child, Britney Spears, all the classics.

Juliet laughed as she undid her seatbelt when I pulled into her driveway. "Thanks for this," she mentioned, gathering her stuff and giving me a side hug goodbye. "You're a lot more fun than Rick."

"Duh," I shot back with a grin.

She smiled at me one more time before letting herself out of the car, and I felt my heart stutter in my chest.

This was it. *I should ask her. Right now.* Before I chickened out and had to wait another day.

Or maybe it was better to wait? Maybe I could just wait until Friday, in case she said no? That way I wouldn't have to see her if she did, because awkward. The weekend could be cool-down time, that way.

Were my palms sweating? Probably.

"Drive home safe!" Juliet said before the door swung closed.

I nodded numbly as I watched her walk up to her front door and pull her keys from her back pocket. She would be inside soon, and I would lose my chance, have to wait until tomorrow.

I was out of my car before I even realized I'd moved, jogging up to her. "Juliet!"

Juliet stopped halfway inside and glanced curiously back at me. Her expression was so open, so easy, but for some reason that just made me all the more nervous. "Um." I shifted my weight from foot to foot, wrung my fingers together. "Um. This Saturday. Go out with me."

It wasn't even a question. I just *demanded* it. Holy fuck.

The corners of her mouth lifted slightly. "Okay," she answered, stepping inside and dropping her bag where she usually left it. She turned to shut the door behind her, then paused when she realized I was still there.

"Okay?" I repeated, and I could barely hear my own voice over the sound of my blood rushing through my veins. "Okay. Okay. I mean, cool. Yeah. Awesome. Okay."

I nodded quickly and turned around to finally leave, but couldn't quite manage. I turned back to her once or twice before I let out a frustrated sigh. "You know I mean...go out with me…like as a date? Like, wear something nice, I'll pick you up a little after four, actual *date?* D-a-t-e. Date. Date date."

Her lips twisted up into the type of grin that looked involuntary. When I still didn't move, her smile got impossibly larger. "I know. Goodbye, Lena."

My heart stuttered again, and I stared at her for a moment, but Juliet didn't waver. Instead, she just patiently waited. Finally, I nodded again, took a few steps backwards, said something that sounded like *great*, and then dashed to my car.

I was mildly embarrassed, but mostly I couldn't stop smiling.

***

"I don't know what to wear."

I smirked as I pulled my curling iron through my hair again, adding another loose tendril before spraying it gently into place. I was probably being too particular with the way it looked, but I was excited.

"Wear whatever you want," I replied, loud enough that the speaker on my phone would pick it up. There was silence then shuffling on the other end that most likely meant Juliet was digging through her closet.

"Bitch, you told me to wear something nice."

I laughed at that and shook my head, using my hand mirror to make sure I hadn't missed any strands in the back. "Jules, you look great in anything, just pick something."

She huffed angrily, made a show of throwing something around, before she very mockingly added, "It would be really nice if someone would tell me where we're going."

"Oh, right, yeah, I totally forgot that I decided to ruin the surprise!" I said as I turned back around, leaning my hip on the counter and picking my phone back up to speak into it. "Think casual, nice. Like something you would wear to a formal school event."

"Ugh." Something slammed down wherever she was, followed by light cursing, and then finally Juliet came back. "Lena Newman, if you take me to school on our—"

My laughter cut her off. "Jules, I promise we're going on an *actual* date. Now, stop panicking, get dressed, and I will see you in an hour, all right?"

"Stop panicking," she mocked. "I'm not panicking. You're the one that's panicking."

It was a childish dig, but one that I let her have just for the sake of ending the argument. The truth was, I *wasn't* panicking. I wasn't even nervous. It was a new feeling. A *good* feeling. I was excited, enough that my heart felt like it was beating too fast, but it wasn't the queasy feeling I'd always associated with dates.

With anyone before, I had been beyond nervous. Like I might screw up or not be good enough. Like I could say something and suddenly they wouldn't like me anymore. Like I had to fit in this mold that I had created, but didn't know how to stay inside of.

Juliet already knew me. She'd decided to be my friend long before I'd decided to make a move. She already liked me. In fact, she liked me enough to agree to go on a date with me. That, instead of nerve wracking, was empowering.

Or I'd just had all fucking week to freak out about it and had finally managed to reach a level of calm.

"Fine," Juliet finally said, "but if I'm not dressed appropriately and I have to change then it's going to be your fault that we run late."

I shook my head. "I'll see you soon."

"Okay," she grumbled, and then the call ended. I stuck my tongue out at my phone even though she couldn't see before going back to getting ready.

I was halfway through my makeup when there was a knock on my door. A glance over my shoulder showed it was my mother.

"You know, I don't think I've seen you get this dolled up in a while," she mentioned carefully, lingering in the doorway. I knew she had to be off to work soon, was probably just stopping in before she left.

96

I frowned at my reflection because I wasn't particularly trying to go out of my way to look nice for Juliet, but I was definitely dressed up. Date dressed up. Which wasn't something my mother knew, of course.

I hadn't intentionally not come out to either of my parents, but I also hadn't made it a priority. Between my own personal confusion and their busy schedules, there just hadn't been time. Not to mention, it was nerve wracking. Worse than coming out to Lacey had been. I had no idea how they were going to handle it.

My mother let herself into my bathroom, ran her fingers through my hair until she picked up a comb and started pulling gently at the sides. "If I didn't know any better," she mused. "I'd say you were getting ready for a date."

I considered what it would be like to just drop the Bisexual Bomb right then. Get it over with, get up, go on my date. But it didn't particularly sound like a good idea. If she took to it badly…

I would *not* miss this date.

"Maybe."

She smiled at me through the mirror before pulling my hair into a half ponytail. "What are you going to wear?"

"My little black dress," I answered. It was one Lacey had bought me a couple of months ago. Simple, long sleeves made out of lace, cinched at the waist, fell to a modest mid-thigh length. I liked it because it was both elegant and casual somehow.

My mom smiled again and dug through my drawers until she found a black rose barrette to clip in my hair.

"You know I love you, right?" she asked as she distracted herself with combing her fingers through my curls again, fixing what I couldn't see. "You're my favorite girl in the whole world."

I spouted off some generic "yes mom" teenage answer even though the simple words sat my nerves on fire. She smiled fondly and dropped a kiss on my head. "Have fun. Drive safe. Don't be home *too* late."

I watched her go before applying my lipstick and standing up to slide my dress on, followed by a pair of hose, black ankle boots, and a matching clutch. One last double check and then I was heading to Juliet's place.

The nerves kicked in on my way there. I rethought our plans over and over again, checked to make sure I had our tickets at every stop light, thought myself into circles before I finally got to the James' house.

Given that it was late in the afternoon, I only rang the doorbell once because I knew someone would be up. Surprisingly, it was Juliet who opened the door. Her gaze didn't find mine first, but rather stuck on my outfit. Like she was assessing that she had, in fact, dressed appropriately.

She looked amazing—of course she did. Her own dress was white, lined in black, hugging her figure down to her waist. She had on a cute pair of designed tights, simple black pumps, and an edgy mid-length black jacket. Her long hair was down like normal, makeup soft, and she was absolutely beautiful.

"Do I look okay?" she asked softly.

"Do you look okay?" I repeated mockingly. "Juliet James, I know you own a mirror."

Her mouth quirked into a small smirk that seemed much more at home on her face before I practically *felt* her give me a once over. "You don't clean up so bad, yourself."

I wanted to kiss her. The feeling slammed into me, and even though it wasn't anything really new, it was the first time I realized it was *real*. And possible. Soon, probably. Hopefully. Holy hell.

"So, do I get to know where we're going yet?" Juliet asked as we stepped away from her doorstep and started for my car. I hesitated, wondering if I should open the car door for her or not, but then I reminded myself that she was a strong, independent woman. Who had been in my car a million times.

Dating friends was awkward. Or I was making it awkward. I probably needed to chill.

"Nope," I answered as we both settled in. She sighed but went for the radio anyway, keeping it low enough that we could have a conversation over the music if we wanted.

The drive to SouthGate was just under two hours, but it wasn't an awkward one. We listened to music, joked around, talked about the usual stuff: school, our friends, the boys, whatever. It went quicker than I expected.

The old mall was one of those city-owned buildings that got rented out for various occasions, and looked hardly recognizable decorated for the show. There were old Hollywood-esque signs, large dark drapes, a red carpet. It was fantastic.

"Babe, where are we?" Juliet asked, and I grinned at not only the pet name but also the mildly annoyed expression on her face. I knew she was really interested, which made it twice as fun. I mimed sealing my lips before we both got out, locked the car, and went inside.

The venue was beautiful. Inside, it hardly looked like it had been a mall. The walls were covered in movie posters—from every single version of *Texas Chainsaw Massacre* to new gems like *Annabel.* In the middle of the opening room there was a display where mannequins were gathered, showing off the outfits from *Beetlejuice.* There were props and statues, photos and filmstrips, and Juliet took to it immediately.

Her fingers hesitantly touched my wrist before sliding down my palm and eventually twining together with mine. I smiled and gave her an encouraging squeeze, even despite the flutter of my heart.

The little encouragement seemed to be all Juliet needed because she was moving suddenly, across the room and tugging her phone out of her jacket pocket with her free hand. She used it to take a picture of one of the original *Dracula* posters. "Did you know Lakyn has a collection?" she asked. "All across his bedroom walls. I don't think you can even see the paint anymore."

"Sounds like you and your band posters," I mused.

"In another lifetime, we would have been twins," she agreed, shrugging before giving my hand another tug and leading the way to more posters. Juliet made it a point to see everything that was up; we laughed over movies that were particularly cheesy, glared when our opinions differed, and bonded over the appreciation of art even when the plot had fallen short.

Eventually we ended up in the queue with everyone else waiting to be let into the auditorium for the main attraction. "Are you going to tell me what we're doing yet?" Juliet asked, acting like the curiosity might actually kill her.

"Um," I muttered, a nervous pinch starting up in my stomach. "It's a fashion show, themed around Hollywood Horror movies. I know your style is a little more goth chic or whatever but...horror movies are kinda *our* thing and fashion is kind of *your* thing and wow, I just realized how lame I am, so we can—"

"Lena!" Juliet was laughing, softly, ducking her head to catch my gaze, which meant it probably wasn't the first time she'd said my name. Her face was soft, open, amused.

God, I wanted to kiss her.

"It's perfect," Juliet promised me, her thumbs pressing against my wrists, and just like that the nerves went away. "Also, the nice lady is waiting for our tickets."

I looked passed her to see a woman with a kind smile, palm patiently outstretched. "Shit," I muttered, pulling my hands free and popping open my clutch to hand over said tickets.

The woman tore off the stubs she needed before giving them back and telling us which door to go through.

It was dim inside, except for the stage which was lit up and decorated in a classic *Rocky Horror Picture Show* style. There was music playing, familiar but not something I could place off the top of my head. No doubt from a good movie.

Somehow Juliet ended up leading the way, her hand wrapped around mine even as we slid down the aisle to our seats. We had good ones, fairly close to the front but off centered. They weren't perfect, of course, I was a high school student, but they were the best I could afford.

People sat around us, I knew logically that was a thing that happened, because the show was sold out, but I didn't see them.

Juliet was too distracting. Excitement vibrated off of her in a way that I'd only seen a handful of times, and it suddenly hit me that she was here with *me*.

This insanely gorgeous, amazingly cool, wonderful person, probably way too good for me…she was all of that and she was sitting next to *me*. She was holding *my* hand in her lap. She was looking at me.

"What?" Juliet demanded.

"You're beautiful," I answered without thinking. She rolled her eyes but I saw the smile that tugged on her face before the lights went down completely.

The show was amazing. There were tons of models, done up perfectly to match the characters they were copying. There was the *Bride of Frankenstein* in a boxy white dress, looking both feminine and imposing. The wives from *Bram Stoker's Dracula*, who walked while the announcer talked about where Eiko Ishioka had gotten her inspiration for the outfits. There were outfits from *The Craft*, all done up in classic 90s, and even some from *American Horror Story*, which were announced as guest pieces.

The show ended with all the usual Horror suspects—Michael Meyers in that awful William Shatner mask and boiler coat and Jason Voorhees with his machete and hockey mask. The last two were Freddy Krueger in his trademark sweater, fedora, and knives—someone had done a speculator job with his make-up and I was really glad when he stayed out longer than the others—and Leatherface with his apron and gloves, and likewise, a truly amazing mask.

When the show ended, all the models walked down the main aisle so we could get one last look at them before the lights went up, and we whistled and applauded loudly.

There was a gift shop opened afterward and Juliet was excited to take a look at the clothes and the high quality costumes. There was stuff we both wanted, of course, but the price tags were a bit high and I'd already spent too much on the evening. There was, however, a stuffed black cat with a blood splattered bow clipped to its ear wearing a *Haunted Hollywood* shirt that I somehow fell in love with. Juliet bought it for me, despite the fact that I told her not to. To go with the theme of the evening, I named it Church after the cat in *Pet Sematary*.

"That was awesome," Juliet commented once we were back in the car, holding Church in her lap while I drove. "I think my favorite were the pieces from *Interview with the Vampire*."

"That's just because it's your favorite movie," I accused as I pulled out of the parking lot behind the rest of the traffic.

"No!" Juliet argued. "I really liked the period pieces!"

"Whatever," I shot back with a playful smile. We continued to bicker for the ten minutes it took to get to *Cuppa Mocha*. It was already late enough we really should have started home, but the lure of muffins and hot chocolate sounded too good for either of us to pass up. Not to mention, I wasn't quite ready to let go of her.

We found a comfortable seat easily due to the hour, curled up and took a moment to enjoy our snacks.

"So," Juliet started, leaning back and regarding me mischievously over the edge of her cup. "Are you gay, or what?"

I snorted and glanced up at her. "Aren't you supposed to have, like, gaydar or something?"

She flipped me off lazily. "I was beginning to think it was malfunctioning."

"Mmhmm." I didn't believe her at all. "I know *you're* not withholding orgasms from Scott, so what all has he told you?"

"To tone down the flirting," Juliet answered innocently. "I honestly didn't even realize I *was* flirting. But apparently you've been dealing with some shit."

I shrugged and picked up my muffin to take a few bites before giving her my attention again. "I don't even think you do have to flirt, Juliet. You're a very sensual person."

She stuck her tongue out at me and I laughed. "What did I tell you about doing that?"

"I do believe I intend to share, this time," Juliet shot back. My heart slammed hard against my ribcage, but her smile faltered before she took a drink. "You're okay, right? With this whole…"

"Bisexual thing?" I supplied, when she couldn't seem to grasp a label herself. She hesitated, then slowly nodded. I shrugged, but nodded myself. "I'm handling it. Little by little. It helps, having Scott to talk to. He, uh, he and Lakyn, they…"

"Told you some things, about me?" Juliet guessed. When I confirmed, she only nodded again. "It's okay, I told him he could. And if you have questions, I can try to answer them."

The deep breath she took between her words let me know that even though she would, now probably wasn't the time to push it. So instead I changed the subject. "So, what do you actually want to do after high school?"

"Fashion," she answered without hesitation. "I've wanted to be in fashion since I was a child. It was something my mom and I did together a lot. You know, the shows we watched, the games we played. Which, let me tell you, are super fun when your mom is actually an actress."

I smiled, unable to help it. It was the look on her face. The pure and utter happiness of talking about something she loved. It made her impossible to look away from.

"I actually want to have my own line. Call it *Ramona & Juliet* or something more lame."

I laughed, and we finished up the hour that way—with easy conversation and light teasing. Being with her was effortless. Even the drive home, late at night and tired, was one of the best trips I'd ever taken.

I didn't want to take her home, but I knew that I had to. And more importantly, I knew I would see her soon.

I walked her to the door out of habit mostly, but I was glad I did if only because Juliet took my hand, as short of a moment as it was. "Tonight was really fun. Thank you."

"It was, wasn't it?" I replied with a grin, before I suddenly realized what position I was in. It was too late for me to go inside without spending the night, but too impersonal to just leave. A fucking hug seemed like a terrible idea, though. "Uh, right, okay. So I will…see you on Monday. Yup. That. All right."

"Lena." Juliet laughed as I went to walk away, but my hand was still caught in hers. She gave me a tug, and when I turned back to her, she was suddenly *so close*. I felt my breath catch as her free hand settled on my hip, and once again, my heart took up its constant goal to try and *beat its way out of my chest*. Her nose trailed across my cheek slowly as she somehow stepped closer to me, and I was frozen. Completely and totally unable to move.

She was giving me time to back out.

I wouldn't dare. God, did I want to kiss her. I felt Juliet smile more than I saw it, blue eyes falling gently shut, a ghost of warm breath on my lips before hers were against them.

The world stopped.

She was soft, her mouth moving smoothly against mine, the tip of a tongue just barely touching mine. It was the best kiss I'd ever had, and as much as I wanted more, it was over.

Juliet moved away from me slowly, her fingers sliding through mine as she murmured, "Goodnight, babe."

"Goodnight," I repeated softly, my head fuzzy, knees weak. I watched her smile one more time as she opened the door, tossed a cute wave over her shoulder, and then she was gone.

For the second time in a handful of days, I left Juliet's house with a smile that refused to go away.

9. BTW, I'm Gay

When the week moved on, it took the last of fall with it. Gone were the flowy clothes we could get away with when the weather hadn't been freezing, replaced with sweaters and layers and beanies. I wasn't a fan of the cold, personally, so I hid under sweatshirts and complained.

Juliet, however, was some kind of Winter Goddess.

It was seriously unfair how beautiful she was.

Winter also brought with it *snow*, which I hated. Most people loved snow, but it was awful to drive in, it was *cold*, and Grant was not a fan of snow days. Which meant I still had to drag my ass out of bed, brave said cold, and go to class.

Granted, Juliet was at school.

Which meant I basically got to pine for her all day.

"Sit with me," I complained, catching Juliet's wrist as she went to move past me. She still tried to keep her momentum, until I wouldn't let her go, then she sighed and turned back to me. She was smiling, despite the fact that she was trying to look annoyed.

"No," Juliet answered, leaning down enough to pat me on the head. That was about as close to PDA as we got in school, which was totally fair. I didn't like it from other couples, so no need to contribute. "If I sat up here I'd actually have to pay attention. I'll see you at lunch, okay?"

I pouted despite myself but let her go anyway. Juliet shot me one more smile before pulling the light blue beanie off my head and onto her own instead. It actually looked better on her, which was ironic considering she was wearing mostly black.

I was so busy watching her take her seat in the very back of the classroom that I barely noticed the look Lacey was giving me. Which was totally uncalled for. "What?"

"I didn't believe you when you told me you were gay," she stated, the look on her face completely flabbergasted. "You are *so* gay."

She shook her head before leaning back in her seat and flipping through her history book with her normal air of disinterest. I blinked at her before she held both hands up in surrender. "Sorry, *bisexual,* damn."

"What?" I asked, and my voice sounded flat even to my own ears. Juliet and I had only been out once, so it wasn't something I had shared with my best friend yet.

Lacey glanced up at me, pausing halfway between flipping another page and finally just letting it fall. "Are you kidding me?" she asked, and gestured between me and the spot Juliet had just stood theatrically. "You are so fucking gone that it's vomit inducing."

I scoffed at that and turned my back on her for possibly the first time ever in that class, distracting myself by sorting through my notes. "I don't know what you're talking about."

I heard Lacey move and I knew her well enough to know that she was probably leaning as far across her desk as she could. "So are you two dating yet, or what?"

I spun around and regretted it immediately, because Lacey's smirk said she already knew the answer. I frowned, glanced over her head to where Juliet wasn't paying any attention to her surroundings—go figure—before answering. "One date. We went on one date. Saturday."

Lacey grinned like she'd won a prize. "Mhmm, and was it *life altering?*"

I glared at her one more time before turning back to my book. "She bought me a stuffed cat," I mumbled just as Mr. Radford got up to start class. Lacey's only answer was a snicker.

The rest of the morning passed rather uneventfully, each class reminding us we had midterms coming up at the end, which was a good thing because it meant our actual work load was small and no one dished out homework.

I wasn't too worried about the tests, because as seniors, if our grades were high enough we got out of them, and I knew most of mine were. Except for French, and possibly Calculus, but even still it could be worse.

Library was as boring as usual, but I got to spend it digging out Christmas books to put on display. Juliet sauntered in early, flopped into the chair backwards and crossed her arms over the desk, resting her chin on them. "Hi beautiful."

"Shut up," I muttered, letting my hair fall in my face to cover what I was sure was an incredibly shameful blush. "Do you think if I put out *Harry Potter*, they'll realize it's not a Christmas book?"

"Probably," Juliet replied, and when I was finally brave enough to glance up at her, she was watching me much too intently. Finally, she smiled. "Hey, do you want to come over after school tomorrow? We can double with the guys. My dad and Rick will be out."

I shrugged, tried to play it nonchalant for about two seconds, then cracked and nodded enthusiastically. "Yeah. Yeah I'd like that a lot."

"Cool," Juliet answered just before the bell rang.

I set out one last book and made my way across the room to swipe my bag off the floor.

Juliet smiled at me one more time. "I don't think we'll do much. Probably just make hot chocolate and watch movies."

"That's perfect," I answered, and gave a pitiful little wave before leaving her to go to English. We didn't do anything particularly notable in there, either, and then it was lunch time.

Juliet was waiting for me when I got out of class, my lunchbox folded in her arms.

Lunch passed in its usual serenity of laughter and way too much sass from a certain cheerleader. Afterwards, we had senior pictures, which I was pretty sure none of us were actually looking forward to. In fact, I had almost forgotten about them.

Lacey, however, was a fan of getting her picture taken, so she happily volunteered to go first. As best friend duties demanded, I made it my mission to stand behind the photographer and make faces at her. She tried to ignore me, but I was pretty sure at least one photo was snapped with her middle finger up as she ran it through her hair. I hoped she bought that one, even if it didn't make it into the yearbook.

Senior pictures were weird if only because, from the outside looking in, it seemed like everyone wore the same outfits. They didn't; in reality the pretty black dresses were actually just a wrap that didn't even reach mid-length.

I changed into my own, pulling the wrap across the tank top I'd worn under my outfit, before finding my way to Juliet. She was dressed too, pulling her hair back so only a few stray waves hung around her face.

I smiled as I watched her and she pretended not to notice, but I saw her roll her smile. "Fix my hair," I demanded.

"Fix your own hair," she shot back.

"Um, I wore a hat today so I didn't have to fix my hair. Someone stole it." My glare eventually wore her down, and Juliet sighed deeply before pinning the last bit of her hair in place and walking over to me.

She ran her fingers through my hair before eventually moving to stand behind me, then I felt her tug it all up and start braiding. It didn't take her long, actually, and then I realized she was braiding around my head, putting a bun down just right behind my left ear, pinning that into place with bobby pins that were coming from who knew where. Then she circled around in front of me again, pulled some tendrils loose. "Beautiful."

"I look stupid," I muttered, meaning the outfit overall. My jeans and snowflake patterned boots did not match the weird wrap thing at all.

Juliet just smiled, her fingers gently touching my temple before sliding down to rest under my chin. She lifted my head like she might kiss me, the way she was looking down at me clearly saying she wanted to.

"Beautiful," she repeated, then gave me a slight nudge toward the line where the photographer was waiting.

Lacey was giving me that *so gay* look again while she handed over her own shawl to another girl, then mimed vomiting when her hands were free. I stuck out my tongue in retaliation.

***

"Stop it!"

Somewhere behind me the little fucker giggled. I looked up to toss a glare Juliet's way, but she was making it her point to ignore me while I passive aggressively shook snow off my arm.

Ironically enough, despite how nice the weather had been until winter pounced, I'd never been in the James' backyard before snow covered everything.

It was beautiful. Tons of space that looked like it needed a dog or something to run around in it, large trees dripping with icicles. A covered patio area sat off to the left.

The patio wasn't too big—maybe the size of a small living room, with bug screen netted walls and cobblestone floors. There was nice furniture lined around, a grill set up, a gas heater in the middle with a bright flame. Juliet was in the corner, messing with a Christmas tree. The real kind, apparently.

"Lakyn!" Scott scolded, snowball in hand, looking for where his boyfriend was hiding behind one of the trees. "Leave Lena alone! You know she doesn't like the cold."

Lakyn groaned, then he popped up from behind the tree nearest the side door, which explained how he'd managed to pelt me without my noticing. "She's being such a sourpuss, though."

"Yeah, well, that's what happens when girls don't get laid regularly," Scott said before throwing his weapon and hitting Lakyn square in the face with it. It was so funny I wasn't even offended at his really, *really* lame joke.

Lakyn wasn't nearly as impressed. He wiped snow from his face and glared.

"You wanna put that theory to the test, see if it happens to guys too," he muttered, and Scott grinned, made a show of stretching out. Even bundled up in winter clothes he was pretty attractive. It was like there was no doubt what his padded vest was hiding. If I knew it, Lakyn definitely knew it. He got to get up close and personal to all that on the daily. "You suck," Lakyn added.

"Actually, I'm pretty sure you do most of the sucking."

"Okay!" Juliet finally snapped, deciding she'd had enough, which was probably a good idea because Lakyn was smirking and I knew that wasn't good. Scott was grinning though, so I figured it was a conversation they would probably continue later. "Lena, what's next?" she asked.

I sighed as I looked down at the text book in my lap. We were officially on the last week of school, which meant midterms but also getting out at lunch every day. I managed to get out of all of my tests except for one. French. Go figure.

Thankfully, I had a high B in the class, so I was getting away with only an oral exam of ten questions. Short, sweet, simple.

It also meant that if I missed more than three I would fail and have to take the written exam with everyone else.

I ran my fingers through my hair and stared at the words as I tried to remember the correct pronunciation. *"Je vais à la... Martinique pour les vacances. Qu'est-ce que... je dois prendre?"*

Juliet was silent as she messed with a branch before tilting her head. "Mmhmm, and what does it mean? Break it down. First half of the question, and then the second."

"Um, 'I'm going to...for a vacation...I'm going to Martinique for a vacation. What do I bring?'" Juliet shrugged in a way that said I was close enough, so I nodded and tapped my fingers against the page. "Fuck if I know. Where the hell is Martinique?"

"The Caribbean," Lakyn answered as he launched another snowball my way. It splattered against the screen this time. I flipped him off, which seemed to lose some of its power with my fingers wrapped in knit gloves.

"Lena." Juliet was looking at me when I gave her my attention again, and she nodded down at the textbook as if to remind me of what I was actually supposed to be paying attention to. "How do you answer?"

I thought about it, trying to find a simple way to answer that wasn't an obvious cheat. Finally, I settled on, *"Prends un maillot de bain."*

Juliet nodded, clearly stating it as acceptable, and then asked for another one. Overall, I was freezing, French was the last thing I wanted to be studying, and the boys playing in the background were distracting. But, it was nice. Just getting to be with them was nice.

The last two weeks had basically passed in a blur. School was boring, too many teachers trying to finish off their lesson plans before midterms officially started and Christmas break hit. The younger kids got it worse, with piles of homework and mental breakdowns. Holidays were stressful.

Most of the seniors didn't have anything to worry about. Juliet had to take the chemistry final, and Georgia had to take a couple, but Lacey and Kiki were both completely free. Which meant we spent a lot of time at school running errands for the teachers or working in the library.

Which gave Juliet and me tons of time together.

Our official second date had been a fun one. Pajamas, hot chocolate, and really cheesy Christmas movies. Lakyn had whined about our choices, but after Scott had curled around him, he'd effectively shut up. And once Juliet finally put in *The Nightmare Before Christmas*, everyone had been officially happy.

It actually wasn't all that different from what we normally did together, but it *felt* different. When we all piled up in the living room Juliet was immediately at my side, arm over my shoulders, letting me settle comfortably in the dip of her collarbone. We fell asleep on the floor like we usually did on movie nights, and there was no awkwardness when I woke up with Juliet's head on my stomach.

That was the difference. That, and the fact that she would press her lips against my temples when the boys weren't paying attention—because lord knew they would tease us to no end— and she let me draw shapes into her thighs with my thumb. And when I left Saturday morning, she crowded me up against the door and pressed three chaste kisses against my lips before her tongue was suddenly chasing my own, and I couldn't breathe anymore.

It still made my hands shake to think about it.

I tried not to actually see her too much during the week, afraid that I was pushing too hard or getting too clingy, so the next Saturday I went Christmas shopping with Lacey. Which was about as disastrous as I knew it would be.

I was a notoriously awful gift giver—the type of person who passed off candles as real gifts and bought coffee makers for people who didn't even drink coffee, just because the couple in the advertisement looked happy.

I'd managed to find presents for my friends fairly easily, even more so for Lacey, who was used to just pointing out what she wanted at this point. The James family was more difficult, and Lacey had dragged me away by my hair when I tried to make a beeline for the candles. Apparently, they were only appropriate gifts for *her* parents, who loved me anyway, and no one else. They had been nice candles, too.

I'd lost it over trying to find something for my parents though, which hit the tail end of Lacey's patience. She'd thrown her arms up when she'd finally had it with me and said, "Honestly, Lena, it's not that hard. Hey, maybe you should get them a cake and put *BTW, I'm Gay* on it."

"You think you're funny," I'd mumbled into my hands. "But you're really not."

"I'm a riot," Lacey had argued. "You don't have a sense of humor."

"Bitch."

"Slut."

She'd laughed me off and told me that—once again—she would handle gifts for the parental figures. She had a real talent for it, somehow.

Sunday afternoon my mother had had off of work, and we'd spent it together getting mani-pedis and overall spoiling ourselves. My father had managed to get off at a decent hour too, and met us for dinner. It was a fantastic way to de-stress.

Then, Tuesday afternoon led me to Juliet's, where I was currently sitting while the boys had a snowball fight and the goddess herself decorated. She made me go through a few more phrases, occasionally perfecting my grammar or my pronunciation, before nodding finally like I'd done good enough.

"When is the test?"

"Before lunch tomorrow," I answered. The morning was split between Chemistry and French for me, which meant I'd spend half the day working in the library with Juliet because I didn't have to take the first test. She would be in there all day, poor baby.

On the upside, we were kept busy, because we had to do inventory and it was a big library.

Juliet nodded and stepped down from the tree to walk back over to me and pick up the ornaments. I grabbed her jacket when she was close, curling both hands into the fabric, smiling at the way the corners of her mouth twisted up even though she tried to ignore me. "Take a break," I muttered. "Kiss me instead."

The smile finally broke free and Juliet rolled her eyes before her hands were on my face. They were fucking freezing because she wasn't wearing gloves, but I found that I didn't mind as they softly traced my jawline, thumbs settling behind my ears before she tilted my head up and leaned down to seal her mouth over mine.

My heart still stuttered in my chest when she kissed me, the world both spinning and standing still at the same time. She was so cold, but the friction eventually started to warm us up.

Somehow my hands found their way to her hips, and I wished I could get a better grip on her.

Juliet tilted her head, getting a better angle, and everything was *so amazing* suddenly. I felt heat pull at my toes, surge through the rest of my body, and I wanted to pull her closer. I wanted to get lost in her. I wanted—

She jerked away with a growl, and it took me a moment to notice why. Lakyn blew a kiss at us while snow fell out of Juliet's hair, and two steps behind him, Scott was holding up his hands in the universal sign for surrender.

Juliet didn't seem to care. She pulled gloves out of her pocket and very calmly put them on, one hand after another, before she looked up at Lakyn and glared. He tried to run, but he didn't make it very far, and in the next second Juliet had him tackled into the snow.

Despite how much I hated the cold, I had to get up and join.

10. "I do not hate Christmas!"

I had a decently sized family, most of whom lived out of state, so Christmas was usually just my parents and myself, sometimes a Skype call with a few of the others, but nothing overdone.

I hadn't seen my father's parents in at least two years outside of a computer screen, but they were visiting. My grandpa was a big man, stocky, bald with old military tattoos and hard eyes. Generally kind, in a gruff sort of way, with high standards and a no-nonsense policy.

My grandma was a short, plump, white haired woman who made too many cookies and liked to pinch people's cheeks, like a character straight out of a family movie. Everyone called her Grandma May, even though her name was Urma. I'd never really asked why.

There was music playing and gingerbread men clasped in the hands of children running about the house. Juliet was there, dressed in an oversized sweater and nothing else, her blond hair pulled back into a messy bun. She was sitting in my dad's favorite armchair with her long legs curled underneath her.

It was an oddly sexy look, because she seemed thrown together. She wasn't even wearing makeup, like she'd just rolled out of bed and put on whatever she found off the floor. Like...

Like she'd crawled out of bed after being with me.

I was both unbelievably smug about that fact and appalled because, *hello*, she was sitting around with my family. But no one seemed to comment on it, so I didn't bring it up either. Instead, I plucked a finger sandwich off the tray on the counter and walked across the room to perch on the arm of the chair next to her.

Juliet was in a deep conversation with my younger cousin, Graham, who was telling her all about his Hot Wheels collection. She smiled when I sat next to her though, and silently moved one of her hands to my lap, twining our fingers together. It was such an easy move, so natural, that I didn't even think about giving hers a slight squeeze before my mother asked me about what our friends were doing for the holidays.

We talked for a while; the world kept spinning around us. Everything felt fine. Until my grandfather stood. He didn't say a word, just crossed the room, put a hand on Graham's shoulder to pull him back, and then reached for mine and Juliet's hands.

Then the living room was quiet, everyone watching as the man pulled our hands apart. He dropped Juliet's dismissively, gave me a look that clearly said I should go sit somewhere more appropriate, and then went and sat back down by his wife.

"Walter," my mother spoke up as she looked between me and my grandfather. He was sipping his tea like nothing had happened, although his shoulders were in a tense line. "What are you doing?"

My grandfather huffed out of annoyance, like he hadn't expected to be asked that question. "They look like faggots, Margaret," he answered finally. "Don't let them pull that shit at home. They'll start doing it in public, too. Disgusting."

I woke up sweating.

And then I curled in on myself and started to cry.

***

The first Friday of Christmas break my friends and I had claimed to exchange gifts before our respective parents got hold of us all. Lacey, as usual, volunteered to be the host. She lived in an old, humble home, with a large living room and *so much food*, so it really was the best set up.

"We're going to listen to Beyoncé and you're going to shut up about it," Lacey threatened when I reached for the remote again. I sighed dramatically, folded my arms under my chest, and slouched down against the couch as much as I could possibly manage.

Lacey gave me a flat look before placing the remote on top of a bookshelf. I could reach it if I wanted to get up, but I think we both knew that I wouldn't get over my laziness just because I didn't particularly care for Beyoncé. Or Christmas music. Or listening to music through the television and not a fucking *radio* or something.

Juliet leaned over the couch behind me, smiling as she handed down a brownie. I glared at it, but the stupid elf hat iced on top of it eventually broke me, so I took it. And ate it. Passive aggressively.

Juliet stayed where she was, elbows braced on the back of the couch, watching Georgia and Kiki bicker over what the sizes of their gift boxes meant. They were all probably better than my presents, but who cared? I didn't. I certainly wasn't nervous or anything. I totally didn't want to return anyone's gift. Nope.

"I can feel your mood from here," Juliet murmured, before I felt her fingers comb through my hair. She smiled when I finally looked at her, crossed her arms and set her chin on them, waiting for me to explain.

Lacey sighed when she came back from the kitchen, a mug of hot peppermint tea in her hands. "She's upset because she hates this holiday and hates being forced to partake in happy events. Because where most people have a heart, Lena has a black hole."

Juliet's mouth quirked into a slightly amused smile. "You hate Christmas?"

"I *do not* hate Christmas."

"Yes you do," Kiki and Georgia said at the same time, sharing a fist bump when they realized they totally twinned out, before going back to looking at their presents like nothing had happened.

I threw my hands in the air and sat forward. "I don't hate Christmas! It's a wonderful holiday! And I love hot chocolate and cuddles and Christmas movies and food! I just don't like giving gifts! There's too much pressure! I don't know you fools that well!"

Lacey seemed very unimpressed and Georgia snickered as she looked up at me. "You really do stress out too much over this. We love you and we're just happy to spend time with you."

"You love Lacey more," I accused.

"She gives better presents," Kiki answered without missing a beat. "So, duh."

Juliet laughed while I turned around and buried myself in the couch cushions, silently declaring that I wouldn't be coming out again no matter what. They were awful and I couldn't stand any of them.

Juliet's fingers went through my hair again, slightly more forceful this time. "Come on, it's not that bad."

"It's *awful*," I complained, and then felt my chest seize up when I realized just whose company I was in. Georgia, for example, whose holidays were always strained due to a broken family, and Juliet, who had to spend Christmas without her mother. "Also, I'm an asshole, and I'm sorry."

Juliet tugged on my hair again and I finally looked up at her. She gave me a smile, one that clearly said I would probably get a kiss, but we weren't out to our friends yet. It was another one of those things. I wasn't consciously hiding it. Everything was so new. So different. Lacey knowing, at the moment, was more than enough. Everything else would come in due time.

"So stop sulking," Juliet demanded.

I nodded because there was nothing else I could say before she left in search of more food. I dropped my chin down on the cushion, watching her go. In the Christmas spirit, Juliet was all about holiday sweaters, but with her own little twist. The one she'd chosen for today was a faded red and green, cut off her shoulders, stringy and hanging well down to mid-thigh, which of course meant she'd paired it with leggings. The sweater was striped, like any typical one would be, but the reindeer on it were skeletons.

Sometimes she was indescribable.

"Jules!" I called out, leaning over the couch so I could try and peer into the kitchen. It didn't really help, but I was in no mood to get up. "Bring me some apple cider!"

She responded by yelling at me to get off my lazy ass and get it myself. I didn't, because I knew she would bring it to me anyway—a fact which she proved when she came back and sat next to me. I smiled when she handed my drink over.

"Okay, can we do this now?" Lacey asked, one hand on her hip, a slightly sad pile of presents at her feet that were paid for by a bunch of high school students. I nodded, content with my apple-y goodness, and was backed up by the others.

Because Lacey was wearing a Santa hat, she took it upon herself to pass out the presents. Kiki and Georgia made a show of shaking theirs, frowning, and offering to switch. When I finally called them out on their shit, Lacey smacked both of them with her hat and glared until they settled down and promised to be good.

Juliet gave me a mildly amused look, her hand falling against one of my ankles when I stretched my legs out across the couch. She smiled to herself, her forefinger drawing absent minded shapes into my skin while Lacey sorted out the last of the gifts.

Opening them was more fun than buying them ever was. We had all gotten Kiki book related items, and each chipped in to treat Georgia to a spa day. Lacey had a habit of picking out her own things and then acting surprised when she got them, but for the first time I saw her seem genuinely curious when she reached for her last box.

"Oh, that's mine," Juliet spoke up. "Sorry, I didn't realize they usually let you pick out your gifts."

Lacey laughed and shrugged before she ripped through the wrapping. Inside the box was a dark pink crop top, somewhat baggy, the sleeves fashionably ripped, a stray blood splatter here and there. In the center was a zombie cheerleader. The caption read *Still cuter than u.*

"I know it's not really your style, but after Halloween I couldn't resist," Juliet explained.

Lacey was grinning so wide I was afraid it might break her face. "Oh my god. This is fantastic. Where the hell did you get it?"

"Uh," Juliet shifted uncomfortably. "I made it."

The room was silent until Georgia let out a low, impressed whistle. Lacey huffed and looked at Juliet with fond annoyance. "Damn, are you even a real person?"

"No," Juliet answered with a smirk, her usual confidence snapping right back into place. "I'm a motherfucking goddess."

Lacey laughed and got up to give her a hug before changing into her new shirt. She wore it proudly, and demanded pictures before anyone else could open their presents.

Juliet went next, and got some very style appropriate pieces from everyone until she landed on my gift. Before I could help myself, I ended up saying, "Um, you don't have to use it for school or anything. You can keep your art stuff in it, if you want. I mean—" Juliet arched her eyebrows at me. "Lacey helped me because I'm really insanely bad at this stuff—"

"Lena," Lacey interrupted, "shut up and let her open the damn thing."

I flipped her off while Juliet went to pull at the wrapping paper. It was just a messenger bag, black, made to look layered and tattered and well used. Lacey and I had spent about an hour finding all the pins of Juliet's favorite bands to cover it with.

Actually, it looked pretty cool, now that I was seeing it again.

"You're such an asshole," Juliet complained, pinching my ankle while she was at it. "I love this. It's awesome."

"Really?" I asked, relief surging through my body. I hadn't even realized how tense I was until it was over. Juliet rolled her eyes fondly, nodded, and then Lacey was—very rudely—reminding me I had my own gifts to open.

I got a new stationary set from Kiki, a cute jewelry set from Georgia, and an awesome Hogwarts sketchbook from Lacey, which earned her a hug. Juliet's gift, however, was definitely the coolest. Inside the wrapping was a makeup pallet, one we had seen at the *Haunted Hollywood* shop.

I looked up at her, shocked.

"Before you freak out, no, I did not disobey the price limit we set. Half of this is from Lakyn, who wholeheartedly agreed you needed a set just to play with. Despite the insane amount of makeup you already own." She tilted her head and grinned. "*Now* do we have enough Halloween in our lives?"

I laughed and reached blindly for her hand while everyone else got up to play with their new things. She met me halfway, twined our fingers together, and smiled again when I thanked her for my gift.

The rest of the night passed with bad lip syncing to stupid Christmas songs, complaints about drinking too much hot chocolate, and eventually Lacey's parents coming home to smile at us all fondly, but remind us that we had to go home eventually.

Juliet and I packed our things up in the backseat of my Camaro before saying our goodbyes, and I probably hugged Lacey three times to thank her for not making me look like an idiot in front of the girl I liked.

We sat in Juliet's driveway for a good thirty minutes just making out, which meant my head was fuzzy and my hands were shaking until I finally slid them up into her hair.

"Thank you for my present," she whispered, each word between another chaste kiss that I tried to follow.

I smiled slightly, drew her in for another before we both admitted that eventually we had to part ways. "Thank you for mine."

She leaned in for one more kiss, then smiled, and slid away from me. I watched her walk into the house with a too warm feeling in my chest, and the knowledge that I was in way too deep.

Unlike in my still fresh and admittedly traumatizing dream, Christmas day was just my parents and myself. It was a traditionally slow and lazy event, had been ever since I was a child. We dressed casually, cleaned up so we would look good in our pictures, and ate breakfast together.

It was an easy morning, filled with jokes and laughter before we pulled up Skype to call the extended family. I tried my best to act normal when talking to my father's parents—it wasn't their fault that Grandfather was the homophobic star of my dream—and *ooohhed* and *awwed* over the gifts Santa had left for my cousins. We opened our own presents afterwards, not that there was much between the three of us. Most of mine were for college, along with money my relatives had sent in.

"So," my mother said that afternoon, sitting on the living room floor and working on putting her new nightstands together. "How are you, Lena?"

It was such an odd question that I glanced at my father, who was sitting in his favorite chair on his laptop. He met my gaze, shrugged, pushed his glasses up his nose and went back to whatever he was working on with rapt interest.

Oh, my parents knew something.

"Fine?" I guessed. I wouldn't say that I *wasn't* close to my parents, but there was definitely a distance there. Our schedules kept us from ever really just sitting down around each other with nothing to do. Light chitchat was almost unheard of.

She nodded while she picked up two different pieces of wood before sizing them up to each other. "How were midterms?"

"I only had to take French," I answered, glancing at the instructions before pointing out the piece she needed. She nodded her thanks. "I only missed one question so that's good, I guess."

My father looked up to give me a proud smile, which I appreciated, but my mother was still working diligently, like the answer to her question hadn't really mattered.

"I ran into Mrs. Barron at the supermarket the other day," she said. I resisted the urge to stick my tongue out. My parents knew about my breakup; something I'd mentioned in passing at dinner that same night. "She said Quin is doing well."

"That's great," I said honestly, sorting out the screws and other bits that would hold the nightstand together.

The silence that filled the room was thick, and I *knew* she wanted to say something more, but didn't seem to know how to go about it.

Until finally, "Juliet sounds like a nice girl."

Oh no.

I dropped a screw on accident, licked my lips and willed my hand not to shake when I reached for it. I managed a shrug that I hoped was nonchalant. "Yeah, she's really cool. I like her a lot."

Oh hell no.

Abort mission.

"I'm sure," my mother replied, and when I glanced up at her, her expression was open, but worried. She'd steeled herself up for this. She was prepared. She knew, one way or another.

My opportunity was *right there*. I could see it. The door was thrown wide open. I had the ability to nod and say "Actually, we've been out a couple of times," and it would be as simple as that. Boom, bisexuality bomb dropped, any questions? It would probably even be easier than telling Lacey had been.

I opened my mouth, but before I managed to say anything nausea slammed into me. My heart started beating so fast it was almost painful, my hands shook, sweat broke out across the back of my neck, and it was getting hard to breathe.

Anxiety.

I wasn't ready.

Abort mission.

"So, I think that we use these weird triangle things to connect piece A and piece B."

***

I spent most of the remainder of break with Lacey, because my parents had to go back to work and Juliet had family down. She showed up on occasion to hang out, and usually ended up dragged along to help with the Parker's annual Christmas program at the church. Mostly it was just me and my best friend, though.

It marked the first time I'd stayed the night with Lacey since coming out. I made the assumption that she would kick me to the couch, but when I voiced that out loud, she *literally* hit me upside the head and asked why I was being an idiot. I mentioned that I thought it might make her uncomfortable, sleeping in the same bed as a half-lesbian.

She replied that if I honestly believed people were born gay, then that included myself. Thus-forth, I had been gay as long as I had known her. If her virtue was still intact—which, it wasn't, but I definitely didn't have it—then she would be fine.

In the end, she was, and we didn't bring up that little misfortune again.

New Year's eventually rolled around, which Lacey and I usually spent together at whatever party she could get us into, but a text from Juliet changed that. Scott had been invited to a Bridgewood party and was allowed to bring whoever he wanted. So we all went.

The party was a blast. Bridgewood kids were known for throwing their money around, so there was a big house, lots of pizza, and more alcohol than anyone—*especially* anyone underage—should ever be able to get their hands on. Lacey and I definitely drank too much, while Juliet and Lakyn seemed much better at pacing themselves.

Lacey and Scott, surprisingly, got on really well. I chalked it up either to the fact that they both had jock brain, or that Scott was just literally the type of person *everyone* liked. His stats were above that of simple popularity. He was honestly a great person, but he was just bad enough that he appreciated Lacey's natural bitchiness.

When the ball dropped, Juliet took my hand and tugged me in for a quick kiss no matter what shape I was in, and then we both put an arm around Lacey's waist and pressed kisses to her cheeks. She complained and shoved at us, but I knew she didn't really mean it.

Scott, of course, was too busy with Lakyn to notice.

It was, without a doubt, the most perfect way to bring in the New Year.

11. Homo Central

Me 7:56 P.M

Can I come over?

Scotty Scott 7:59 P.M

Sure.

I sighed out of gratefulness that Scott always had his phone on him while I pulled on my jacket and left the house. There was snow on the ground, but thin enough that the grass peaked through, the weather tolerable even with the sun gone.

I'd managed to make it through the holidays no worse for wear, but there was a dream still in the back of my mind and my mother's ever-growing cautious looks to deal with. I was anxious, and I needed someone to talk to about it.

The James' still had family over, which put them only mildly out of commission. Scott was at home with his parents, and I figured he could use a friend just as much as I could.

For some reason, I felt like I should have known better than to expect Scott to be hibernating in his room like any *normal* teenager. When I got to his house I found him on the freaking roof. He grinned at me, waved, then cupped his hands around his mouth to call, "There's a ladder on the left! Come on up!"

I blinked at him owlishly, considered asking him if he was serious, but he was already up there so *of course* he wasn't playing around. "Is it icy?"

Scott shook his head so I sighed, took a moment to question my life choices, then made my way to the ladder. I tested it a few times, wondering if this was how I was going to die, and started climbing.

The ladder was stable, at least, so the hardest part was transferring from it to the actual roof. Scott was there to help, taking my elbow and guiding me.

"What the hell are you doing up here?" I asked once my footing was solid. Scott shrugged and led the way to where he had been sitting.

"Some of the lights went out," he explained, gesturing to the Christmas lights that went around his roof. "I was taking care of it and then just decided to stay."

Scott kicked his feet out before folding his arms behind his head and lying down. He looked up at me and smiled. "So, Len, what's up?"

I sighed and drew my knees up, hugging them to my chest and staring out at the street below us. There were Christmas trees lit in windows, old snowmen barely hanging on, everything bright in the early darkness. "I think my parents know."

"Ah." Scott got it immediately. There was no question about it, he just *knew*. He sighed softly and I twisted my head to look back down at him again. "Well, you're not exactly subtle about it."

"Shut up!" I groaned, running my fingers through my hair. I sighed again before dropping my forehead on my knees. "Sorry that all of our talks are about how gay we are."

He laughed and I heard him move next to me, a peek confirming that he was pushing up on his elbows. "Lena," he said, waiting for me to look at him completely. "It's okay, all right? It's nice having someone to talk to about these things with. I don't mind being that person for you. Juliet was mine for a while, so it's a fair trade."

127

I smiled, then turned my attention back out toward the winter scene below us. "How did you do it?" I asked finally. "Come out, I mean."

Scott was quiet for a very long time, and when I looked at him, his attention was on the stars above us, face shadowed. He took a deep breath, let it out, and did it again before speaking. "Not well. My parents are very conservative, traditional people. *Gay* wasn't just a word we didn't say in my house, it was almost a bad word. I was scared, mostly. I didn't want to disappoint them and I *liked* my easy life, you know? I shoved myself so far back in the closet that it stopped hurting. I had a reputation, plans, I didn't want to be gay. But you know, eventually, it gets too hard to lie to yourself. Especially when you *want* things. And I wanted someone. I wanted Lakyn.

"I fucked up," he said. "And I honestly think that part of the way my parents reacted was my fault. They never wanted me to be the kid that slept around in high school, you know? I was supposed to be a gentleman, wait until marriage, that sort of thing. No girls in my room, no shut doors. But I..."

When he sighed and sat up, I let my legs drop to a crisscross position so I could focus on him better. He rested his arms on his knees, kept his attention toward the skyline. "You know I've mentioned before that I snuck around with Lakyn. I'm not just talking stolen kisses behind the school, or dates where I told my parents I was hanging out with the boys. I mean full on lying. Saying I was single, or had a crush on some chick in another grade. Not only having sex, but having sex *in their house*. I blindsided them, you know? I think it really hit them that...not only did they have no idea *who* I was, but that I was also a liar and that I didn't respect them."

"Scott—" I said softly, but he held up his hand and shook his head.

"I'm not making excuses for them, or even saying that the way they reacted when it did come to light was *okay*. I'm just saying it probably could have been better, if I would have done something differently. If I would have actually *told* them, the

128

way I told my friends. They're decent people, just uneducated and misguided."

I licked my lips slowly and nodded. My heart was pounding like I was watching the most dramatic part of a movie and couldn't look away. "What happened?"

Scott sighed deeply. "First of all, I didn't come out of the closet. I left the door open and got myself *thrown* out. And I don't recommend it. It fucking sucks."

"Noted," I said.

Scott's chuckle was broken, but a chuckle nonetheless.

"My dad caught us together. Lakyn and I were having problems. We'd probably been together for a good four or so months before he told me to get my shit together or he was gone. And I use the term *together* lightly, only because we were doing a lot of off-and-on."

"Because you didn't have your shit together," I guessed.

Scott cracked a smile. "Pretty much. Anyway, I'd finally made my rounds. I told my best friend, Matt. Then the football team and anyone else I deemed important. I was feeling good, so one weekend my parents were out of town and I called Lakyn. I told him to plan to stay over, and we could talk. *Really* talk."

"Fuck," I muttered. "Your parents came home early, didn't they?"

"Oh yeah," Scott replied with a dry laugh. He ran a frustrated hand through his hair, took a breath, and sighed deeply. "In the middle of the night, because their flight had been delayed. Lakyn and I had talked for hours, but finally decided to go to bed because it was late. We didn't even...we were just *sleeping*, which is the ironic part of all this, really. But, as you know, my pajamas are just pants and Lakyn usually strips down to his boxers. So, that's how we were found, all tangled up in each other because Lakyn's a cuddler."

"That doesn't surprise me," I admitted, and for the first time since he'd started talking Scott's smile was genuine.

"I guess it was too much for my parents to handle all at once. They'd come in expecting me to be awake. It was only midnight—they wanted to let me know they were home. Opened my door and...I'm sure it looked bad. Keep in mind, they would have been pissed even if it'd been a *girl*."

There was a look in Scott's eyes that I'd only seen a handful of times in my life. A certain type of sadness. It was one Georgia had carried around for a long time when she had just gotten pregnant and was having trouble with her family. Something I vaguely recognized when Lakyn was sitting alone and thought no one was paying attention to him. It was the look of a kid who knew there was something in them that wasn't accepted by the people who were supposed to love them the most.

"That's why it's easier to come out to your friends first," I muttered, realization hitting me. Scott looked up, waiting for me to explain. I cleared my throat, reached in my jacket pockets for my gloves. "Um, why it's easier to come out to your friends. Because they choose to be in your company, so, like, they chose to love you instead of being forced to? And, if they leave, it doesn't hurt as bad as..."

"When it's someone who says they'll love you always, *no matter what*, does it?" Scott finished. He nodded and looked up at the sky again. "The last time I spoke to my dad, *really* spoke to him, was two years ago. He'd grabbed Lakyn by the back of his neck that night to pull him out of my bed, and Lakyn has problems, you know? *Especially* then. His parents were awful, and he's walked through hell to recover from that."

I nodded slowly, because even though I didn't know the details, I knew Mr. James was Lakyn's guardian, and there was a reason for that. I'd heard enough snippets and seen enough little things to gather it was a *big* reason.

"And I just *reacted*. I woke up because I heard him scream. This...fucking *worst* sound I'd ever heard in my life. He scratched my chest to shit trying to stay with me, and then he was being thrown into my wall. There's still a crack, right by my bookshelf, where his shoulder hit."

I winced, shook my head, blinked back the damn tears that threatened to fall. Lakyn was strong—I had no doubt about it. I'd seen him wrestle with Scott, keep his own, but there were lines that should have never been crossed, and no teenage boy deserved to be thrown around by a grown ass man.

"So," Scott continued. "I jumped out of bed and I just started pushing him. My dad. Out of my room, away from this boy I was so in love with. Screaming over and over again for him to *never* fucking touch Lakyn again. I'd never laid a hand on my father before, or vice versa. He's *not* a violent person. Something in him just fucking snapped that night.

"Anyway, my mom burst into tears and my father started yelling about how he raised a boy, not a *fucking fag*, and there was talk about getting me help and I don't even remember it all. I just remember there was so much going on and all I could see was Lakyn. Standing inside my bedroom, eyes wide as hell, and while my entire world was falling to pieces he mouthed *I love you* and that was it. I drove him home that night, and it was the first night I actually met Mr. James. I did it right that time. Like the amazing person he is, Mr. James let me stay with them for a month before my mother finally called and begged me to come home."

"Why did you go home?" I asked, unable to stop myself. I had to admit I wouldn't have blamed him, if he hadn't. I knew just from texting him that he wasn't happy at home. Where Lakyn wasn't welcome. Where being *himself* wasn't welcome.

Scott shrugged. "Because they're my parents," he answered, and I knew it really was that simple. "I love them and I *want* them to be a part of my life. I *hope* they will be, someday. And if that means I have to be uncomfortable for a while, I will be. Because I hope seeing my face every day will be a reminder of what they're missing out on."

A silence fell around us then, because there was nothing I could think of to say, nothing that would be of any good, anyway. The night was loaded with all the things that meant too much to us, too much of who we were. We shared this thing that made us different and pulled us together all the same.

Finally, Scott asked, "How do you think they'll take it?"

I shrugged slightly, let out a long breath to help the nerves that reacted to that question. "I don't know. My dad was raised a lot like how you described your parents but, he's not a very reactive person, about things? I think unless I was like seriously hurting myself, nothing I do could *really* bother him. Confuse him, sure, but he's not going to hate me or anything."

Scott nodded. "And your mother?"

I hesitated. "She's the one giving me the looks, you know? And I can't decide if it's because she's just waiting for the affirmation or praying that she's wrong."

Scott nodded slowly, took a moment to process this information. "Well, in the grand scheme of things, I'd say you've got it pretty good."

"Yeah," I muttered, nodding because I knew he was right. "It's going to be awkward."

"Just for a little while," he promised. "Tell them, give them time to process it, and eventually, they'll accept it as their new normal."

"Think so?" I asked as I leaned over and dropped my head on my shoulder.

"I hope so," he answered.

"Thanks for being my person, Scott."

He chuckled, and then a warm arm went around my shoulders, and we spent the rest of the night counting the stars.

***

Of course, school started back up again, but I didn't complain too much because it meant getting to see Juliet on a daily basis again. Not to mention, the first day itself was pretty relaxed because most of the teachers were dealing with the aftermath of exams and those could get hectic.

The seniors ended up pulled together for serious talks about college, scholarships, financial aid, and what needed to be done. Of course, they'd been shoving higher education down our throats since junior year, but it was the second semester now and that meant shit was getting real.

Lunch was a good time for us all to finally catch up. Georgia and Chris had fought over Christmas and visitation rights, and she was very *not happy* that his mother had demanded Rose split the holiday. Apparently the entire fiasco had ended in a petition to get new court papers drawn out, which did not sound fun.

Kiki, whose family didn't celebrate holidays in general, spent the break skiing a couple states over. She had a few new bruises, but seemed proud of herself nonetheless. Pictures were exchanged and stories were told that we all laughed over like we hadn't seen each other for years.

It was at the end of the day when Juliet approached me, grin on her face, asking me to join the family for dinner. I'd already had plans with Lacey, to finish up some college applications, and to my surprise, Juliet invited her, too.

Lacey originally said that she didn't want to submerge herself in Homo Central, but after the *wildly* unimpressed looks Juliet and I both gave her, she insisted that we couldn't appreciate her good humor but eventually agreed.

Which was how the three of us ended up at the James house, sprawled on the living room floor with the boys and more official-looking forms than any of us knew what to do with. Well, at least most of us. Lakyn was incredibly uninterested in it all, so he was perched on top of Scott's back, clad in basketball shorts and one of his hoodies that actually fit, playing on his Game Boy.

He was uncharacteristically quiet with the addition of Lacey to our group, but as usual no one really commented on that. We still functioned just fine, and Lakyn either tended to himself or stayed lost in whatever game he was playing. It had taken him a while to warm up to me; I doubted Lacey would be his new favorite person any time soon. Though she did seem to be Scott's.

Scott was the one who seemed to be having the most problems filling his sheets out. After a while he groaned and dropped his forehead against the ground, laying there like the work had officially killed him. Lakyn glanced up from his game just long enough to make sure that wasn't actually the case, then decided nothing was worthy of keeping his attention.

"I hate this," Scott explained. "I am so not good at this. *Explain why you deserve to go to our school.* How the hell do I answer that? Who the hell is that vain?"

"Lacey," Juliet and I answered at the same time. Lacey removed her pen from her mouth like she might argue, but then realized we were right so she just shrugged instead, going back to reading her own pages.

Juliet leaned over our circle to pick up what he had been working on last, eyebrows rising as she thumbed through the pile. "Jesus, Scott. How many schools are you applying to?"

"All of them," Lakyn answered for his boyfriend, still not looking up from his game.

Scott sighed and lifted his head, folding his arms up under his chin. "I'm not like the rest of you. I don't have a fucking clue what I want to do with my life. I'm not incredibly smart. So I'm just trying to get in *somewhere*."

"Why don't you just take a year off?" Lacey asked, tucking her hair behind her ear and shrugging. "Lakyn's only a junior, right? Chill and you can both go together."

Juliet shook her head. "Lakyn's Advanced Placement. He'll not only graduate a year early, but with college credit, too. And, if I'm right, he's already been accepted to three schools."

Lakyn glanced at her over the top of his game screen and nodded. "California, New York, and Pennsylvania."

"Which is where these are all to," Juliet murmured at the pile of papers, even though there were more than just three college applications there. I had a feeling that Scott was most likely applying to any school remotely close to where Lakyn would be. They'd gone to the same school for the last two years of their relationship and were beyond committed. Of course they didn't want to split up.

That thought made me realize something, and I tapped my pen against my own papers while chewing on my bottom lip. I'd already finished my applications and Juliet and I were quite new, but college was just around the corner.

"What?" Juliet asked, head tilted in a notably exasperated fashion. "What is that face?"

Scott chuckled softly until Juliet shot her next look his way. "That's the *holy crap, is it too soon to worry about whether me and my girlfriend should go to the same college or not?* look."

Juliet blinked at him, then twisted her attention back over to me. She looked like the idea honestly scared her a bit. "Seriously? Please don't make us one of those couples that U-haul. We can totally go to different colleges and stay in a relationship. Long distance is *not* that hard in this day and age. Plus, we both have family back here—it's not like we'd never return."

"U-haul?" Lacey asked, looking completely confused that there was a word in the English language she didn't know.

At the same time I asked, "Couple?" if only because we hadn't *officially* titled ourselves.

Lakyn chuckled softly, not looking up from his game. "It's a term used for lesbians who move too fast. Usually because they actually move in together after, like, a day of knowing each other."

Juliet nodded at Lacey to say that Lakyn's definition of the word was accurate before she looked at me and shrugged. "I wanna be your girlfriend. Do you wanna be mine?"

I couldn't help but grin, resisting the urge to duck my face and let my hair hide me. Juliet seemed far too amused, and I realized she knew my answer before I even had to say it. I did anyway, nodding excitedly before she crossed the distance between us and sealed her lips over mine.

"Oh my god," Lacey muttered dramatically. "Rainbows everywhere, gay exploding all over the place."

Lakyn snorted as Scott dropped his head again, laughing so hard his shoulders shook. Juliet rolled her eyes and I smiled despite myself, throwing my arms around her neck and drawing

135

her in enough that she had to plant her hands on my thighs to keep from falling over.

"Here Scott, let me help you with these." I heard, more than saw, Lacey gather the papers that Juliet had taken from him earlier and subsequently abandoned. "Now, let's talk about your skills."

We spent the next couple hours working on tying up loose ends. I was mostly filling out the last of my scholarship applications, as well as packaging up some sketches and portfolios. I'd applied to mostly art schools, and a few two-year colleges just to make my parents happier. Juliet was working on some fashion schools, which meant her applications were much more interesting than the rest of ours, but I tried to stay out of her business.

Lacey worked hard with Scott, which caught Lakyn's attention enough that he had put down his game and was leaning over his boyfriend's shoulder, reading everything secondhand and making comments on occasion when Scott said something he didn't agree with. Which seemed to be a good thing, oddly enough. Scott really wasn't vain enough to talk himself up, even on paper.

I hadn't actually realized how long we'd been there until Lakyn's stomach growled so loud we all heard it. He wrapped his arms around his middle, groaned pathetically, and rolled off of Scott completely. The rest of us shared amused looks, finished whatever we were working on, then climbed to our feet to stretch out.

"Baby," Lakyn complained from the floor. "I'm hungry."

"I know," Scott replied, kicking at him playfully. "Come on. Let's go find something to cook."

"I don't want to cook," Lakyn grumbled as a reply. "I just want food to magically appear."

I had to agree with him, realizing we probably should have been smart enough to order pizza, especially after a glance at the clock said Mr. James and Rick would be home soon, definitely expecting dinner to be on the table waiting.

"Come on, Lace," I muttered, pushing her over slightly as we all went toward the kitchen. "Help us cook."

Lacey grumbled something under her breath that I was sure was more swears than anything else before she eventually pulled herself off the floor and followed us. In the end, we made spaghetti, and Scott complained about having to use the canned sauce because he was used to making it homemade but didn't have the stuff. Still, it was a quick and easy meal. Lacey helped make garlic bread to go along with it, even though she was very unhappy about the whole thing.

Lakyn spent a lot of his time wrapped around Scott, small smile on his face, and I found out quickly that their clinginess was contagious. I tried my best to keep my hands to myself, but Juliet was too fun to touch, even if it was just drawing my fingers across her shoulders every time I passed her.

Lacey rolled her eyes. *A lot.*

Mr. James and Rick made it home just as we were finishing up, looking exhausted. Apparently having the shop closed for a week meant angry customers and overwork, and spaghetti was the best part of their day.

Lacey said grace, folding her hand into one of mine while I twined my fingers together with Juliet's, sharing a soft smile. It felt different, sitting in her house as her girlfriend. Not her friend, not someone she was dating, but someone *important*.

It was good. I liked it.

In that moment, I realized there wasn't much left in life that I wanted. I had good friends, some that had even passed the line straight into family, and suddenly my future didn't seem so blank.

12. "No intent to seriously maim or kill."

Lacey continued to help Scott with his college applications, a process which spread into financial aid and how to get scholarships and everything else that his parents probably should have been helping him with. A particularly frustrating session ended with her bringing that up, and when Scott winced like she'd slapped him, Lakyn promptly told her to shut her whore mouth. In typical Lacey fashion, she'd appreciated his bitchiness and had not torn him to pieces for that. It was still the only thing he'd ever actually said *to* her.

As January began to disappear, we got increasingly busier. Between college preparations, homework, and actual school, getting to go on dates was unheard of. Even when we finished our work early enough to do something, we were usually too tired.

February brought with it lots of teachers shoving the SAT and ACT tests down our throats, and reminders to get shit done as soon as possible. Lakyn and I had both already taken ours back in December and had good enough scores not to worry about them, but Scott hadn't taken them at all and Juliet wanted to retake one of hers for a higher score.

We tried to help them study, but it just ended up with us eventually getting kicked out, so we spent a lot of time binge watching *The Walking Dead* together or making snacks for our significant others—an effort that was seriously underappreciated. For the second month in a row, active dating became too complicated. It wasn't even unusual for Lakyn to fall asleep sprawled in Scott's lap, despite what promises were made for when the other boy finished his work.

Their breaks were spent laying around and playing video games. Our favorite thing was making pallets on the floor like we did for movies, stretching out on our stomachs, and staring intently at the screen well into the middle of the night. Juliet tended to settle herself comfortably in the grove of my lower back—something she'd picked up from her cousin. She was a lot nicer than Lakyn though, who I quickly learned was a dirty, *dirty* cheat.

He didn't actually care who won the game as long as Scott didn't beat him. He would cover his boyfriend's eyes or drag his fingers through Scott's hair in an oddly obscene way. There were even occasional kisses, gropes, and *moans* that I tried—and failed, mostly—to erase completely from my memory.

It was a Saturday after the tests and we were gathered in the kitchen arguing about what to cook for a late lunch, when Mr. James finally walked in. He'd slept late due to having the day off, and frowned at each of us in turn as if we'd done something seriously upsetting.

"No. I can cook for myself today. You four need to get some vitamin D and do something other than sit around all day."

"Don't be ridiculous, Daddy," Juliet muttered, a bit of bite in her tone that suggested she didn't particularly like her father's choice of words, while Lakyn looked unimpressed. Scott turned his back on the situation, pulling out food at what looked like random before Mr. James took it and put it right back.

"I'm serious," he insisted. "None of you have been out of this house in over a month. No father would be okay with his children staying indoors, alone, with their partners that often."

Scott opened his mouth, a smirk on his face that stated whatever he was about to say was probably highly inappropriate, but Mr. James pulled him into a headlock before he could go there. "Yes, Scott, I am well aware that no one under this roof will end up pregnant. That is *beside the point.*"

Lakyn turned a bright shade of red, followed by Juliet, although Scott just laughed. Mr. James pushed him away before leaning his hip on the counter and very literally shooing us out of the room. Juliet shot him a friendly glare, but the effect was highly dulled by her still-pink cheeks and we walked away dejectedly.

"Well," Scott muttered once we were in the hallway, arms crossed over his chest and leaning back against the wall. "Where to?"

We all considered for a moment. There weren't any movies that we wanted to see. We were hungry but not starving, and the weather was actually nice. It was still cold, but the sun was out, which meant jeans and light jackets were cutting it.

Eventually, it was Juliet who spoke up. "Mini golf?" she offered.

I laughed, thinking she was kidding, but Lakyn shot me a sinister look that had me immediately regretting that thought, and I wondered briefly just what I was getting myself into.

***

Of course the three of them didn't play regular mini golf like normal, *sane* human beings.

Scott drove us to the arcade in his jeep, blaring music and scaring the shit out of Juliet and myself when he decided Lakyn's mouth was much more interesting than the road, but we made it in once piece, somehow. We drew our funds together and bought a couple of day passes that got us into all of the events— discounted, due to the time of the year.

We hit the mini golf course first, which started in a small room that allowed us to pick what color clubs and balls we wanted. Scott was swinging a green one made for his height before the workers left us alone. Then he grinned and drew it close like it was a microphone. "The rules are," he said dramatically. *"There are no rules."*

Lakyn rolled his eyes, although his overall expression was fond, while Juliet was busy being way too serious about choosing her own club. "Liar," she muttered, giving a pink one a few swings before deciding it was worthy.

Scott chuckled and dropped his club to the ground, leaning on it and smiling. "All right, real rules: No biting"—a look shot at Lakyn, who mumbled something suspiciously like *not what you said last night*— "no intent to seriously maim or kill. Don't let anyone score more points than you. *Do not* get us caught."

I was alarmingly unprepared for what they called Extreme Mini Golf.

"Should we do teams?" Lakyn asked as we walked outside, dropping his purple ball onto the starter point of the first hole. He flicked his dark hair out of his face and looked up at his boyfriend. "You and me, and the girls? Don't want to accidentally hurt one of them."

Somehow, I still thought they were kidding around, but Scott nodded with all seriousness and stepped up behind Lakyn. "All right, Lena, just watch this round, and then you and Juliet can go. Cool?"

I glanced at Juliet, and then just nodded. She was smirking at me, far too amused for my liking. "Please tell me you think regular Mini Golf is boring?" she asked.

"As fuck," I answered. "That's why I didn't actually think you guys were serious."

"Well, welcome to Extreme Mini Golf," Lakyn said, lining his shot up. "Where we break just about every rule possible and try not to get kicked out."

I shot a glance at Juliet again, who just grinned at me and nodded. They weren't joking then. Lakyn took a swing, too powerful, and the ball soared to the end of the course but didn't fly off. It also went right over the hole, almost like he'd done it on purpose.

Scott dropped his ball down next. "Now, each person gets one uninterrupted hit. If you get a hole-in-one, you win the round, simple. If you don't, then you get to fight for it. A hole-in-one is ten points, anything made after the fact is five. You can use your club and your feet, but only your hands if you manage to knock your opponent's ball off the course completely. Also, remember not to get too violent, kids. Accidents happen."

Then he swung, and the moment his ball stopped rolling he and Lakyn were both on the course within seconds. They used their feet mostly, either trying to kick their own ball in or block the other's from going anywhere. It was an understood fact that if the ball got out of reaching distance the clubs had to be used again.

It was fascinating to watch, mostly because they were laughing like it was the most fun thing they'd ever done before. Lakyn was more ruthless than Scott, but eventually it was the older boy who won, blowing a kiss at his boyfriend before jumping down and heading for the second pair.

"Ready?" Juliet asked me with a grin.

As it turned out, Extreme Mini Golf was a fucking *blast*. The second Juliet and I started the game, I was laughing so hard I could barely breathe. She was faster than me, but I was determined, and we fought over those meaningless points like they might change the world or something.

As soon as I got the hang of it, it was somehow even better.

The hardest part was playing it cool when someone else stumbled upon us. Sometimes it was a park attendant, and one had only watched in mild concern when I had picked Juliet up. She'd screamed, which had caught his attention, when I twirled her around. She was laughing so hard she was crying, so the man just shook his head at our dropped clubs and glanced at Scott and Lakyn like he knew better, but wasn't going to question it. He obviously didn't get paid enough for his job.

Occasionally we ran into other players, usually because we caught up to them, but on particularly difficult holes, someone else would catch up to us. When that happened we'd calm down, whistle idly, and let whoever it was pass us by. Usually we'd have to slow down for a bit in case we got turned in.

Like with video games, Lakyn cheated here, too. He jumped on Scott's back once, bit at his neck, and literally shoved his hands down his pants when we were hidden under the waterfall. Scott cursed out loud on that one, and Juliet did the honors of covering my eyes for me. As usual though, Juliet had a tendency to pick up on her cousin's traits, and at one point snuck up behind me and clasped both hands over my boobs. It shocked me so bad I hit my ball hard enough that we never found it.

It was, without a doubt, the most fun game I had ever played in my life. By the time it was over, and the eighteenth hole had eaten the others' balls, we were sweating and exhausted, so we made our way to the cafe and ordered hotdogs and sodas before collapsing in a booth.

While we ate, they told me horror stories of how much they'd ended up hurt before. Juliet had taken a nasty spill a couple of years ago that ended up with her hip bruised so bad she couldn't sleep on her side for a week. One time, Lakyn had split his hand open and ended up with stitches. He was very proud of the scar, but Scott took the opportunity to explain *that* was why there were rules.

All in all, it was a good date, and we were all glad we'd taken Mr. James' advice and gotten the hell out of the house.

***

"My father wants to have dinner with us. Tonight."

My grip wavered on the tongs I was holding and Juliet immediately grabbed my elbow to stabilize me. She was trying not to smirk, I could tell, but she was also failing miserably.

I took a deep breath and side-eyed her. "That is not something you say to a girl holding glass over a fire, Juliet."

She shrugged before letting me go and using her own tongs to grip the other end of the glass rod and twist it upward slightly. The chemistry lesson of the day was how to use fire to shape glass, and we got to keep whatever shapes we made. Juliet and I were both fairly artistic, so we had curvy Ls and Js, a heart, and were currently working on a flower.

"What does he want?" I mumbled, helping her by holding the finished part out of the flame so we didn't twist too much. Juliet shrugged, too focused on her work, but I could give her time. Eventually, she looked up at me again. "He wants to talk about us, doesn't he?" I asked.

She nodded, and together, we moved the glass to a new section to be heated. "Look, I'm never going to be that person that outs you without your permission, but he sees us at home. He knows we're together, and when he asked I wasn't going to lie to his face."

I glared down at the half finished flower we had. Lacey had taken it upon herself during lunch two days ago to out me to our friends. It had actually been amusing, looking back on it, but I'd probably be mad at her for a bit longer.

Georgia had come in complaining about Chris. It'd been a perfectly normal story that I'd only half listened to about how he'd gotten them lost because he was a stubborn man and refused to ask for direction. She'd shaken her head, stabbed her burrito, and said, "So we wound up going the other way for *hours*."

"Speaking of going the other way," Lacey had mentioned, completely nonchalant. "Lena's a lesbian now."

At first, I hadn't really realized what she'd done. I'd snapped at her for not knowing the word *bisexual* and told her if she refused to use it in the future, I was going to stab her in the face with a fork. It was Juliet who caught my attention, eyebrows raised, reminding me that there was a bigger issue at hand.

Lacey got another lesson in *things you aren't supposed to do to your gay best friend* but it was done and over with. I'd never been one to cry about spilled milk so I just faced the music. Georgia had only shrugged, mentioned that she'd gotten pregnant at fifteen and she definitely had no room to judge.

Then she'd gotten much more interested, demanded to know if I was seeing anyone, and Juliet had sighed in mild annoyance before silently raising her hand. Of course, then it was all about Lacey and Georgia bonding over how in the hell they had *missed that*.

Kiki, surprisingly, had been the one who wasn't okay with the entire ordeal. She'd just gotten up, walked away, and I hadn't seen her since. Not at lunch, not in class, though I knew she had to be around. I decided not to push the issue, but it'd stung.

I sighed and ran my free hand through my hair, shaking my head. "I don't know, Jules, I'm not even out to my parents yet and..."

Juliet's gaze caught mine and she nodded before we finished off our flower and sat it on the cooling pad. She turned her back to the rest of the class, leaning against our desk and searching my face.

"I will," I promised, looking up at her. "I *want* to. I'm getting there. What Lacey did was a bitch move but I had planned on saying something; she just pushed me over the edge. I just keep thinking about my parents. I probably should have told them before I ever asked you out. It's just..."

"It's hard," Juliet finished my sentence, and I sighed and nodded. "I get it. Trust me, I know how hard it is. And I'm not saying you have to tell them today or tomorrow or this week. But why not start off with my dad? He already loves you, he's beyond accepting; he just wants to have a nice dinner and talk about how much he adores us. Okay?"

I knew that she was right. Mr. James was probably the best person to start on this road with, and he was good practice for my own parents. So I nodded eventually. Juliet smiled, squeezed my hand, and then picked up another glass rod. "So, should we be like every annoying teenage boy on the planet and make a dick?"

"You're disgusting," I muttered.

"You love it," she shot back.

I did.

I really did.

"Okay, but we're giving it to Scott and Lakyn."

"Duh."

***

145

"Why are you so nervous?"

"*I'm* not nervous, *you're* nervous," I grumbled under my breath, drawing my gaze up from behind my menu. Juliet's mouth twisted up into a sly grin as she settled back into her seat, lifting her wine glass for a drink. It was filled with iced tea, but *Cleo's* was a very nice restaurant with a very specific tone to it. Alcohol or not, wine glasses were a must.

She, of course, looked absolutely stunning in a gorgeous black dress. Her bright blond hair was done up in an elegant ballerina bun, makeup more natural than usual, and jewelry simple. She was the picture of elegance.

She was also smirking at me like the damn cat that ate the canary.

I sighed and dropped my menu, folded my arms over the table and glared at her. She sipped at her drink innocently before setting it aside, giving me her full attention once again, and gesturing for me to go ahead and explain.

"I'm *not* nervous," I repeated. "I just…"

"Want him to like you?" Juliet asked. "Want to make a good impression? Lena, sweetheart, you've already done those things. It's just dinner, okay?"

I tried to ignore the fact that the pet name made me feel all warm and fuzzy inside as I shook my head and played with my bracelet so I didn't run my hands through my hair and ruin all my hard work. "Yeah, but not as your *girlfriend*, Jules."

Juliet leaned across the table and took one of my hands in hers. "That's right," she said. "My girlfriend. Trust me, this is a happy dinner, babe. Stop worrying so much."

I held her gaze, finding something there that seemed honest and put me at ease before I nodded and sat back again. Juliet kept my hand and before long her father was entering the room. He caught her gaze and waved before making his way over.

"Hello, Lena," Mr. James greeted politely as he sat next to me. I gave him a tight little smile, and under the table Juliet's foot nudged mine. It was a simple reminder that she was there, and I had nothing to be nervous about.

Dinner, of course, went wonderfully. I'd eaten with Mr. James a good majority of the past few months, I knew him and he knew me. He never said anything about my sexuality, never made me feel weird about it, never asked just how long Juliet and I had been together. I wondered if it was something he'd already talked to Juliet about, or if he simply didn't care.

With dinner usually being such a big event at the James' house, it was odd to have all of his attention, but nice all the same. And then the inevitable turn of events eventually happened once desert hit the table.

"So, Lena. Do you remember the first night you spent at my house, when I asked if you were seeing my daughter—"

"*Dad!*" Juliet sounded scandalized while I choked on my water, and even though she hadn't been there during that conversation I had a pretty good feeling she knew what he'd said. "He's joking, Lena. Dad, tell her you're joking."

Mr. James grinned at me in a way so similar to Lakyn that I was honestly surprised he wasn't actually the boy's father. "I am. I'm joking. Kind of. If you two are having sex in my house, I expect you to have done the research and to be proceeding so *safely*. That's the boys' rule, and it will be yours as well."

"We're not," I managed to get out while Juliet shook her head slowly.

Mr. James seemed mildly impressed as he nodded and happily went for another bite of cheesecake. "Do your parents know?"

I took a drink of my water just to keep from choking again before I answered. Juliet pressed her foot to mine again, drawing her toes gently up the curve of my calf and then down again, which was surprisingly reassuring. Finally, I shook my head. "No, not yet."

He hummed in acknowledgment and nodded. "Well you know you're always welcome at my house, if the need is there."

That I did, and was forever grateful for.

13. This or That

Coming out, as it turned out, was still a big deal. I had been nervous about coming out to myself, downright scared about coming out to Lacey, but my *parents*? That was an entirely different ball game. Part of me realized that I should have known that, given the obvious avoidance of the subject and the Christmas incident, but denial was a river run deep.

The dinner with Mr. James had helped somewhat. It calmed my nerves, reminded me that I had a support system if all went to hell, and gave me an idea: Approach uncomfortable topics with the promise of food.

After Friday night, I spent the entire weekend at the James' place, hanging out with Juliet and the boys. Now that her father was completely in the know, some little barrier between Juliet and myself lifted. We were touchier at home, more cuddly. The boys teased us, of course, but we could throw it right back at them.

"How did you come out?" I asked Juliet one night, when we were all gathered in the living room with *Saturday Night Live* playing in the background.

She and I were cuddled on the recliner, my back pressed against her chest, one of her arms thrown over my body so I could play with her fingers. I tilted my head onto her shoulder so I could look up at her while I waited for her answer. The boys, who were on the couch, looked up too, even though I was sure they knew the story.

"To my parents?" Juliet asked and I nodded. "I didn't have to," she admitted. "Heteronormativity wasn't really a thing growing up. My parents were always really open minded. When I was in grade school one day my mom asked if there was anyone I had a crush on. I told her Lizzy Mann had the most beautiful brown eyes I'd ever seen. And that was just kind of that. I didn't really think it was weird until..." She trailed off.

"Until I started hanging around so much," Lakyn offered up. "Because my parents were dicks."

He and Scott high-fived over that, though we all knew it wasn't really a funny subject. I wanted to ask them, just for ideas, but I knew Scott's story. Lakyn's, I was sure, would break my heart. In fact, I was almost certain *any* of Lakyn's stories would break my heart.

"Anyway," Juliet continued. "Once I was old enough Dad gave me the sex talk—which was the most awkward day of my life, mind you—without even mentioning boys. He'd honest to God done the research to get it from a lesbian perspective. I've never thanked him for that, but I probably should..."

"How did your dad get to be so cool?" I asked, unable to help myself. Said sex talk wasn't really a conversation I would have ever wanted to have had with *my* father, but I admired Mr. James for going the extra mile.

Juliet was silent before she shifted and ran the fingers of her free hand through my hair. "His best friend in high school was named Roderick Haggard. When he was born, he was called Raleigh because... I don't want to say he was born in the wrong *body*, but definitely with the wrong parts. So, people thought he was a girl. His mom was really supportive, and when he was in middle school she started helping him transition. But it put a lot of stress on his family. His parents separated, his little sister refused to talk to him, he lost a lot of friends. One day, he went home early, to tell his mom he made it onto the baseball team, and found her crying. I don't know why or whatever, Dad never told me, but apparently he called him that night and said he was really sorry. He was just tired of hurting people, but he had to hurt one more." She sighed heavily. "Dad didn't realize, at the time, that he was the last person Roderick hurt. His suicide note just said, '*tell them I'm sorry, for everything'*."

149

"Shit," I muttered, feeling my heart seize up. I couldn't even process the level of emotions, not enough to voice out loud. I couldn't even find any other words. *"Shit."*

Juliet nodded while I shook my head and squirmed to cuddle up into her some more. "I think, mostly, Dad just wanted to create an environment where no one ever felt like the world would be better off without them. Where no one thought the only way to stop the pain was to stop existing at all. To never feel that alone, like they had nowhere else to go. And my mom was just really loving and really nurturing. I don't know if she was always *that* open minded or if that was something they grew together. But they did it. They were a pretty awesome parenting team."

A silence fell over the room, but it wasn't necessarily uncomfortable, just there. Juliet didn't talk about her mother a lot—in fact, I'd never heard her say so much about her at all. I expected to feel on edge after all that, but I just felt oddly calm. And sad that Mrs. James was a woman I would never meet.

"When I was ten," Lakyn spoke up, twisting around to lay on his side, pulling Scott's arm over him like a blanket. "Aunt Lily caught me in her bathroom trying to paint my nails black. I was so scared I was going to get in trouble. But she sat me down and painted them for me. She was the first person I ever told I liked boys. We talked for *hours* over nothing at all and everything."

Juliet pressed a kiss into my hair, slow and lingering. "You would have liked her," she mumbled, and I nodded. There was no doubt in my mind that I would have.

We spent the rest of the night going over coming out stories, ranging from hilarious to dead serious. Mostly we tried to stick to the former, if only because the latter was hard to deal with. Even though he'd had it rough, Lakyn had some hysterical pieces; which was only unsurprising because he was a little shit.

That weekend gave me the confidence to face my own parents. Even if I made an underhanded decision about how to do it. Getting my parents' undivided attention had always been difficult, but there was one thing that had worked since I was a kid: scheduling a meeting.

They both had hour and a half lunches, so it was fairly simple to call up their offices and request that they both meet me at the Chinese restaurant downtown. It was an unspoken rule that if I went through their jobs, I actually needed their attention. I had nothing to do but sit back and wait.

The waiting was the worst. For the first time in my life, I almost understood why people smoked, and even though I definitely wasn't going to go find a pack of cigarettes, I did have alcohol. Hotel brand mini-fridge bottles Lacey and I had stolen a while ago and hidden under my bed.

I threw one back like a shot and tried not to feel guilty about the fact that I was drinking before noon. Then I got dressed in my favorite outfit, threw my hair into a messy ponytail, and drove across town.

***

My mother arrived first, looking perfect and put together as always in a pantsuit, carrying the briefcase I'd gotten her for Christmas. She looked frazzled as she sat down in front of me, swiping free strands of hair out of her face before pulling off her sunglasses and setting them aside.

"Lena, darling." She smiled at me, sighed, and seemed to relax. "Why aren't you in school?"

"It's a college day," I answered, looking up from my menu. "Since I don't plan on staying local I didn't have to join them, so I have the rest of the afternoon off. Hi, Dad."

He nodded as he joined our table, which was circular, giving us all a fantastic view. I had chosen it on purpose, so I wouldn't end up feeling cornered if things went south.

There was a flurry of activity as the waiter came by to introduce himself, pass out menus, and get our drink order. That was followed by an awkward silence long enough that we had our beverages before anyone spoke.

"Seriously, honey," my mother said, "what's so important that it couldn't have waited until this weekend?"

I delayed answering by taking a drink, considering my options. I was aware that it probably wasn't nice of me to drop the bisexuality bomb during their day, but at the same time, it gave me a bit of protection. They had to keep their emotions in check because they had to go back to work, which also gave them hours to process, and it gave me a perfect excuse to hastily exit the conversation if needed.

So, yeah, I was being a bit of a bitch, but I ignored that fact. Because if I didn't do it now, I probably wouldn't ever.

Not to mention I'd already put everything into place—there was officially no backing out.

"I have to talk to you both about something," I stated as the obvious. "But I think we should order first."

So we did. The restaurant was one of our favorite places to eat as a family, even if that was a rare occurrence. We generally had a habit of ordering the same thing every time we went there, even though we looked at the menu and pretended like we weren't going to.

I forced us all into small talk about college and school until our food came, and my mother surprisingly let me. I had a feeling she knew exactly why I had wanted them to meet me, and she didn't want to talk about it anymore than I did.

Finally, our food was there, the waiter was gone, and there was nothing keeping me delayed. I took a deep breath, and faced the music.

"So," I started off. "I know things have been a little strange lately. I've been going through a lot. Had a lot on my mind. But, um, everything's cleared up now and I'm ready to talk about it."

My father glanced up, but I was willing to bet he'd stuffed his face with noodles as an excuse not to talk to me. My mother, however, was intently working on mixing her rice and chicken like the ratio had to be exactly right.

I sighed slightly. "I know you know about Juliet. I don't know how much you know, but I know that you know."

That was a train wreck of a sentence.

Fucking smooth, Lena.

I figured it had been my fault, in the long run. It wasn't like my parents had ever actually been around Juliet, but I talked about her. A lot. At some point, I assumed my mom recognized the *way* I talked about her for what it was. And, of course, it was possible Quin had run his mouth to his mom, who had said something to mine. I doubted it, but not enough to rule it out as a possibility.

My mother didn't say anything, but she did shoot my father a sharp look. He sighed, his expression clearly stating he wanted to be just about anywhere else. "Lena, it's *fairly* normal to experiment. I've heard people usually wait for college for that, though."

"Dad," I interrupted, gently enough that he let me. "I don't even…I promise you, I'm not. I didn't just wake up one day and go, 'Huh, let me pull out my sexuality and play with it.' I've done the research; I've put in the work. And it's important enough that I'm bringing it to you."

My mother sniffled like she was holding back tears, even though her expression said no such thing. She took a moment to eat, sighed, then said, "I just don't understand. You date boys, Lena."

"I do," I agreed. "I like boys. I will continue to like boys. But as for right now, I'm dating Juliet and I really, really like her."

My mother shook her head, tucked a few strands of hair behind her ear. "Where did this even come from? Lena, if she put…*ideas*, in your head, you can tell us." When I looked like I was going to argue with her, she pressed on with, "You've just never mentioned liking girls that way before, Lena."

"Not true," I pointed out, thinking back on Scott and his parents—likewise, *gay* had never really been a word in my house growing up. Not good or bad, just simply not there. "I wanted to marry Princess Jasmine when I was five."

My mother blinked at me. "I just thought you wanted to be her."

"No." I shook my head, because I remembered that fairly clearly. My father had explained to me that girls couldn't marry girls, and although *technically* he hadn't been wrong, as a child I had believed that to mean girls couldn't *love* girls.

My father sighed and rubbed at his temples, but my mother was looking at me with that same expression she'd had during Christmas. She was ready to listen, but she was *scared*. "I just don't understand."

"It's called bisexual, Mom. And it doesn't make me any different than I always have been."

My father let his hands drop to the table, and he and my mother shared a look for a long time. The silence stretched on to the point that we all eventually went back to our food.

Finally, it was my father who spoke. "If you still like boys then why not just be with boys? That would make your life so much simpler."

The words caught me off guard, and I blinked at my dad before shaking my head. "I don't think it would, though? I mean, that's a whole part of myself you're asking me to ignore. It'd be like if all my friends like vanilla ice cream and you were telling me I couldn't tell anyone that I actually like chocolate?" On the list of metaphors, it was definitely not the best, but I figured I was doing all right. "I'm not gay if I'm with a girl and straight if I'm with a boy. It's not *this* or *that*. It's always going to be there. Bisexual. Constantly. No matter what, end of story, take a bow."

For a while, my father just looked at me, and then eventually he gave me a nod.

I sighed and sat back, feeling tense and overall uncomfortable. "I just want to be happy, and she does that for me."

No one said a word after that, which I was almost grateful for. Lunch ended and they went back to work.

It hadn't been perfect, but it hadn't been awful.

That alone gave me hope.

***

Things at home certainly weren't *bad* as the week moved on, but they were awkward. My mother was tense, my father didn't

154

quite know what to say to me, and overall I found myself missing the comfort of a time before I had come out. Mostly though, I felt lighter, freer, and that kept me from regretting anything.

Because my parents worked a lot and school was busy, avoiding each other wasn't really a hard thing to do. Friday after school, I packed a bag to stay at the James' place, left a note, and didn't plan on being back. I knew they wouldn't bother calling me home, if only because no one would be around to make sure I stayed there.

I had, of course, let Scott and Juliet know when I had done it, so by the time I got there I was surrounded by hugs and bittersweet congratulations. Given that my parents were only distant and not cruel, I almost felt bad being in Scott and Lakyn's presence and feeling hurt over their reactions. It was Lakyn who hugged me after that, told me that I deserved to feel whatever I was feeling, it didn't matter who had it *worse*. All that mattered was I'd done it.

I spent the entire weekend there, drove home incredibly late Sunday night, showered, and crashed without even attempting to make conversation with my parents. Then the entire cycle started all over again.

By Thursday, I was holding Juliet's hand as we walked down the hallway. She'd slowed at first, made a show of looking between our hands and me, then asked if I was sure that was something I wanted to do.

I'd shrugged and said, "Why the hell not?"

As it turned out, the answer to that question came in various forms. Most people didn't give a flying shit, a few people just stared, but Quinton Barron, of course, had to make a scene.

It happened in English, which he had right before me so we occasionally crossed paths. He was on his way out when he dropped his backpack on my desk, followed by his hands, then glared at me as he never had before. "Seriously? How long have you been a fucking dyke, Lena?! What was I, your cover up?"

"Quinton," I said slowly, hoping to stop whatever this was. Instead, he made a show of throwing his backpack across the room, followed by my books. I jumped, then slid out of my chair and walked out of class.

Mr. Patterson called after me, but I didn't stop. I walked all the way to library, throwing the doors open with too much force and refusing to cry. Juliet didn't say anything, just watched as I crossed the room until I was behind the desk, then I sat at her feet and stayed there. Eventually she got up and got *Harry Potter* for me.

Kiki brought my backpack and books to lunch. She hesitated, looked at me and Juliet both, then sighed. "I don't agree with homosexuality. But that's something I was raised with and I care for you both. So, I'd like to still be your friend, if that's okay?"

After the day I'd had, I couldn't find it within myself to say no, so I'd just nodded and Juliet pulled Kiki's usual seat out for her.

Then, for the first time in forever, we had a normal lunch period.

Friday afternoon both of my parents were home, because it was my dad's one day off and my mother had gotten in early. It was the first time I'd *really* been around them since the restaurant, and we ended up in an argument.

My mother wasn't comfortable with me spending the night at Juliet's house, which my father backed up by explaining they'd never let me sleep over at a boyfriend's house—why would this be any different?

I saw their point, from a skewed sort of perspective. But after the week I'd had—after all the negativity—I was craving the safety of the James' house and the ability to just be *myself*. I explained this as best I knew how, but it just led to more concerned glances and confused expressions.

We weren't sexually active; we weren't even alone most of the time, because Scott and Lakyn were generally around. I even said I'd sleep on the damn couch, handed over Mr. James' number and said they could call him if they wanted to discuss it.

It was probably the most *rebellious teenager* moment I'd ever had, and maybe that fact alone was what eventually led to my parents letting me go.

I was still stressed by the time I made it to Juliet's place. She took one look at me, and then decided we were going out.

***

Juliet was sitting on the edge of her bed in a pair of denim shorts over lace tights and a crop top. I stopped short, stared at her for a moment, because I'd almost forgotten just how thin she was under all her normally baggy clothes.

Her crop top was characteristically too large, hanging off her shoulders and dangling across her body, decorating the subtle curves of her breasts and her smooth, flat stomach. I licked my lips slowly and managed, "I didn't know your belly button was pierced."

Juliet smirked as she pulled on her combat boots and gave a nod toward her closet. "Feel free to grab anything you want."

"I mean, boobs, though," I answered with an eyebrow wiggle, which got a pillow thrown at me.

"Pervert," Juliet laughed.

"You love it," I accused as I grabbed my own jeans from my bag, tugging them on and letting myself in Juliet's closet. She had an array of tank tops I liked, all in larger sizes with the arms cut down to about waist length. I grabbed an orange one that read *Cray* in big, block letters and pulled it on before dropping one of her flat billed hats on my head.

Once we were both dressed, Juliet held out her hand expectantly and we had an entire argument without words before I eventually sighed and dropped my keys in her palm. She grinned too triumphantly for my liking, then led the way downstairs.

"Why don't you have a car, anyway?" I asked as I climbed into the passenger seat, feeling very out of place. "Your dad owns a dealership. I know he can afford to get you one."

Juliet shrugged nonchalantly. "I crashed three, so Daddy said he wouldn't pay for another one."

157

I gaped at her and she laughed as she pulled out of the driveway, heading to the highway and then out toward Bridgewood.

The drive to the city wasn't a long one, but once we got there, Juliet took a lot of back roads I'd never been on before, including one or two alleyways and an old parking garage. There were other cars, but seemingly no people or other buildings.

"Is this the part where you tell me you're a serial killer and I have to choose between joining you or having my body found in a dumpster?" I asked.

Juliet snickered as she killed the engine, leaned over to give me a quick kiss and murmured, "You're adorable," before getting out. I followed her, reminding her to lock the doors as she led the way to an elevator in the corner. There was a faded rainbow sticker over the buttons that seemed innocent enough, but Juliet ran her fingers over it almost fondly.

Once we were inside, we went down, and after the first ding I felt the floor vibrating under my feet. Suddenly, it hit me where we were. "Seriously? An underground club?"

She grinned at me and nodded. "An underground *gay* club."

When the doors slid open, there wasn't much to look at—just an open hallway with two women guarding the entrance. They wore matching dark blue dresses; one held a change bag and the other a stamp.

They didn't ask for IDs, but looked us over pretty good before both of our hands got stamped. "Stay out of the alcohol, but have fun ladies," one of the girls said before waving us aside. Juliet's fingers twined with mine and she gave me a little pull, dragging me with her.

The hallway was long, the music getting louder with each step—something more techno than an actual song of any kind. Eventually we were in a club without any real warning. It wasn't much to look at—high ceiling, large open space. There was a huge bar set up on the far wall, a DJ in the corner who was using the acoustics to her advantage, and a few tables and chairs lining the perimeter. It wasn't packed exactly, but there were enough people that I knocked shoulders a few times as Juliet pulled me deep into the middle of all the gravitating bodies.

"Where are we?" I asked, leaning in to be heard, watching the lights overhead bathe everything in shades of pink and purple. There were men and women, but not men *with* women. In fact, every couple was same sex, foreheads pressed together or lips locked, hands on hips or lower backs. It was the first time I'd been around that much gay *in public*, and it was fucking fantastic.

Juliet grinned at me and pressed her cheek against mine as she answered into my ear. "*The Rainbow Room*. It's about the best gay thing we have close to home. It's strictly eighteen and over but they'll let you in younger as long as you don't touch any alcohol and stay out of trouble. Lakyn found it a while ago."

"This is awesome," I gushed, and it was only then I realized I was the only person standing still, because Juliet threw her arms around my neck and stepped up closer to me.

"Lena," she breathed against my ear, a bit of a chuckle in her tone. "Shut up and dance with me."

It was easy to get lost in it. The music quickly started to feel like it was matching the beat of my pulse, the heat became addicting, the noise blocking out any memory of the real world. I'd never been much of a dancer before—outside of late nights with Lacey and a few drunken mishaps—but it was easy with Juliet. It was easy to follow her lead.

Because she was fucking awesome at it, of course. She was all sway, perfect rhythm, hair tossed over her shoulder and body easily following the beat. My hands found their way to her hips eventually when I stepped in time with her, so close it seemed like every part of ourselves were touching.

I snapped my gaze up to see her smirking down at me and I couldn't help but lean in for a kiss. She met me halfway, soft lips capturing mine. The hours faded away, all I became aware of was how she felt against me, the music pumping through my veins, soft skin splayed underneath my fingertips.

Before long we were both laughing, and when the music changed to something more pop-ish, we decided we could survive without being completely plastered to each other. Juliet was a hair dancer, which meant she tossed her blond waves every which way possible while she jumped to the beat. I just watched her mostly, occasionally getting my hands on her when she got close enough.

At some point, we fought our way across the floor to the bar, ordering waters and gulping them down so fast we nearly lost half of them on our shirts. Juliet laughed and shook her head, grabbed the back of my neck and pulled me in for another kiss. It was too harsh, too frantic and needy, but I didn't have it in me to not completely return her desperation.

When she pulled back, she was grinning, covered in a thin sheen of sweat, blue eyes bright and mischievous.

I loved her. I loved her so much.

"Thank you," I finally said, leaning in for another kiss. "For being so fucking amazing."

"Of course," Juliet answered, then winked before she dragged me back to the floor.

14. "Do you want to get diabetes?"

February came to a close with the turn of a season, and spring brought with it warmer weather that finally allowed us to shed a couple of layers. Flower prints replaced the earlier winter patterns, which generally made the hallways more colorful.

Except for Juliet James, of course, who thought blacks, grays, and whites were considered festive enough. And, generally, moods were brighter.

School fell into an odd mixture of busy and slow, depending on the teachers. Half of them were determined to dump a load in our laps to get through their course plans before spring break, and the other half were just as lazy as the rest of us. Mostly we did the homework that the first group dished out in the second group's classrooms.

"I think Chris and I are going to take Rose to the aquarium over the break," Georgia said, picking disinterestedly at her taco salad. They were getting along better these days, which made her more willing to let him be around. "She's in this weird fish phase and it's not that expensive. I think the tips I made over Christmas should cover it."

Kiki looked up from her book long enough to tilt her head, brows knitting in confusion. Things hadn't quite returned to normal with her, and I doubted they ever would, but she was as friendly as ever. Which, admittedly, wasn't very. "Aren't you scared of fish?"

"Terrified," Georgia answered without missing a beat. "But they'll be in, like, tanks and stuff, right? They can't get to me or anything, right?"

Juliet was giving her a look so disbelieving I wished I had a camera so that I could capture it.

"Shut up. It's a legitimate phobia, all right?" Georgia snapped at her.

Juliet held her hands up in surrender, smiling slightly. "I didn't say anything."

Georgia stared at her for a while longer, but finally shook her head and sat back. "All right, seriously, someone else. What are you guys going to do over the break?"

"I'm writing a screenplay for the theatre club," Kiki announced, and then shrugged when we all turned to her. "It's no big deal, just a little interpretive thing. But I get to work with the director, which is kind of cool."

"That's awesome," I complimented, and she offered me a slight smile in return.

"What are we going to do this year?" Lacey asked, directing her attention to me. "I'd assumed you were going to spend it with the Q-bag so I didn't even think to plan."

I snickered at the nickname Lacey had given Quinton since the beginning of the week. It had started out as douche-bag, of course, but a slip of the tongue one day had ended up mixing it and his actual name and then the combination just stuck.

He was still acting a fool, unfortunately, but there wasn't much I could do about that. No one else bothered Juliet or myself, after the initial shock. In fact, after we came out, a few other couples did as well. Some girls in sophomore year and a pansexual boy in our grade. I didn't know any of them personally, but it was nice to hear the stories floating around.

"I don't know," I admitted on the subject of break, shrugging a bit. Lacey and I usually spent it together—last year we'd driven into the city and hit up all the outlet malls. But with everything that had happened in the last few months, I hadn't planned.

The dessert line opened up, which was a rare occurrence at Grant. Georgia asked if we wanted anything before she got up and left, dragging Kiki along with her. Juliet watched them go before she turned back to Lacey and me. "So, the boys and I are going up to Opal Resort for the week. You should come with us."

Opal Resort was upstate, a good five or so hour drive, but it was a beautiful place. It was one of those all-inclusive type deals. The hotel itself looked like a palace, the pool was amazing, there was tons of open space and certainly enough things to keep a group of teenagers busy for a week.

Lacey scrunched up her nose and sat back in her seat, crossing her arms. "Hmm, let me think… A week locked in with a bunch of half-naked homos and absolutely zero adult supervision, *or* coming up with a decent lie to cover being alone all week and never changing out of my pajamas? Decisions, decisions."

Juliet gave her a look I was beginning to associate with any time Lacey made some stupid homo joke, while I just flipped her off.

"Seriously," Juliet continued. "Come with us. The boys like you, and it's not like you can go to Opal and *not* have fun."

Lacey sighed deeply, looking at her nails like this conversation was the biggest disruption to her day possible. "I'm not disagreeing with you, but can you talk about being a *serious* fifth wheel? I mean, really."

"She kind of has a point," I muttered. "Scott and Lakyn can't keep their hands off each other."

And Juliet and I were new, but we also didn't get a lot of time to just be a couple without anything else distracting us. Spring break was basically a free for all, and obviously I was all in.

"Matt is coming, so he's fifth wheeling it too," Juliet mentioned.

Lacey's eyebrows shot up in interest at that one, even though I knew she was trying to somewhat play it cool. She'd never met Matt, but when Scott mentioned being friends with him, she had lost her mind. Only to me, though.

"Matt Alvarez?"

Juliet gave a nod. "Yup. He's Scott's best friend, horribly single, and I'm sure would be more than happy to keep you company."

Lacey stared at her, then nodded once the girls came back with cookies and passed them around. I chuckled softly and shook my head at Juliet, who just offered me a shrug before we finished off our lunch.

***

The last weekend that month was the first time Juliet and I had the entire house to ourselves, which happened completely by chance. The private schools in the surrounding area were having an athletic banquet out of town, which meant Scott was gone for the weekend and Lakyn was, obviously, his plus one. Saturday there was a car show a few states over that Mr. James had left for Thursday afternoon, and wouldn't be back until the following Monday.

Which left Rick. By the time we got to the house after school, everyone else was already gone, and he was on his way downstairs. There was a duffel bag thrown over his shoulder and the smuggest smirk I'd ever seen in my life on his face. Which was saying something, really, because I knew Lakyn James.

"Where are you going?" Juliet asked as we dropped our school stuff by the door.

"Carla's," Rick answered with a grin. "Dad's not home, the two assholes aren't home, so I figured I'd do my part to help my little sister get laid."

I could feel myself going red, but Juliet just elbowed her brother in the ribs.

He chuckled as he grabbed his keys off the rack, then turned back to us, grinning. "Have fun gaybies."

The door shut behind him and the silence was deafening for a few moments before Juliet laughed awkwardly. A second later I followed, and then we were both practically in tears.

"No pressure," she joked.

The thing was, with the house being empty, we could literally do whatever we wanted. Within a half hour, we had the sound system in the living room turned up so loud we could hear the music through the whole house; had destroyed the kitchen with the things to make brownies, and were wearing whatever we wanted because no boys were going to come in and bother us.

Which meant Juliet was in only an oversized tank—white and thigh length, with the Joker and Harley Quinn embraced on the front—and a backwards cap. I was wearing my *Bates Motel* tank and undies set, hair thrown up into a messy bun, sliding around the kitchen in my socks.

"No, nu-uh, the cinnamon ice cream is only good with apple pie," Juliet decided when I presented it to her. I pouted immediately, because the cinnamon was my favorite, but I spun around and slid it back to the freezer anyway. "Don't we have vanilla?" she asked.

"Nope," I answered, tilting my head as I realized something else. "Or chocolate syrup. Scott and—"

"Lakyn?" Juliet finished, shooting me a grin over her shoulder. "Probably."

I shook my head at that and reached back into the freezer, wondering if that was a sex thing or an innocent snack thing. Knowing them it was most definitely the former. There was mint—which, gross—and some peach sherbet that didn't sound like a good idea at all.

"What about milk chocolate?" I offered.

"With brownies?" Juliet asked incredulously while she pulled the pan free of the oven. She dropped them carefully on the stove before reaching for a pack of toothpicks to check them, which apparently they passed because she twisted around and crossed her arms. "Do you want to get diabetes?"

"I don't think it works like that," I shot over my shoulder with a grin, then something caught my attention. I grabbed the bottle of whipped cream out of the fridge and held it up triumphantly before kicking the doors shut with my feet. "No chocolate syrup, no edible ice cream, but we do have whipped cream." How the boys hadn't gotten into *that* was beyond me.

Juliet grinned and made grabby hands for it, but I was already popping off the top and giving it a shake before aiming for my mouth. Only half of the dollop made it, however, because Juliet reached out and jolted my grip just enough that I ended up spraying my nose instead.

"Jealous bitch," I complained.

She grinned at me before she leaned forward, going for the tip of my nose and very literally kissing the whip cream off of me. She grinned, licked her lips, and then shrugged.

"We're going to play that game then?" I asked, shaking the can one more time before aiming for her cheek. Juliet closed her eyes and tilted her head, but that just gave me reason to lean in and lick the stripe of sugary goodness off her face.

And then it was *on*. She made a grab for the can but I laughed and turned away, darting across the kitchen. She was on my heels in a moment, but instead of going for it, she grabbed me, pulling me into a kiss easily. I complied, all too willing to have her mouth on mine, and didn't realize she was a *cheater*. She had the bottle out of my hand before I ever knew what happened.

There was whip cream being sprayed on my neck, hands on my bare hips, and her tongue was so much more sensual dragging across my skin than I ever could have realized. She trailed it all the way to behind my ear before her teeth captured the lobe, tugging on it gently.

"Still wanna play?" she asked.

I could hear my pulse thumping, feel a thrill run down my spine, and realized that it was nothing I had ever felt before. Not with Quinton, not with any of the boyfriends before him. No, this was something only Juliet got. I nodded as I leaned in for another kiss, taking the can the same way she had from me, then pulled back and drew a line down her arm.

At some point we ended up on the floor, Juliet stretched out below me, her tank top pushed up over her head, tangled somewhere in her arms. It was the first time I'd ever had her like that, spread out, completely on display. She looked oddly comfortable for someone who was lying half naked on the cold kitchen tile, with a girl her size straddling her thighs.

Juliet was astoundingly beautiful. Her skin was such a perfect pale, her black lace underwear set contrasting wonderfully. The ring looped through her bellybutton was a simple heart, nothing flashy, yet I still noticed it. Everything about her was *breathtaking*.

"You're staring," she murmured, peering up at me through her lashes. I just smiled at her before shaking up the can again, drawing a line from her navel to her bra. She sighed when I chased it with my mouth, arching into my touch ever so softly. I could do this for ages.

I went to get more when she shook her head, pushed herself up and took it from me. She drew a line from the neck of my tank to the hollow of my throat, and then leaned down. Her hot tongue sliding between my breasts brought a surprised gasp out of me that I couldn't have stopped even if I wanted to.

I heard the can drop to the floor beside us before her hands were on my hips, pushing up under the thin cotton and touching skin as of yet unexplored. Having her hands on me seemed to jump start my pulse again. She was so soft, so careful, as her touch moved up my sides until they found my breasts. At first they rested on either side of the curves, until one of her thumbs moved, dusting over a sensitive spot that made my breath hitch.

"Jules, Jules, wait." I was breathing hard by the time I finally pulled away from her, shaking my head slightly. She brushed a few quick kisses against my cheek, her hands falling back to my hips, and somewhere I heard her ask if I was okay. Gently. Patient. "I'm just not ready," I admitted, realizing that we could very well end up having sex right there. And although I was sure it wasn't something I would regret, it also wasn't something I was ready to just *do*.

She searched my face for a moment, before it seemed to dawn on her. "You've never...?" When I shook my head, she nodded, pressed a few comforting kisses along my jawline. "Okay, it's fine. Seriously, no pressure. Do you want to keep—"

"Yes."

Juliet laughed, but despite her words, a moment later her tank came off, which was fine—it had been in the way for quite some time. For a while we just sat there together, exploring each other's bodies, finding out what made the other one tick. But bras and panties stayed on, and some territory remained uncharted.

Between kisses and whipped cream, we actually got hungry, and after a while, pulled ourselves to our feet. I shivered when Juliet stopped me to lick a bit of extra cream off the back of my ear, then laughed and put some much needed distance between us.

She called and ordered us some pizza, and then we set to work cleaning up the mess we had made, which somehow was actually just as fun as making it. There was lots of getting distracted going on, before the doorbell eventually rang.

Juliet stole one more kiss and grabbed her shirt to pull back on. It was just long enough that one could assume she was wearing shorts under it, and it was dark enough outside that I was almost certain no one would be looking hard enough to realize she wasn't.

We ate together in the living room, legs intertwined, pulling up Netflix to feed our *Hemlock Grove* obsession, sharing pizza and eventually the brownies that had been so neglected before.

All in all, it was the most amazing weekend of my life, and when we eventually fell asleep together, I realized I regretted nothing that had happened in the last few months. Because nothing was better than this moment.

***

"Hey, Mom."

I'd nearly walked right passed her office on the way to my own room, barely seeing the door was open and managing to catch myself before I was too far away. She was at her desk, leafing through papers, glasses balanced on the edge of her nose, but she looked up at me.

"Lacey and I want to go to Opal for Spring Break this year, that cool?"

"Sure, darling." My mother answered on what I was willing to bet was instinct more than actually processing what I'd said. I nodded and gave a thumbs up before moving on, but she called me back with a quick, "Lena!"

In the hallway, where she couldn't see me, I sighed and dropped my head back on my shoulders. We still hadn't really talked since I'd come out, besides the argument, so I wasn't sure what to expect now. I backtracked through, sticking my head around the doorway.

My mother gestured for me to come in while she took off her glasses, which meant I was probably in for an actual conversation. I nodded and sat in one of the extra chairs, waiting for her to speak.

"Will Juliet be going?"

"Yes," I answered honestly. "As well as her cousin and a couple of other friends."

My mother nodded slowly, considering. That look was on her face again. Vulnerable, open, but still defensive of something. Like she was ready to hear me, she just didn't know how to listen.

"You care about her a lot, don't you?"

"I love her," I admitted. "I've loved her since the first day I saw her. I've never believed in soulmates but if I did, I'd think she was it."

My mother stared at me a while, trying to piece her words together before she finally nodded. "I believe you."

"Well, generally speaking, Mom, I'm not a liar," I responded dryly. That got a chuckle out of her, at least, and I smiled. "I don't know how to explain it to you, if that's what you're looking for. It just feels *right*, to be with her. It's like watching a romance movie and *finally* understanding what the hell they're going on about. I want to spend every day watching her smile and hearing her laugh. I just want her around me, all the time, just...*present*. Even if she's not interacting with me."

It was getting too personal, so I stopped and shrugged.

"It's not the life I saw for you," my mother admitted with a sigh.

"It's hard, I know that. I've seen the damage first hand, but I stand by what I said the other day: pretending is harder. I'm good, like this, and I really am happy."

My mother smiled then stood up and motioned me over to her for a hug. I went willingly, and the moment her arms were around me, stress I hadn't even realized I was carrying floated away. I could feel tears coming on as I instinctively nuzzled into her shoulder.

"I will always love you," she promised, pressing a chaste kiss to my forehead. "My brave, strong, beautiful girl. Your father and I... we're going to learn and... we'll get there, we will."

I wasn't sure how long we stood there before she eventually patted my back and moved away. "Your dad and I have Wednesday afternoon off work. You should invite Juliet over. I think it's time we meet her."

***

"Why are you so nervous?" I mocked, but if the look Juliet gave me was anything to go by, she definitely didn't find it as ironically funny as I did. "Oh, come on, Jules."

She shook her head as she went back to looking at herself in the Camaro's visor mirror. She'd toned herself down for the evening which meant shorts, boots, and an oversized black shirt.

"*I* actually have something to be worried about," Juliet pointed out. "Your parents probably hate me already on sheer principle. I turned their straight little angel all upside down. What a bitch."

I sighed, but knew she did have a bit of a point. Dinner with my parents definitely wasn't going to be as fun as dinner with her father had been. "They do not *hate* you. And at least they're trying?"

"Mm," Juliet mumbled, but she sighed and gave me a nod. "What are we going to do if this goes south?"

170

"Go back to your place, where your father will pamper us and restore our faith in parental figures," I answered with a grin. "I wonder if he ever gets tired of having so many people to love all at once?"

Juliet snorted at that and snapped the visor back into place. "Please, as if. It's like my father's goal in life to love all the wayward children."

I chuckled as I pulled my car into the driveway, but the temporarily dissipated tension came back in full force once we were parked. Juliet was generally a relaxed, confident person, but at that moment, I realized she honestly *was* nervous.

"Hey." I gave her hand a bit of a tug until she turned toward me, and then leaned in to press my lips against hers. It was a short and sweet kiss, just a reminder and something to calm her down. When I pulled back, it was only far enough to rest my forehead against hers. "We can do this."

"Right," Juliet answered. "It's no big deal or anything."

"Exactly." I stole one more kiss before we nodded at each other and finally got out of the car.

Juliet had been to my house on the rare occasion, so there wasn't a tour I had to give once we walked inside, but it was the first time she was meeting my parents.

I found my mother in the kitchen making sandwiches. She looked about as nervous as Juliet probably felt, but there was still a smile on her face. "You must be Juliet."

"Yes," my girlfriend answered simply, then fumbled awkwardly before finally offering a hand.

My mother took it with another smile. "Nice to meet you, sweetheart. My name is Margaret."

"It's nice to meet you," Juliet greeted politely.

She was ready for my father when he finally showed up, shook his hand promptly and introduced herself. When asked what she would like on her sandwich, I was the one who managed to say we would make our own, which she seemed thankful for.

Actually sitting down to eat was when things got weird. We didn't say Grace, for one thing, which threw Juliet off. I shrugged apologetically, but couldn't do anything about it, and then conversation was difficult to grasp.

"So," my father started, picking at his sandwich before looking up at Juliet. "You're a lesbian then?"

"*Dad*," I muttered, more shocked at his bluntness than anything.

He seemed apologetic as he glanced between mine and Juliet's somewhat taken aback expressions. "I'm sorry, was that rude? I was just curious."

"It's okay," Juliet said, her hand landing on my thigh reassuringly under the table. "Yes, I am a lesbian. Yes, I've known since I was a child and do believe people are born that way. Yes, my parents know and are accepting of it. And yes, I do care very much about your daughter."

There was a beat of silence, and then a couple of nods when my parents realized they didn't have a question Juliet didn't cover. I ran a hand through my hair, sighed, and then my mother asked, "So, when exactly did you two, um, begin..."

"Dating?" I asked, trying to figure out where she was headed. The word seemed to make her uncomfortable, but she composed herself and nodded. "A couple of months ago, about the beginning of Decemberish."

Juliet shot me a mildly amused look, like she didn't believe for a second that I wasn't aware of the exact date I had asked her out. I shrugged, and after that things leveled out. My parents focused on Juliet after that, the usual questions one asked when trying to get to know someone: family, school, future plans.

Unsurprisingly, she was vague, even about school plans. She answered questions politely, but the information was sparse, which made it obvious just how much she actually shared with me these days.

We kept our distance from each other, except for the occasional light touch or shared smile. It was nice, for my parents, but harder than I would have expected it to be. Being together was so much easier at her house, where nothing had to be second guessed. It was oddly sobering, and a reminder that sometimes the real world just sucked.

We made it, though, and when dinner was over, my parents seemed more comfortable. Goodbyes were insanely less awkward than hellos had been, but I was still thankful for the chance to drive Juliet home.

"You okay?" she asked, once we were shut up in my car.

"Are you?" I shot back, and after a moment of consideration, she gave a nod. She seemed tired, but not hurt, which meant the evening had been a success.

We shared a quick kiss before leaving, and caught her father in the front yard tossing a football around with the boys when we got to her place.

Mr. James smiled at us and nodded toward the house. "There's ice cream, if you need it."

"You're amazing," I declared, and got a smile and a hug for it. I didn't stay long, just for one cup, but Juliet cuddled up to me, head resting on my shoulder, and I couldn't help but smile and press a kiss into her hair.

Yes, the night had definitely been a success.

15. Token Heterosexual

"You are *actually* an asshole."

"Are you two fighting already?" Scott asked as he walked out of the James' house, Lakyn's bags tossed over his shoulders. He arched an eyebrow at where his boyfriend was sitting on the hood of his jeep doing absolutely *nothing* useful except stealing my M&M's.

Lakyn huffed as he popped another piece into his mouth. "I don't know what she's complaining about. I'm adorable and completely innocent."

Scott snorted and rolled his eyes. "Yeah. Right. Lena, if you murder him, I won't tell the cops you went to Mexico."

"Please, I'll run to Canada," I retorted, trying to grab the bag of chocolate back, but the little fucker was fast and quickly dodged. "No one will think to look in Canada."

"It's cold in Canada," Juliet pointed out as she walked over and snatched the bag from Lakyn's grip with practiced ease. She leaned in and gave me a quick kiss before handing it back to me. "No candy is safe anywhere near him."

Yeah, that much I had figured out. I kissed my girlfriend once more because I was grateful, then stuck my tongue out in Lakyn's direction. He repeated the action before the sound of another car pulling up stole our attention.

Matt's mother, blessing that she was, had handed over her Dodge Durango for our trip to Opal. It was a large, bright red monstrosity, but it would comfortably seat all six of us and hopefully hold our luggage.

That last part was questionable. There were three girls and two gay boys going on this trip.

"Hey guys!" the man in question called as he hopped out of the car, stretching his arms up overhead.

I'd only ever hung out with Matt Alvarez once, at the Bridgewood football game a while back. The sling was off his arm now and his grin was almost as large as Scott's as they clasped hands and pulled each other into a bro-hug.

"We good to go?"

"Yup," Scott answered. "Lacey should be here soon, so we can start loading up I think. Lakyn! Get your cute little ass over here and help!"

"Don't call me cute!" Lakyn retorted, but he slid off the hood of the jeep anyway and went over while Matt opened the hatch. They dragged all our bags inside like gentlemen. Already it was taking some maneuvering, and Lakyn ended up in the backseat of the car directing them on how to stack.

"This is going to be a disaster," Juliet muttered as she draped an arm around my waist, resting her chin gently on my shoulder. I chuckled softly and tilted my head against hers comfortably while we watched.

It was a Friday afternoon, so we would get to the resort late— probably in just enough time to unpack and possibly hit up the pool, or watch someone try to get drinks out of the bartenders. But we had all week at the resort, so a lazy evening wasn't one wasted.

The weather was nice, which was a plus side. It was warm enough I had a feeling the approaching summer heat was going to be killer, but still cool enough that we weren't melting yet. That meant clear skies which was good for driving. It was only a five-hour trek, though I was sure between bathroom breaks and food, it would probably stretch passed that, because we were a pretty high maintenance group.

Lacey was the last to arrive, parallel parking in front of the house like a boss. She climbed out looking stellar as ever, even in yoga pants and a *Spring Breakers* crop top, her long hair pulled up into a ponytail, and obscenely large sunglasses perched on her nose. "'Sup, homos."

"'Sup, twat," Lakyn shot back without missing a beat, grinning as he pulled himself out of the back of the Durango. Lacey popped an annoyed bubble of gum at him in response, but otherwise let him win. Which seemed to be the usual game those two played. Lakyn only ever acknowledged her presence to throw insults her way.

Lacey went for me first, making a general shooing motion at Juliet. My girlfriend huffed in irritation but let me go so that I could hug my best friend.

"Hey Lace!" Scott greeted, leaning around from the back end of the car. He looked slightly worried, probably about the space issue. "I hope you didn't bring much."

"Me?" Lacey asked and then shook her head and went back to her own car. She dragged out one suitcase and a small duffel before locking up. "Please, I intend to wear as little clothing as possible this week."

There was a thump and then Matt emerged, rubbing the back of his head while I hid a laugh in Juliet's shoulder. Lacey tilted her sunglasses to get a better look at him, which was an obvious once over if nothing else.

"Matt Alvarez," she guessed, even though we all knew she knew exactly who he was, before offering her hand.

"Yes ma'am," Matt replied as he leaned over to take it.

"I'm Lacey," she introduced. "Otherwise known as the token heterosexual."

Matt laughed. "Wow, I feel like we have so much in common already."

Lacey's grin was almost predatory. "So, Mattie Boy. Got anything against casual sex?"

The pair had everyone's attention by that point. Juliet did a double take, Lakyn looked over his shoulder, and Scott stopped packing long enough to watch.

Matt looked taken aback at her brashness, but shook his head. "Not a thing."

"STDs?" she asked.

"Clean as a whistle," Matt answered, grinning. "Got tested a few months ago. You?"

"Same," Lacey replied, pulling her stuff over to Scott. He took it from her after a moment, and nodded at Lakyn to help him add it to the pile.

Once they were busy, Lacey turned back to Matt. "Wanna bang all week?"

"Totally," Matt replied with a breathless chuckle.

"Cool," Lacey grinned before she pushed her sunglasses back into place and then went to climb into the passenger seat. Because everyone else was so shocked, no one thought to stop her. Matt did a fist pump before he ran around to the driver's seat.

Juliet shook her head and glanced over at me. "Did that...actually just work?"

"Straight people are *so* weird," Scott decided as he slammed down the hatch, double checked to make sure it actually clicked into place, then gave it a pat.

"Fucked on the first date," I pointed out as I walked passed him, dragging Juliet with me. I was pretty sure he mumbled something about when the hell I was going to let that go, but then everyone was in their seats and it was time to get going.

***

The drive was interesting, to say the least. With Matt and Lacey in the front seat together they were mostly playing twenty questions, much too personally because they obviously wanted to know who exactly they were going to be bumping uglies with. It was gross and yet I couldn't help but listen on occasion.

Scott and Lakyn were in the very back, either completely quiet or arguing with each other under their breaths. After the first thirty minutes or so, Lakyn crashed hard, cuddled up into Scott's side, and Scott either listened to his iPod or spoke up when general conversation filled the car.

That left Juliet and I in the middle of everyone. We were playing a couple of games worth of slap-jack because we were going old school. It was the best way to stay entertained without getting lost in our phones or something.

Eventually, however, the questions from up front were hard to ignore.

"Isn't your father a preacher or something?" Scott finally spoke up. Lacey looked at him through the review mirror. "Is he okay with you being so…?" he trailed off.

"Promiscuous?" Lacey finished for him. "He doesn't know. At least I haven't told him. Because, yes, he is a preacher, which means that yes, he believes sex before marriage is a sin."

"You don't?" he asked.

"Lacey believes sex is a social construct," I answered. "That as long as two parties are consenting and safe, there isn't a reason why they shouldn't enjoy their time together."

It was something she'd been saying ever since we were young teens. I'd never really seen her negotiate in action until now, but I'd known about it. She'd always been loud spoken about having a sex drive and refusing to be ashamed of it.

Lacey nodded and asked Matt. "Speaking of safe, condoms?"

He looked at her guiltily. "Uh, no. I kind of figured I'd be flying solo on this one. Birth control?"

"Of course," Lacey replied as she settled back down in her seat. "But you're still wrapping. I'm sure the gift shop will have us covered."

"*Straight* people," Scott muttered again, sounding just as lost as he had the first time.

Suddenly, Juliet was undoing her seat belt and was turned around so fast it almost gave me whiplash. "You two had *better* be using protection, you little shits. I swear to God I am not even kidding, if I find out—"

I'd never heard her so pissed before. I was basically pressed up against my window, staring at her in shock. Juliet was a perpetually calm person, her voice never even rose, but she was almost yelling at this point. She only stopped when Lakyn silently pulled out a whole train worth of condoms from his pocket, blinking at her sleepily

There was a beat of silence and then we were all laughing so hard I ended up doubled over, clutching at my side. The real tears started once Lakyn complained that he'd been having a really good nap and all of us had ruined it for him.

Halfway there, we stopped at Wendy's for a bite to eat and a bathroom break, mostly because Juliet was doing the potty dance and threatening to kill someone if we didn't pull over soon. We made an annoying spectacle of ourselves while we lounged around one of the booths in the back and tried to throw French fries into each other's mouths, which only succeeded in making a mess. We cleaned it up though, because we were decent fucking people.

Scott drove from that point on, though Lacey refused to give up her passenger seat. So Matt sat in the back with Lakyn, talking about video games and occasionally getting into very heated arguments over whatever they were playing. Juliet and I spent most of it making out, deciding to be the annoying couple for once. It was a lot of fun. Ten out of ten would do again.

Around eight, Lakyn climbed out of his seat and into the middle of mine and Juliet's, which was accomplished only by pushing our heads apart and then wiggling himself uncomfortably between us. Juliet shoved at him, but it didn't seem to help much. "Are we *there* yet?" he whined.

"Almost, baby," Scott promised with a soft chuckle.

True to his word, not even twenty minutes later, we were pulling up in front of the resort.

Opal was a beautiful place. It was situated just outside of the city limits so it was close enough to still be convenient, but far enough away to feel more like a vacation spot. The building was longer than it was tall, a bright white color, with shining opal columns. Scott drove us under the port where the valets were waiting.

He handed over the keys, then we were all falling out of the vehicle, either erupting in stretches or going to grab the bags out of the back. One of the workers brought us a cart, which made things so much easier, even if it was piled so high we couldn't actually see over it.

The lobby was huge, all high ceilings and brilliant architecture, lavish armchairs, rugs, chandeliers. There were a few guests out and a couple of staff around the front desk. Scott went ahead of us to check us in while Matt pushed the cart.

We were on the fifth floor up, which made the elevator ride rather interesting because no one wanted to wait for another one, so we all squeezed in and got to know each other real good, real fast. Lacey somehow ended up pressed into me, so I wiggled my eyebrows as suggestively as I could manage. "Wanna switch teams?"

She tried, she really did. I could see her face contort to attempt to be flirty back, but she just couldn't do it. Eventually, she shook her head and said, "Ew, gross, *no homo Len!*"

I laughed as Juliet wrapped her arms around me from behind. Then she was tugging me away from my best friend, pulling me down the hallway. Scott was running, Lakyn trailing right after him, until they reached the double doors at the end of the hall. A swipe of the key and we were officially in our room.

The suite was *huge*. It opened up to a hallway and then the living room, which was large and square. There was a sectional couch separating it from the kitchen just behind it. There were two armchairs, a desk in the corner, and a flat screen TV with a set of drawers underneath.

Matt dragged our luggage there; Lakyn helped him take bags off and drop them onto the floor while the rest of us explored. The kitchen was fairly small, granite and wood, but it had a large fridge and a stove, so that was a plus. It was, of course, well stocked with appliances, and had the usual coffee and tea set up. There was a dining table in a nook off in a corner, with enough place settings for eight, so that rocked.

There was a total of four doors scattered about. One led to a large bathroom, with two sinks, a toilet, a standing shower, and a bathtub. I sincerely hoped it wasn't the only one because again, three girls and two gay boys.

Seriously. Poor Matt.

There was a total of three bedrooms. With king sized beds. *Score*.

"Guys!" Scott called, catching all of our attention. We circled back to him appropriately and he handed us each a hotel key. "We each get a bedroom but please remember these walls are probably even thinner than the ones back home. Lace, Mattie boy, the couch pulls out to a bed if you guys want to separate but..."

Lacey looked over at Matt. "Do you snore?"

"Nope," he answered, popping the *p* and grinning.

"Cool," Lacey nodded. "You can sleep with me."

Scott nodded as he grabbed his bag off the pile on the floor. "All right then. I say we go have some fun and eat out. Tomorrow we'll go grocery shopping and shit. Sound good?"

***

It was late enough by the time we finished dinner that the pools had mostly cleared out, but thankfully did not close for a few more hours. The guys all wore the usual swim shorts, Scott's decorated like a comic strip while Matt's were just *Batman*. Lakyn's were black, but the edges of the legs were covered in Pokemon. He was the only one wearing a shirt out of them—a long sleeved rash guard—and like Juliet, I was surprised at how good of shape he was under all the layers he usually wore.

Before we left the room, Scott managed to trick him out of it. It wasn't really fair, in my opinion, because he'd tugged the other boy's shirt off while they were mid make-out, but once he got it off, I realized why Lakyn had been wearing it in the first place.

Scars. I'd never really assumed Lakyn wore so many hoodies for a reason, but suddenly I understood. He was covered in them. They were thin, healed, and barely visible against his fair skin, but they were there. Marks gathered around his shoulders, hips, and even across his chest. Some crossed and intersected, and it was like he'd just taken a razor blade to his skin and went to slashing.

From where I was, I could hear Scott when he pressed a kiss to Lakyn's ear and told him he didn't have to hide them, and then I saw the scars on Lakyn's wrists. They were long healed, but loud, bright white, vertical lines. Suicide attempt scars.

Lakyn gave in, and didn't put his shirt back on, but as we walked to the pool I hung back with Juliet. She searched my face then sighed. "He's okay," she promised.

"Is he?" I asked, barely managing to keep my voice from cracking. I *knew* Lakyn's past was rough, but I'd never imagined. "Jules."

"There's a lot of scars, I know," she answered. "But he really is all right. Therapy, man. He worked his ass off."

Juliet shrugged before she looped her hair up on top of her head, and it was easy to get distracted then, because *of course* she looked amazing. Her bikini was dark red plaid, the top doing wonderful things for her boobs, the bottoms with a little skirt attached. The ring in her belly button had a mermaid attached to it and…

And I just wanted to stare at her. Maybe hold her down and suck hickeys into her hips.

She caught me after a moment then grinned and shook her head. "Come on," she said as she took my hand, pulling me off with her.

We chased the boys, all jumping into the pool with cannon balls. Lacey tried to save herself, claiming that her hair was really too well done to get wet, but she wasn't paying close enough attention and Scott got a hand around her ankle, jerking her in with the rest of us.

She was pissed for only a moment.

We swam around for a while, generally being dicks to each other, either splashing or dunking. Matt was the hardest to get down, and it took almost all of us piling up on him before he finally gave in.

Somehow, we eventually ended up in a game of chicken. But, as it turned out, Juliet and I couldn't hold each other up. Didn't really matter how hard we tried, we just couldn't pull it off. At least not while walking.

"Ugh," Lakyn complained. *"Girls."* He gave a sigh as he fell off Scott's shoulders, then swam over to Juliet and myself. He disappeared for only a moment before coming back up with Juliet securely seated on him. Scott turned his attention to me and when I shrugged, he went under and I got myself situated.

The game was only fun for a good ten or so minutes though, because Lacey was unbearably competitive and Lakyn was a cheater. And also, apparently, very good with his toes, because Scott dropped me in order to save his swim trunks.

***

There were fingers dancing across my stomach, every so lightly, and lips brushing over my cheek, following a trail down to my ear. I smiled despite myself, turning my face into my pillow. "No," I mumbled. "I don't want to get up."

Juliet chuckled lightly and I felt the bed move as she resituated herself, and then her mouth was against my neck, drawing lazy, open-mouthed kisses down my throat. Her hand splayed against my hip, warm and soft, before she slid it up my side.

"Come on Lena, we've got lots to do," she muttered against my skin.

I rolled over finally, smiling at her, and she sat down on her legs and brushed hair out of my face before leaning down for a kiss. "Morning breath," I reminded her, halfheartedly, but she ignored me and pressed our mouths together sweetly.

It didn't last long before she was up, patting my thigh and heading to the bathroom situated in the corner. I sighed and ran my hands up through my hair before I followed her.

We threw clothes on before going downstairs with everyone else to grab breakfast at the hotel restaurant. It was a buffet, which Scott seemed to take much too seriously, but he was the one who reminded us we actually needed to buy groceries instead of spend all of our money there. So we pulled some funds together and he and Juliet left for the store.

Matt and Lacey disappeared sometime after that, which left Lakyn and myself. We contemplated going back to bed; on the way to the elevator, though, we noticed an arcade, and *obviously* that was a much more attractive idea. We were killing it at Dance Dance Revolution when Juliet and Scott found us about an hour or so later.

We helped them unload and then all hit the pool. Around the time the sun was going down Matt and Lacey joined us, his arm thrown over her shoulder and she cuddled into his side like they were actually a couple. They announced they'd found a place to rent bicycles and asked if we wanted to tag along.

The boys were in, so Juliet and I climbed out too, tugging shorts on over our bottoms and slipping into our sneakers. The jocks of the group decided they obviously had to race, and after some pretty heavy coercion and what I was willing to bet was a promise for sexual favors, Lakyn joined in.

Juliet and I shook our heads and watched them take off, with Lacey in the lead for the time being, even though I knew she'd eventually burn herself out.

"*Jocks*," I muttered, trying to channel my inner Scott.

Juliet laughed and we rode together in comfortable silence, occasionally swerving as close to each other as we dared.

"Kiss me," she demanded at one point.

"I'll crash!" I replied as scandalized as I could. Juliet wasn't having it though, and leaned over and kissed me anyway. It ended with us mostly laughing because it was definitely a lot harder than it seemed.

But that was all right. We didn't really mind anyway.

***

"You want to play what?" Lacey asked incredulously, eyebrows arching over her sunglasses.

"Extreme...golf?" Lakyn answered, at first confidently and then trailing off in a question. The game had obviously been invented for mini courses, and didn't quite have the same ring to it without the extra word.

Scott considered before finally giving a nod of approval.

"Oh no," Matt said quickly as he climbed out of the golf cart and shook his head. "No, we are not playing that *fucked up* game. No way. I refuse to be a part of it."

Lakyn rolled his eyes dramatically while Juliet gave me a look and muttered, "Pussy." I chuckled and hit her arm in reprimand, but that didn't seem to do me any good because she just grinned.

Lacey was looking at the golf course with blatant disinterest. None of us were actually golfers, but it was a nice day out and the pools had all been full, so somehow we'd ended up at the resort course. "What the hell is Extreme Golf?" she asked. "How can *golf* be extreme *anything?*"

"Yeah, that's exactly what I said my first time," I answered, and Juliet laughed as her arms went around my waist before she pressed a kiss into my cheek.

Matt was still shaking his head as he pulled down the bag of clubs. "It's these three psychopaths' way of beating up on people and outright cheating without actually getting into trouble for it," he explained, then shot the teens in question a look.

They all played innocent, of course.

As it turned out, Extreme Golf was a lot harder and less fun when there was actually a whole field worth of playing land and not just a small section. New rules quickly started appearing and it didn't take long before Lacey lost her cool and she and Matt were both out.

Even though she'd lost voluntarily, Lacey was still a poor loser, and she mumbled under her breath the whole time about how *actual* rules were important and made things more fun. We ignored her until Scott took a nasty fall and ended up smacking his head against the ground so hard we all winced.

Lacey was much too smug about this but we all settled down and tried to take the game seriously after that. Unsurprisingly, it was just too boring, and Juliet decided it was more fun to try and distract me. I couldn't really argue with her.

No one actually won.

***

"We're on vacation!" Lakyn complained loudly from the couch, half on it and half on the floor, throwing his boyfriend the most annoyed look I'd ever seen.

Scott grabbed his T-shirt and pulled at it hard enough to snap his boyfriend's ass when he crossed the room. "That doesn't mean we get to skip out on gym day."

"But *vacation*!" Lakyn wailed, burying his face in his arms. I could actually see where he was coming from, really, but Scott and Matt were both already heading for the door.

Scott sighed and hung back as Matt led the way out. "Lakyn!" he called, and when his boyfriend gave a grunt of displeasure, he sighed. "Fucking against walls is *really hard* when we're out of shape!"

Lakyn sat up with a snap and asked, "Will you keep your shirt off?"

"Yes," Scott answered with a laugh.

"Sold," Lakyn said as he jumped up, grabbing his shoes on the way to the door and pulling it shut behind us.

There was a beat of silence before Lacey turned to Juliet and myself, flipping her hair over her shoulder. "Spa day?"

***

Our week of absolute freedom passed with a theme of idiotic fun that I honestly hoped we wouldn't grow out of. We saw outside movies and danced at parties, swam and joked, pushed each other around and stole kisses with our respective partners. It was probably the most fun I had ever had.

Our last night there was a campfire party, with an open bar and an assortment of s'mores. Matt and Lacey took it upon

186

themselves to get us booze, because he looked the oldest and she was not above using her boobs to get what she wanted.

We each ended up with a margarita, sitting around one of the small fires and enjoying the nice weather. Juliet leaned back against my chest and I dropped a kiss on her head as she got comfortable.

"Did you finish up your college stuff?" Lacey asked Scott, and looked proud when he told her he had. Then Matt went on a tangent about how stressed he was, and we could all agree with that.

"Okay, can we not?" Juliet asked, shaking her glass at the others. "I am so *sick* of college talk. Please, anything else."

"Okay," Lacey decided, and sat up from where she was pressed against Matt's side. "Let's play Never Have I Ever. I'll go first. Never have I ever...mmm, smoked weed."

Everyone took a drink except for her and myself. Juliet didn't surprise me so much, but I was shocked by the boys, who just shrugged.

Matt offered an, "I'll try anything once," explanation, and Scott nodded in agreement.

"All right, never have I ever been in handcuffs," Matt said. Juliet flipped him off lazily as she took a drink, and then so did Lakyn. My eyes went wide and he made a show of licking his bottom lip then biting down on it, sending me a wink. Kinky fucker.

"Lena?" Lacey asked.

"Sure," I agreed, and regarded my glass as I thought. I grinned, and because I hadn't been able to take a drink yet, sacrificed myself. "Never have I ever kissed someone of the same sex."

Everyone took a drink except for Lacey, who regarded Matt like he had personally betrayed her. "What the hell, I thought we were in the same boat!"

Matt shrugged. "What did I just say? I'll try anything once, and I wanted to make *sure* I was straight! I mean, Scott seems to *really* enjoy the gay thing! I wanted to make sure I wasn't missing anything."

We all laughed at that and eventually got up for s'mores. I refused to move, so Juliet brought me one back, sat down in front of me and actually fed it to me. It went horribly, of course, because s'mores are messy, but she licked chocolate off my bottom lip so I figured it could have gone worse.

Scott at some point threw out, "Never have I ever been in love," and I didn't drink even though part of me wanted too.

Juliet's eyes were on me, and I smiled at her slowly. Because yes, I had been in love.

But I hadn't told her yet.

16. "We're loved infinitely."

Going back to school was uninteresting in the way first days back usually were. The feeling spread well into the week as teachers worked to get their lesson plans back in order and students got back into the swing of things.

March came to a wrap with a feeling of finality settling on every senior's shoulders. The year was almost over. College acceptance letters were rolling in by the dozens, a new group of teenagers celebrating every day. Or, unfortunately, the occasional glum face of someone who didn't manage to get into their dream school.

My own letters came from Iowa, California, Ohio, and New York. I wasn't dead set on any of them, except that I liked the beach and Lacey was going to Rhode Island, which would put me close to her if I chose New York.

It became a bit of a topic at school, especially over lunch time. Lacey was extremely excited, and even though Kiki was staying local, she couldn't seem to quit talking about it herself. It was Juliet who eventually mentioned that we should probably chill out, because Georgia didn't get to go. Even though I knew she loved her daughter more than anything, I could also see her mourning the life she had left behind, so we took Juliet's advice and calmed down a bit.

Scott managed to get into a school based in California himself, and we were all so proud of him it ended up in a celebration of sorts. There was cake, which Lakyn shoved Scott's face in, but everyone just laughed it off.

Juliet didn't talk about college much. In fact, she seemed to avoid the subject. If someone asked her where she was going, she simply stated that she still had letters coming in. It was mildly irritating when she did it to me too, but it wasn't particularly a fight I wanted to have.

Overall, however, things were good. My parents were doing their best to get to know Juliet, and she was doing her best not to shy away from them. The boys were happy, and always fun to have around, and Lacey had adapted to being a part of our friend group more than I could have ever hoped. Spring break had brought us all closer together, and I was loving it.

My relationship with Juliet was near perfect. We'd settled into a routine, and things with her were just easy. There wasn't any pressure and rarely any awkwardness.

Juliet had a thing for matching underwear, which was awesome because I just usually threw on whatever I could find and what was comfortable, but I could definitely appreciate the aesthetic value when she was stretched out on her bed in nothing but dark purple lace. Her pale, creamy skin made the perfect canvas for me to practice with my *Haunted Hollywood* kit.

She was letting me paint on her stomach while she watched some movie, and I was deeply concentrated on the creepy treeline I was working up her abdomen, when I got distracted by the tattoo on her wrist.

The infinity symbol was small, situated diagonally, and although it had been there since I'd met her, it'd somehow fallen off my radar. I put my brush down and sat up, reaching for her hand. "Jules, can I ask you a personal question?"

Juliet glanced over at me. "Since when do you ask for permission?"

I shrugged, running my thumb over the tattoo. "Why an infinity symbol?"

Juliet was quiet for a while, her attention moving back toward the screen even though I knew she wasn't really watching it anymore. "Lakyn and I both got one after my mom died. They weren't as cliché back then but they were *slightly* illegal, given our age."

"Just slightly?" I asked, and Juliet shot me a look. I smiled innocently, and I knew she wasn't actually annoyed with me.

"She used to say, *I'll love you infinitely*. It was sort of her tagline. After everything Lakyn and I went through, we got the tattoo to remind us, I guess."

"He tried to kill himself, didn't he?" I asked, remembering the scars I'd seen over the break. I knew the answer, but Juliet's nod was still a shattering confirmation. "Did you?"

"No," she replied, exhaling thickly. "It never got that bad for me. Understand, Lakyn didn't just lose his parents—they were *awful* to him. In the scheme of things, that boy has been through hell and back. He was already falling apart when Mom died. And I couldn't handle the shift of attention, when he was around. Maybe it was selfish—"

"You lost your *mother*, Juliet," I interrupted, twining my fingers together with hers and giving her hand a squeeze. "You're completely validated in *however* you reacted to that."

She gave me a sad smile and sighed. "For about a year after she died I was just in shock, you know? Numb. I just kind of existed, moving from one place to another, there but not really focused. Every moment I was in already felt like a memory. Like it wasn't really happening to me."

She paused, and I settled on the bed next to her, keeping her hand in mine.

"At the tail end of fourteen...my emotions came back in technicolor. It was like getting shot or something. Everything just *hurt*. And I wanted that numb feeling back, you know? So I did anything I could to get it—took anything anyone gave me. That was about the time Lakyn moved in. Things were rough, for a while. But there's something about hurting when someone else is. Not being alone. One day he just took my hand and pulled me up and I knew we were going to be okay. We're survivors, and we were going to make it." She twisted her wrist in my hand, glanced at the tattoo on her skin. "So that's why, I guess. We got it as a reminder that we're never alone. We're loved infinitely. Not just by my mother, but the rest of our family. Our friends. Our partners."

I smiled and brought our hands to my face, pressing kisses against whatever of her skin I could reach.

I loved her.

***

Mid-April was the moment it really sank in that everything was changing. Pictures for Graduation invites were being taken, plans were being made, and prom was being thrown together. Thanks to our extracurriculars, Juliet and I both ended up on the committee, but it was easy enough to spend our Art period doing decorations.

It also meant finals, for the last time, at least for High School. As usual, I'd gotten out of all of mine except for Chemistry, which put me in a bad enough mood that the boys avoided me any time I was at the James' place.

"I hate this subject," I groaned Wednesday afternoon, dropping my elbows on the table and irritably running my fingers up through my hair.

Juliet made a sound of agreement across from me, hard at work on her History essay. Her expression mimicked what I felt, which was absolute despair.

"Can we just make out instead?" I asked, pulling my fingers through my hair and glancing up at Juliet. A grin tugged at the corners of her mouth, but she kept her attention on her work. "Please?" I added.

"Do you want to fail?" she asked, her foot playfully nudging against mine. I sighed, dropped my forehead against my textbook, and let the silence drift around us.

Part of me actually wanted to say yes. If I failed, I wouldn't have to worry about college or about trying to be an adult or anything of the sort. I could just retake senior year and...

Crazy talk. I had reached the level of delusion that demanded a break. I couldn't do any more studying. I closed up my stuff, threw it into my backpack, and tried to pretend that I couldn't see the way Juliet was looking at me.

192

"I'm not going to make out with you."

"Fine."

She almost set her pencil down over that. "Okay. You can go play some video games if you want, I think the boys are in their room."

I shook my head and after a moment Juliet shrugged, as if she didn't care what I did or didn't do. Which was a lie, but I didn't bother calling her out on it. Instead I slid out of my seat, circled the table, and decided to take a page out of her metaphorical book.

As it turned out, being a distraction was fun.

I started with her hair, moving it across her shoulders before leaning down to draw soft kisses from the spot below her ear down her neck until her shirt got in the way, then back up again, tracing the outer shell of her ear with my lips. She didn't react other than to tilt her head slightly, to give me more room.

I went slow at first, same treatment to the other side, hands braced on the back of her chair, following her jawline and pressing up under her chin. She sighed in annoyance at that, because she had to look up, so I chuckled softly and moved back again.

Then I drew my fingers up her sides, oh so slowly, from her hips to the curve of her breasts, following the line of her bra around the front of her, never *quite* touching. She shook her head and I went back to her neck, a bit more intent this time, open mouthed kisses. When I went to her sides again, this time it was up under her shirt, feeling the softness of her skin. It was *addicting*.

"Lena," she breathed, and I knew she was trying to sound irritated. She turned her head, reached a hand back to tangle into my hair, and dragged me down for a kiss. Her mouth was warm against mine, tongue insistent, and I knew I'd won.

Somehow, she'd managed to move in her chair until she was sitting sideways, and was tugging me toward her. I had to let her go, but her hands were cupping my ass to pull me closer, and I really couldn't complain about that.

I pressed a knee between her legs, which made it easier to be near her, hair cascading between us. She smiled against my lips as she went in for another kiss. My hands moved to her face, drawing her in, while her fingers danced along the edge of my waistband. I wanted her hands on me so bad I almost pulled out of the kiss to tell her so, and then her touch slipped under my jeans.

And god, was *that* amazing.

For the first time, I understood the things Lacey said about sex. The insatiable desire, the absolute craving for *more, please, touch me*. My skin felt like it was on fire, but I couldn't quite decide if Juliet was making it better or worse. All I knew was that I wanted her touching me, and I wanted to touch her. All the time. I wanted to lay her out and relearn all the parts of her that I loved to look at with my tongue. I wanted to make her feel good.

"Hey, girls—"

I pulled away from her, probably slower than I should have, but I still managed to move in time to see Lakyn walk into the doorway. His hands were over his eyes and Juliet laughed before she pressed her face into my chest, hands sliding to my hips.

"I was *going* to say we should make something for dinner, but... But. *Hey*—don't you two know we're not supposed to have sex in the kitchen?"

Scott came around the corner right after him, and his expression turned smug as he took in the scene. He leaned against the wall by his boyfriend, biting down on his lower lip and raising his eyebrows suggestively.

I shrugged innocently as I backed away from my girlfriend. "We're in the dining room."

"We eat on that table!"

"Pretty sure that's what they were about to do," Scott muttered. Juliet snorted, and I watched Lakyn try to figure out what he meant before it suddenly clicked. His eyes went wide, and Juliet laughed before she gave me a push toward them.

"Please, like you guys haven't ventured out of the bedroom," she muttered. "Take Len and go cook. She's distracting me."

I stuck my tongue out at her, but decided it probably was best not to mess with her work ethic, so I kissed her cheek as I led the way into the kitchen.

Lakyn followed me, complaining about his purity and things he couldn't unsee. Scott and Juliet laughed so hard at that she ended up having to take a break anyway.

***

May came slowly, and then all at once. The last month of senior year, the last month of high school, the last month where the excuse, "My mom said no" would still be applicable.

It was real, and we were done.

Bridgewood's prom was a week before ours, so I was around to see the boys off to theirs. Lakyn wore a fucking red suit, and even though I thought it was mildly ridiculous, he looked very good in it. It fit him, for one thing, and he fixed his hair out of his face. It made him look older, and somehow even more like his cousin.

Scott wore the traditional black, although his tie did match his boyfriend's suit. They pinned white rose boutonnieres to each other's jackets, and Mr. James shed a tear even though he never owned up to it. There were tons of pictures, of course, and memories made.

Georgia and Kiki weren't attending our own prom, the former because it wasn't really her scene anymore and the latter because she hated dancing and crowds. Juliet and I had both decided to go, if only because it was a milestone we felt we deserved. Lacey, of course, was all for that.

Getting ready for prom included the three of us, a marathon of chick flicks, DIY spa activities, and a touch of champagne that her mother gave us permission to drink. We called it an early night, but were up at a decent hour to do our hair and makeup together.

We went to our own houses to get dressed, and I was pleasantly surprised when my mom had the day off so she could help me get ready. It was like being a child again, playing dress-up and talking about princesses, except real, because I would be seeing my princess soon.

Mr. James brought Juliet to me, only so I didn't have to go out of my way in my dress and heels to pick her up, and it would be easier for everyone to get pictures. It was his first time meeting my parents, but there was very little awkwardness, if only because it was impossible for *anyone to* dislike Mr. James.

None of that was important once Juliet walked in.

She was *breathtaking*. In typical Juliet fashion, her dress was all black, the skirt made up of layers upon layers of tulle, the top a faux corset type with buckles crossing at her waist. Her jewelry was all dripping crosses, her makeup dark but beautiful, her long blonde hair practically glowing as it fell around her.

I was awestruck, frozen, and somehow I was sure I managed to tell her she was beautiful, the word falling off my lips like it was something rarely said.

Juliet smirked at me slowly. "You clean up pretty good yourself."

"Asshole," I muttered, but somehow it sounded like something much more caring than that.

There were corsages, of course, red roses draped in silver lace. We took turns helping the other put them on, trying to ignore the cameras going off around us. My mother was the one who continuously demanded more, and didn't even look away when Juliet finally kissed me. Mr. James had a picture of it, I was sure.

Prom was held in one of the local hotels, and while we'd made most of the decorations in class, I hadn't seen the actual set up. It looked good, though. Silver and gold, black and white—a *Vegas Nights* theme with poker chips and money.

We got our official prom pictures taken first, in front of a backdrop of the Vegas skyline and next to the infamous welcome sign. The photographer stuttered over the idea of posing two girls but Juliet did the job herself.

They turned out really well, and I was beyond happy when we stepped down and ran into Lacey, some football player hanging off her arm and looking good if not a bit lost.

"Hey!" she greeted happily, letting him go to get us both in a hug. "You two look great!"

She did as well of course, completely stunning in a form fitting white dress that looked amazing against her dark complexion. She took us to mingle for a while, but we lost her somewhere amongst the crowds.

Juliet and I danced to a few songs together, mostly the faster stuff but the occasional slow song here or there. I lost my heels halfway in, and even though Juliet's feet weren't bothering her, she took off her combat boots as well—for the safety of my toes.

Lacey and her date joined us at some point when we were taking a break. We laughed, drank too much punch, and ate half our weight in baked goods before running off into the *Casino Room* to play games. Lacey dominated at anything with cards, I won a few rounds of ping-pong, and Juliet caught three hundred dollars in the money machine. Mostly because she was a dirty cheater and shoved the bills down the top of her dress.

Lacey was crowned prom queen, of course, and one of the football guys was crowned king. They managed a decent dance together, but Lacey was so outspoken about winning that she might as well have been crowned alone, because he faded away.

Two hours later, I felt like I was dying, arms wrapped tightly around Juliet's waist, head resting on her shoulder while we swayed to every stupid love song the band played. She smiled and pressed kisses against my temple and whispered sweet nothings in my ear.

We went back to her place that night, showered and changed into our pajamas, curled up in bed and fell asleep watching a movie.

It was the perfect ending.

17. One Hour. Twenty-Two Minutes. Five Seconds.

After prom there were only a couple weeks of school left, mostly for finals and a last ditch effort to get one's shit together. The lull in activity meant too much free time, and teachers often sent the seniors out to finish up Graduation invitations or fill out order forms for the big day.

By the end of the first week, our cap and gowns were in, which meant we all had to gather up to try them on and do a quick rehearsal for Graduation night. It was a serious evening, a few people even cried, but my friends and I were all smiles.

"Well, bitches" Lacey said as we finished up, pulling her hat off her head. "We actually made it." Juliet's fingers laced through mine, and we both grinned. It felt like we'd all come such a far way from the beginning of a year, and the end didn't seem like something to be sad about.

That weekend Lacey spent at the James' house, which meant we all camped out in the living room and kept the entire house up all night with our laughter. We planned our outfits, ate too much food, and decorated our caps together. That lead to Lakyn and Juliet getting into a glitter fight, and Lacey popping off one of her usual gay jokes.

When Mr. James came downstairs to tell us all to can it, he teared up and Juliet and Lakyn hugged him even though he promised there was only 'something in his eye'.

***

"Oh, good, you two are home—come talk to me!" Scott demanded the moment Juliet and I walked into the house, raising his voice loud enough that we could hear him from the kitchen. We shared a look as we dropped our stuff by the door before heading in there.

We'd gone to the movies after school with our friends, so the boys were already working on dinner. Lakyn was sitting up on the counter, pulling apart raw chicken breasts, while Scott chopped away at vegetables with more aggression than needed.

"Hey guys," I said as nonchalantly as possible. "What's up?"

"Lakyn isn't talking to me," Scott replied, lifting one shoulder in a shrug. "He's mad at me or something."

Juliet snickered as she walked in, ruffled Lakyn's hair like she was proud of him, grabbed a water out of the fridge and rested her hip against the counter. "What did you do?" she asked, grin playing on the edges of her mouth.

Lakyn was the one who answered, throwing his hands up in the air. "We want to get an apartment for college, right? So, I'm like, hey baby, you know what else we should get? A cat. Because cats are fucking awesome. But this *dickweed* over here—"

"Dickweed?" I mocked, eyebrows rising in interest, but everyone moved right past me because obviously that wasn't the important part.

Scott dropped his head back on his shoulders and groaned as he let his knife go. "I didn't say we *couldn't* get a cat! I just said dogs are better!"

Lakyn snorted and then turned back to his chicken with new ferocity. Juliet and I shared another look, shook our heads, and then helped them make dinner.

The whole ordeal took longer than usual; despite the fact that Lakyn claimed he wasn't speaking to Scott, he couldn't help but mumble something under his breath. Scott would get upset, try to start a fight, and then walk out for a moment while Lakyn flat out ignored him.

"Cats are assholes!" Scott complained at one point with a whine in his voice. "I already have to deal with you! I don't need to be outnumbered!"

Lakyn smirked at that and slid the pan into the oven, shut it, and then gave Scott his attention again. "All right I'll give you that, but they're less needy than dogs. We can leave her food out and she won't eat it all, we won't have to entertain her all the time, we can go on a trip and she'll be fine. She can just chill and do her own thing and we can love her and it will be *wonderful*. Because cats are wonderful!"

Scott narrowed his eyes, opened his mouth to pop out an argument, but Juliet spoke first, "What's the matter, Scott? Afraid of a little pussy?"

Lakyn choked on a laugh and Scott turned his glare onto her, pointing a finger. "I hate you," he decided, and looked at his boyfriend with a sigh. "And you're infuriating."

"You love me," Lakyn replied, stepping up to nuzzle his way into Scott's arms. "And you would love our cat too. Don't play."

With the fighting seemingly over, I went to rest my chin on Juliet's shoulder while she stirred the macaroni, wrapping my arms around her waist. She brushed a kiss against the corner of my mouth, but otherwise focused on her work.

We managed to set the table just before Mr. James and Rick got home, and since the boys had managed to put aside their cat argument, everyone was in good spirits. Mr. James said grace that night, letting us all clasp hands before he bowed his head.

"Father God," he started. "Thank you so much for this last school year. For Scott and Lakyn, continuing to hold each other up always, and for bringing Lena into our family and protecting her on her journey. Thank you for everything you have done for us, the love and support you have provided, and the meal we are now about to eat. Amen."

The conversation of course went right to graduation, which almost started the boys back on their cat argument, but somehow Rick managed to keep everyone on course from stories of when he had been our age.

Eventually, Mr. James looked at me, smiled politely and asked, "Have you picked a school yet, Lena?"

Juliet glanced up at me slowly, watching while I tried to answer. Finally, I shook my head, tapped my fork against my plate. "Not really. I've narrowed my choices down but I haven't sent word out yet."

"Getting a little close, isn't it?" Rick asked, chewing thoughtfully on his next bite.

I shrugged, but nodded, because I knew it was. It was just harder than I'd expected it to be.

Lakyn brought up the apartments they'd been looking at, which carried the rest of the conversation until we were done. The boys disappeared upstairs pretty fast, but Juliet lingered until her father and brother had cleared most of the table.

When she looked at me, she sighed and pushed a hand up through her long blond hair. "I need to talk to you."

***

One hour. Twenty-two minutes. Five seconds.

Complete silence.

Juliet was sitting on the edge of her bed, long legs crossed, hands in her lap. She was picking at the black polish on her thumbnail, but otherwise she hadn't moved at all, like she wasn't completely aware of just how long it had been since either of us had last spoken.

The information was sitting between us, spread out in neat little pamphlets, letters, notes. Perfect and pristine and I knew they were never meant to do any harm. On another occasion, in another way, maybe I would have picked them up and leafed through them. But not now, not like this.

One hour, twenty-six minutes, thirty seconds.

"London," I finally managed, and even though my voice was rough and my throat was dry, it was still the loudest thing in the room. Like I'd pushed over an entire bookshelf rather than just spoken. I swallowed, licked my lips, tried again. "London."

Juliet searched my face in a way I'd become oh so familiar with, hesitated, then gave a small nod. "London," she confirmed.

London, where she had gotten so many scholarships it wasn't even funny. London, which had one of the top fashion schools in the world.

London, which was over *four thousand* miles away.

I pushed myself up off the bed, because suddenly I felt like I couldn't breathe. There was a heaviness in my chest I wasn't sure I could deal with even walking around. Still, I paced around her room, running my shaking hands through my hair.

When she'd brought me upstairs, pulled everything out, tried to explain to me, everything had come out in a rush of words that I'd barely managed to understand. Finally, she had sat down, let me process on my own, but the silence had just stretched on.

When I stopped walking, it was to lean back against her door, fold my arms under my chest, find her gaze. She was guarded, ready for anything, but I just felt defeated.

"You should have told me earlier. It wasn't like you didn't have opportunities to, Jules."

Juliet blinked fast, looking up and away from me, and it took me a while to realize she was fighting off tears. Her voice confirmed it when she spoke, cracking in that telltale way. "I didn't want to fight about it. Didn't want to lose you or, or, or…taint our time together. The last few months were already so busy and I, I, I…" She closed her mouth, shook her head, unable to keep talking like that.

Watching her nearly break took me down a few notches, and I sniffled myself as I stared at one of the posters on her wall. *Evanescence.* Good band. I tightened my arms around myself more and took a deep breath.

Eight minutes. Forty-three seconds.

"I couldn't stand the idea of you leaving me over it, so I…I'm selfish. I tried to warn you about that."

I glanced over at her again, but she was decidedly not looking at me. I could hear an old piece of advice that never seemed to leave the back of my mind—a friend's voice telling me *do it right*.

"I know you talk to Scott," I muttered. "That alone should have taught you a better way to deal with this."

Juliet sighed thickly, rubbed at the back of her neck with one hand. "Yeah, I know."

Three minutes.

"We talked about this, though," she tried softly, like she was afraid if she spoke too loudly, I would leave right then. It was probably because I was by the door.

I moved, slowly. Back to the bed, even though I sat as far away from her as I could. I just couldn't deal.

"About being long distance. Not having to cling to each other to make things work," she added.

I stared at her, caught between the knowledge that she was *right* and the feeling of being taken completely off guard. "Well, I didn't know at the time that we were talking *across the world* distance, Juliet! I didn't even know you were applying outside the country. You should have *told* me. You could have told me."

"I know," she muttered, her shoulders drooping dejectedly, fingers curling around her toes. My stomach churned at the thought that I didn't want to be without her.

"I thought long distance meant plane rides that would be a pain in the ass, but possible. Long weekends spent together, school breaks, holidays."

"I know," she said again, quieter this time.

"You should have told me," I said, because it felt like no matter how many times I did, the point wouldn't ever get across. "I would have been shocked, but I would have gotten over it. I would have been happy for you. This is an amazing opportunity, but you just…"

"I'm sorry."

One hour, forty-eight minutes.

At some point, we finally laid down, staring at each other, the distance between us across the bed already feeling like too much.

Juliet's hair was down, falling over her face in a way that usually annoyed her, but she'd done nothing about. Eventually I couldn't take it anymore, so I reached out to lightly draw my fingertips across her cheek, taking her hair to slide over her shoulder.

"They really like you down there," I mentioned, my gaze straying to the letters that we were almost laying on now. I'd read them, of course. All of them. The words may have blurred, but I'd still taken my time, getting all the information I could. Juliet gave a small nod, and my lips quirked into a smile I didn't quite feel. "I'm not surprised."

Juliet was private about her work, but I'd seen the insides of her sketchbook, the stuff I'd known she was sending out with her applications.

I focused on tracing the well memorized lines of her face for a while, slid my thumb across her bottom lip. I loved her.

"I *am* happy for you," I mentioned, making sure to catch her gaze. "I know it doesn't seem like it right now, but that's only because I'm in my own head. I'm happy for you. I'm proud of you."

She smiled at me before she blinked unfallen tears away and rolled out of bed. She went for her pajamas, so I got up with her, pulled out the pair of familiar cheetah print silk.

We changed, brushed our teeth, combed our hair. Juliet went downstairs and made us hot chocolate, even though it was warm outside. I opened the windows to let the breeze in, felt some calm wash over me at the smell of rain heavy air.

After a while, we ended up sitting on the floor with two poster boards in front of us, one labeled *Pros* and the others *Cons*. We stared at each other until someone was brave enough to go first.

It was me, finally. I wrote *care about each other* under the first. Juliet nodded in agreement, but inhaled sharply through her nose when I wrote *4k+ miles away* under the other.

The next hour played out like that. We said very little to each other, not even bothering with questions or opinions, just started writing. The pro section ended up filled with things like *skype exists, letters are fun, phone sex is a thing, trust each other, emotional bonding, we're committed, summer breaks.*

But, likewise, the con section filled up just as fast. *Time-zone differences, busy lives, no physical intimacy, lonely, travel expenses, won't see each other much.*

Once we were done, we fell silent again, and for once, I couldn't bring myself to count the minutes.

Juliet leaned forward and circled *we care about each other* a few times, and when I nodded she leaned in to kiss me.

That had to be the most important thing.

We got up with the plan to go to sleep, but my hands started shaking again as we cleaned off the bed. My stomach hurt, my eyes were heavy, and I froze as the reminder of how far she would be stared at me.

"You know," Juliet said carefully. "There are other schools in London. I looked it up briefly. Art schools, good ones. I mean..."

I didn't answer her. Mostly, I didn't have the finances to pull that off. My parents were upper middle-class, but they weren't ready for expenses like that. My scholarships would cover some of it, but not enough. Not to mention, I hadn't *applied*, I hadn't put in the work or even considered it.

Two hours and fifteen minutes of getting in bed and getting out, closing the windows and opening them, listening to music and watching a movie, cuddling and staying away from each other. It was an endless cycle of back and forth, over and over, covered in silence.

"I'm not ready to follow you around the world while you chase your dreams," I admitted finally.

Juliet looked at me again, pillowed her head on her folded arms. I knew she got it, that we could end up with regret, or resentment, and neither of us wanted to be there.

She sighed softly and turned her back on me. "I can't stay here while you figure out yours."

***

"Jules?"

"Yeah?"

"Hold me. Please."

Epilogue: "Can we all just agree on what a hot couple they are?"

Juliet and I broke up that summer, and despite that, it was the best summer of my life. It wasn't something we talked about more than once, but instead was a decision we reached in early morning darkness, staring at each other from either side of her bed, hands held and fingers twined together.

College was a new experience, full of twists and turns we couldn't predict. In the end we decided we would rather split on our own terms than be forced apart by something else.

We made our decision and placed it somewhere in the back of our minds, unreachable until the moment it absolutely had to be dealt with. Until then, Juliet and I were determined to enjoy each other, and the rest of our time together.

Graduation was a day filled with laughter, tears, friends and family. Lacey was valedictorian, which surprised everyone except for her teachers and closest friends. She gave her speech with her head held high and more honor cords around her neck than anyone could actually count.

It was a beautiful speech too, filled with heavy topics and the belief that a person was much more than the stereotypes they were labeled with. Lacey Parker was a beautiful girl who looked amazing in a cheer suit, but was also incredibly smart and willing to go after what she wanted. The bitchiness that had gotten her through high school was going to make her absolutely lethal as a lawyer.

When the salutatorian got up, he'd rubbed the back of his neck awkwardly and started with, "Well, I'm going to *try* and follow that." Everyone laughed and he did a good job, in the end.

Our hats went into the air and that was it. We were done. We hugged our friends, our parents, a few teachers, and then we packed our gifts away and walked out of our school for the last time.

The next day we went to Bridgewood Academy's graduation, and Juliet and I mostly played on our phones between Matt, Lakyn, and Scott's names. Lakyn and a handful of other kids were commended on their hard work and presented with not only a high school diploma, but a college associates as well, which put him ahead of the rest of us, despite his age.

Then summer was finally in full force. The James' owned a cabin upstate that was only a couple of hours away, so we spent a lot of time there, absolutely loving the fact that we could do anything we wanted and no one was around to give a shit. It was usually just the four of us, but occasionally Lacey would join, and sometimes Matt. As far as I knew, those two weren't even friends, but anytime they were thrown together, they acted like newlyweds.

On June 26th, the Supreme Court legalized gay marriage. Scott, who had already been planning to propose in July under fireworks, threw that plan out and did it right then and there. I cried, Lakyn cried, and the realization that their marriage would be *legal* hit us all. Mr. James held a barbeque that night. Everyone came, and no one cared that the photos we got of the occasion were on an iPhone.

The weeks passed in a blaze of movies, pool days, snow cones and lemonade. We took trips to water parks and had water gun fights in the back yard. There were murmured secrets around campfires, kisses and wandering hands under the stars. There were homemade popsicles and smoothies gone wrong, tans and sunburns, and everything else in between.

The day I finally told Juliet I loved her was completely an accident, chasing each other through a slip-and-slide and laughing so hard we could barely breathe. The words caught her by surprise and she froze before I'd even realized what I'd said. When she looked like she was going to say it back, I put a finger over her mouth, shook my head, and asked her not to.

For the Fourth of July, we got a whole group together and went into the city to watch the fireworks display. Lakyn and Scott came, along with Matt who predictably latched onto Lacey, and Georgia, with an amicable Chris and Rose in tow. Their little one was dressed in an adorable tutu and pigtails, and quickly stole the show.

It was a day full of running around in short shorts and tank tops, passing out sparklers, and eating funnel cakes, even though the boys complained it was going to ruin our appetites for their cookout. Juliet let some girl at a booth paint red and blue streaks in her hair, and I got a temporary tattoo of stars down my neck that she made a habit of tracing with her tongue once they dried. The night had ended with us all sprawled out on blankets, watching the colors pop through the sky.

August came too soon, and brought with it the admittance that things would never be the same. It was filled with last minute college preparations, packing, and tears everyone tried to hide.

Juliet was the first to leave, because she had the farthest to travel and a time change to get used to. I spent her last days lying across her bed, watching her pack what hadn't already been shipped, stealing kisses and sharing small smiles. We talked like she wasn't going to be gone forever, kissed like it wasn't the last time, and when she went to the airport, I went to Lacey.

I spent that night curled up in her arms, crying my eyes out, and Lacey petted my hair and fed me cake, and it wasn't okay, but it was pretty close. Then we got in our last days together and she was off to Brown.

I, however, was headed to California. It'd happened after Lakyn had mentioned that our chosen schools were fairly close to each other, and if I was willing to put in a bit of commute, I could easily live with them. The irony never failed me that out of the entire James family, they had become my permanent fixtures.

We ended up with two cats, much to Scott's utter dismay. After one trip to the pet store, Lakyn had immediately fallen in love with a fluffy white beauty, who was promptly fitted with a pink bow and named Marie, because *Aristocats* was always appropriate. I hadn't intended to walk out with a kitten myself, but after passing a feisty black one I'd decided he had been too perfect to leave behind. I named him Church, after a stuffed animal from *Haunted Hollywood* that could be his twin.

The three of us didn't do badly together, already practically used to living with each other after a year's worth of sleepovers. Lakyn immersed himself in psychology and sociology classes, and although Scott hadn't known what he wanted to do with his life, he found a serious niche in the kinesiology department. Of course, he also ended up on the football team, but college games weren't that bad and Lakyn eventually managed to teach me the rules.

I took every art class I could get my hands on, trying to find something I liked enough to do for the rest of my life. Oddly enough, it happened outside of the classroom in October, while I was volunteering at one of the local haunted attractions doing cast makeup. I was noticed by someone who worked in Hollywood, and pulled onto a new path. I excelled in my cosmetology courses after that, and in a few years, ended up with my work on camera.

As people tend to do after high school, I fell apart from my old crew. Kiki, as far as I knew, was doing well but keeping to herself. Georgia ended up working for a realtor, and she and Chris had finally drawn up a real custody agreement. Rose was a beauty, and often the star of many holiday cards I received.

Lacey, of course, forever remained my best friend. We talked at least once a week and even though I missed her fiercely, she was often around during long breaks and for stretches of the summer.

Juliet and I eventually lost touch. It happened slowly, and painfully, at least for me. At first we tried, with phone calls and Skype when she stayed up late, then letters and the occasional postcard, before eventually we had to let go.

She came home rarely, more interested in spending time traveling Europe, and no one really blamed her. I saw her during family events and holidays, but it was never for very long. Sometimes I caught the boys Skyping with her and told them to say hi, but otherwise, I let her fall out of my life. I avoided, so that I didn't have to deal with the fact that it hurt.

The first time I went on a date with someone else, I felt guilty—because I knew my heart was thousands of miles away or because I felt like I was being unfaithful to Juliet, I wasn't sure. Sebastian was beautiful, though—dark hair and thick eyebrows, tanned skin and a stunning smile. He played guitar and sang in Spanish, loved the beach and loved my art, but I didn't have it in me to give him a chance.

One day I came home to cinnamon rolls in the oven and a shifty pair of roommates, and it was Lakyn who eventually cracked first. Her name was Theodora Wells and she was completely stunning. African skin, natural curly hair, freckles cascading across her cheeks. I could see why Juliet liked her, and even though I knew they must have been dating, it wasn't real until Scott said it out loud.

Part of me expected to be jealous, sad, or even angry. But all I really felt was free. I could date.

It started with nothing serious. Rebounds, lunch dates, coffee here and there, occasionally a movie. There was a girl named Erica for a few weeks, who was wickedly beautiful and full of passion, and Naomi for a few months who was smarter than anyone I had ever known and absolutely lovely.

And then there was Sebastian, who came back around and promised me it was the last time he would. After only a few dates, I fell for him hard. We bonded over things like strange art and bisexuality. He taught me how to surf and I taught him how to survive horror movies. My parents loved him, although I was pretty sure it was only because he was a boy.

Theodora and Juliet broke up two years later. Their relationship had been serious enough that Juliet brought her home to meet her family one Christmas, and that Lakyn had spent an entire week locked in his bedroom talking to her.

Sebastian and I were together for a good six months after that, but at some point, we realized we hadn't actually been a couple for a long time. Somewhere during our relationship we'd slipped into being best friends, and after a couple of laughs and some beer we decided to call it quits. He stayed in my life, of course, because he was too close to all of us not to. Unfortunately, that gave my parents reason to believe that we could still end up together, but I didn't let it bother me.

The boys got married when we were twenty-three. School had settled down and they had enough money they could comfortably afford their honeymoon to Orlando Studios, and a quick trip to Disney World—that was *apparently* much better than Disneyland which they could visit at pretty much any time, but my opinion didn't matter. They told me so. A lot.

The months leading up to their wedding were hectic and full of misplaced stress, which made living with them a complete *blast*. Their fights were as trivial as always, of course, and seemed to center around the fact that Lakyn couldn't be normal if his life depended on it.

He wanted to wear a lime green suit, which Scott was having absolutely none of, but when his taste shifted to pure white, we all laughed so hard we actually cried. Somehow they agreed on the traditional black, although they decided to wear superhero themed shirts under them.

Scott's best man was Matt, who he'd stayed in touch with over the years, and even though he'd made some good friends at college, no one could rival him.

Lakyn asked Juliet to be his best woman, which marked the first time I would see her in person in three years.

***

"I can't believe they're finally getting married," Lacey said from where she was tying bows on the backs of chairs. There were a lot of chairs, and a lot of bows, and I'd stopped helping a long time ago. So had Sebastian, who was shamelessly staring at Matt's ass and trying not to laugh every time he caught my eye. "How nervous are they?" she asked.

212

Matt snorted and bent over farther to fix what he was working on, and I watched Sebastian try not to fall out of his chair. "Scott's terrified he's going to fuck up something trivial and Lakyn's going to leave him at the altar."

Lacey looked amused. "They've been engaged for *years*. Is he fucking serious?"

"Pre-wedding jitters," I replied with a shrug. "Everyone gets them. Honestly, I'm surprised Lakyn has kept it together so well. Then again, he doesn't really have the same perfectionist bone Scott does."

Their wedding was going to be beautiful. It was small, mostly just friends, given that they didn't have a lot of family. The James' that Lakyn actually spoke to were in attendance, as well as a few of Scott's cousins. Scott still had a relationship with his parents, but it had never stopped being strained, so neither of them were coming. His mother had sent him a card and some money, though. Otherwise, it was just people they had met at college and Lacey and Matt.

It was outside, almost beach-front but not quite, rustic but simple and cute. The reception was taking place at a nice hotel, and everything was coming together perfectly. It was going to be a good night.

"Lena!" Lakyn's voice sent me scrambling out of my chair, and I grabbed the bow Sebastian handed me without missing a beat.

"I'm working!" I said quickly, sliding the bow over a chair and nodding along. Matt laughed, but I didn't even bother sparing a minute to flip him off.

Lakyn stopped short and stared at me for a moment like he didn't understand what I was doing, then shook his head quickly. "I'm not *Scott*, Len. I don't care what you're doing right now! I have a problem. I need your help."

"Oh, pfft." I dropped the bow and sat back down, waving at him to tell me what he needed.

Lakyn pulled his bottom lip between his teeth and chewed at it nervously, which was when I realized something might actually be wrong. Fuck, I hoped he wasn't having second thoughts. Even the other three were looking at him with worried expressions when his silence dragged on.

Finally, he sighed. "Juliet's flight got delayed again. I...I don't think she's going to make it on time and I need someone to pick up her job. Would you...?"

"Oh." Thank *God*. I stood quickly and pulled him into a hug, doing my best to rub the tenseness out of his shoulders. "Lakyn, of course. I'd be honored to, absolutely."

He relaxed after a moment, nodded nervously, and I pressed a kiss to his cheek before I promised him that it would all be okay. He said he trusted me and left, and then Lacey was getting up and bossing Sebastian back into working as she took my hand and pulled me away. We had exactly four hours to find me a dress that would match the color scheme.

It only took one, and Lacey hung around to help me get ready before running off to take care of herself. Matt found me in time to pass off Scott's ring, and I tucked it safely in my dress pocket before searching out Lakyn.

The last time I'd seen him in a suit, it'd been bright red and he'd been a teenager. Now, I could see how much he'd grown over the last few years. His shoulders had broadened out, his jaw-line was sharper, and even though his hair was still long, it stayed out of his eyes for good these days. Most importantly, though, he was glowing with happiness.

He caught my gaze in the mirror and grinned when I went to fix his hair. It was messy in a way that said he'd probably been running his hands through it, but he didn't look all that nervous. "You doing all right?"

"I think I might piss my pants," he admitted. "I really, really love him, you know?"

I laughed at him, told him I damn well hoped so, and then we were at the ceremony.

As predicted, it went perfectly. They had both written their own vows and I had never been so thankful for waterproof mascara in my life. I could barely see even as I signed my name as their witness, and they were kissing and everything was so *right*...except for the fact that Juliet wasn't there.

***

Two hours later at the reception I was standing on a chair, champagne glass in hand, ready to talk to a room full of the happiest people I'd ever seen. Scott and Lakyn were still covered in cake icing, and I grinned as I watched Lakyn lean over to lick some off his husband's cheek. It'd been a great day. "I didn't exactly have a speech planned because I was just filling in last minute, so this will be short and sweet. I met Scott and Lakyn when we were all in High School, and to this day I have never seen anyone more in love than those two assholes. They're the people who remind me every day that love actually exists, and I'm constantly thankful for that. I'm so glad they were able to get married today, and that I was able to be a part of it. Also, can we all just agree on what a hot couple they are?"

There were claps and wolf whistles and although Lakyn blushed he still grabbed Scott and pulled him in for an almost-too-dirty-for-public kiss. I laughed and lifted my glass for the toast. "I think I can speak for everyone here when I say we wish you guys a lifetime of happiness. Ladies and gentlemen, queers and token heterosexuals...to Lakyn and Scott James!"

Matt helped me down before giving his own speech, which was planned out and longer than mine had been. It was full of jokes and stories of when the boys first got together that I'd heard before but had never lost their humor. I cheered along with everyone else, but somewhere in the middle of it, I caught sight of blond hair.

A wave of panic washed over me and I found myself unable to look, afraid that it would be her and afraid that it wouldn't be at the same time. My heart felt like it was in my stomach, which was stupid. I'd been prepared to see her before the flight delays, had thought about it over and over again, but suddenly the reality seemed impossible to deal with.

Just breathe, Lena. Just open your eyes, casually look up, and—

Oh. Dear. God.

Juliet.

She was sitting between her brother and father, wiping at tears of laughter, just as stunning today as she had been the first time I'd ever seen her. Her hair was short, a wavy bob that framed her face. She still lined her eyes dark and wore bright red lipstick, but her dress was simple and black, matched with a pair of pumps that did great things to her legs. She had more tattoos now, beautiful lines and pale colors, and a few new piercings.

Blue eyes landed on mine, and after a moment the corners of her mouth lifted into a small, shy smile.

Suddenly I was eighteen years old again. Curled up in Lacey's arms and crying my soul out because the love of my life had gotten on a plane and *left me*. The memories hit me in vivid detail. What it had felt like the first day she didn't call, the first time I didn't get a *good morning* text hours in advance, the first time her conversations started being rushed.

How the missed Skype dates and forgotten letters left me feeling empty in a way that none of my favorite things could cover up. The spiraling pain of having to see her at family functions, pretending like I was okay and our breakup had been the mature, adult thing to do. That it was great to be "just friends".

Having to watch her leave *again* and *again* and *again*. Having to deal with the aftermath of her being so physically close and yet still so far away. With her being gone days later, just like that, across the fucking ocean.

As much as I'd tried to hide it, those few moments a year had been heart wrenching. I'd shoved it down, packed it away, because most of the time I'd believed we'd done the right thing. I'd believed that chasing our own dreams and finding ourselves had been the right decision. But then I'd hear the sound of her voice over the phone as she talked to Lakyn, see her face on the computer when I walked by, and it would all go to hell. It would hurt too fucking much to be right.

I'd had to let her go.

I'd had to move on.

I'd had to forget her.

I'd had to.

I'd needed to be my own person and I'd never regretted that, but I regretted not knowing her at the same time.

I remembered pretending like it wasn't hard.

The announcement of Scott and Lakyn's first dance jerked me out of the past, and I managed to focus on them long enough to clap with the others, but when people got up to join them, I found myself looking for Juliet instead. She was sitting alone by then, and I wasn't sure if that made it easier or harder, but my feet carried me towards her anyway.

My heart was pounding and my hands were shaking, but somehow I still managed to say, "You made it."

Her smile was small again, and she was watching me like *she* wasn't sure what to expect even as she used her foot to push a chair out. I took it gratefully, trying my best to cover the fact that I wasn't sure my knees would manage to hold me up any longer.

I wondered if she was different. I hadn't seen her in so long, I only knew about her life in bits and pieces of overheard conversations and Instagram posts. I wondered what she was doing, if she was with anyone—

Just like that my mouth went dry, I couldn't breathe, and I wondered if I could handle it if some pretty girl walked around the corner and sat next to her, asked me who I was. Would I even be able to answer her?

I should have stayed on the opposite side of the room.

Juliet tucked her hair behind her ears. "I stumbled in about the time they were starting their vows. I thought about going up there but," she paused, "you looked happy and capable, so I left it alone."

Three years. It'd been three years since I had seen her, and longer than that since I had *really* spoken to her. I lived with two of the people she was closest to in the world, saw her father almost as regularly as I saw my own, and somehow I had managed to lose her. *I* had done that. *I* had let her go.

"I'm glad you're here—everyone is," I admitted, and even though I felt like I was saying it for the boys, I knew I meant it just as much for myself. As nervous as I was, it was good to see her. It was good that she had made it for such an important event. Her grin was stunning, and I had no idea how I had survived without it. Why I had even tried? Any number of the times she had gotten on a plane I could have ran after her, told her I loved her and asked her to take me with her. Grand romantic gestures had never been my thing, but I *could* have. I should have.

There was only a moment of awkwardness before we found our rhythm, and then starting a conversation was easy. Just like that we picked up where we had left off, like time had stood still until we'd found our way back to each other. Everything felt *easy* with her, we didn't have to work at it, or try to be impressive, or even really think. And suddenly we were down a bottle of wine and laughing so hard our mascara was ruined.

Scott and Lakyn joined us before they left for the honeymoon, and for the first time in a while I felt whole. Lakyn got emotional when it was time for them to go, and hugged me before he latched himself onto Juliet. Scott shook his head, wrapped his arms around me tight, and said, "Thanks for being his person today."

"Yeah, well, it was the least I could do," I murmured, then kissed his cheek and let him go. "Be good. Don't lose him. Enjoy your trip."

There were waves and happy tears that followed them out of the building, and then Juliet turned a smirk on me and asked, "More drinks?"

"More drinks!" I agreed, and we were back at it. I doubted it surprised either of us when we realized how close we were, and I couldn't even say for sure who moved first, but then we were kissing. And we spent the rest of the night kissing, relearning old territory, feeling like we were teenagers again and all the years we'd spent apart were non-existent.

When I woke up the next morning my head hurt a little, but the most beautiful girl was lying next to me. Her lips quirked into a smile long before she ever blinked those bright blue eyes open. "Hi," she whispered.

I was pretty sure I was dreaming.

"Hi," I whispered back, and Juliet smiled as she leaned in for a kiss. I tilted my face just out of her way, and I knew I had to be awake then, because— "Morning breath, Jules!"

She pressed her face into my neck and laughed, and even though her voice was muffled I heard her ask, "You still worry about that?"

"Well, it's gross," I defended.

She kissed me anyway.

We laid there for a while, unbothered to get up and do anything with our day, not really talking but not really silent either. She kept one hand in mine, the fingers of the other constantly moving against my skin, like she was painting a picture.

I didn't care enough to keep track of the time, didn't really care about anything but her, didn't care if we said anything at all. At least until I heard her murmur, "By the way…"

I rolled over to look at her, my mouth opening to ask 'what?', but her finger slid across my lips, stopping me from saying anything at all. She smiled, expression amused. "I love you, too."

I kissed her, and in that kiss I felt the puzzle pieces of my life fall into place. A void that I had been refusing to admit was empty finally filled, and I realized then that I'd been waiting on it since the summer that I'd been eighteen. I had no idea what tomorrow would bring, but right then it didn't matter. I still loved her. She loved me. And in that moment, I had everything in my arms that I had ever needed.

Just Juliet.

This is Charlotte. Thank you for reading Just Juliet. I hope you enjoyed the book! Please spread the word by leaving a review on Amazon!

61626008R00134

Made in the USA
Lexington, KY
18 March 2017